T I M E

A N D   L I G H T

A NOVEL BY

W I L L I A M   B O R N E F E L D

Borealis is an imprint of White Wolf Publishing.

White Wolf Publishing
780 Park North Boulevard, Suite 100
Clarkston, GA 30021

Cover Photograph by William Bornefeld
Cover and Interior Design by Michelle Prahler
Printed in Canada

For Mary

"You can't be too careful."

—H. G. Wells

Twelve more or less well-known photographs are described herein and other allusions are made to photography. But this is not a book about taking pictures any more than *The Big Sleep* was about the detective business.

THE PILL

In the spring of that year strange new plant life began to appear and flourish on the arid plateau around the dome. The occasional outside patrol would come upon this new vegetation and report its unexpected presence through channels to the Central Committee. No one much cared. Life in the dome was so pleasant and so well-regulated that the Outside had been almost forgotten. But Chief Executive Hayes called a meeting, during which small cola drinks laced with brain stimulant were served; after three hours it was decided that a scientist would go out from time to time, collect samples, and make a report. No one volunteered.

Hayes had once been a leading scientist but now preferred the relaxed, club-like atmosphere of the

absolute-upper ruling class. He was like everybody's
uncle and smiled a lot. He smiled now and said:
"How about Dr. Noreen? I have always expected
great things from Noreen, but lately he's been in a
kind of rut. Well, aren't we all, as far as that goes?
I don't mean to criticize." He smiled again. "We'll
send Noreen. He's a very bright man, one of my
former pupils, and very level-headed. He'll do a
good job and we can count on him. I've always tried
to help this fine young chap along the upward path
toward leadership and this may just be the
opportunity he needs. Yes, Noreen's the man. A bit
too sober and strait-laced, but I've known him for
a long time and I've always liked him."

Someone said, not too seriously: "Of course, but
why send out one of the fair people?"

"Why not?" Hayes said, and no one could think
of anything else to add and the meeting was
adjourned.

This is what everyone knew:

The domed city Fullerton was about five miles
long, more ovoid than hemispherical, on a high
plateau near the thirtieth parallel. It was home to
The Family of Man, who, if they thought about it,
which they didn't often, knew they were the last
survivors on the planet Earth.

Outside, ugly radiation raged. No one knew how
long. No one cared any more. The Family of Man
felt safe. A thick translucent hide of non-toxic,

leaden plastic hung down on chains from the dome's strutwork. It was the border to the half-life-country. Only the sun's light and warmth got through.

It had always been like that. Everything remained the same in the dome year after year. The necessary science and technology had evolved and peaked centuries ago. Only what was needed was kept in place. There was no growth, just maintenance of the status quo. Nothing better could be imagined.

During the day, Fullerton bustled. Its narrow streets and moving walkways were filled with people. Small air-propelled vehicles zipped around as if they were on important missions. Each person had his or her own rank in society, a place to live and a specific job to do. Some citizens referred to the dome as the Garden of Eden, which was also a popular midtown restaurant that looked out over the central park of the same name.

The Family of Man used the word *happy* without shame. They were happy because they took the pill. No one knew what it was like to be unhappy, because of the pill. The government gave you the pill, as much as you wanted. You could ingest a little or a lot, as long as you took one pill a day. No one wanted less.

The pill made it possible for a lot of people to live close to each other and to endure small living quarters and still have a good time. It was an aphrodisiac as well as a calmative. It guaranteed robust engorgements, including enormous, sustained erections. Multiple orgasms were the norm.

The pill had been around forever, almost as long as the dome, and had survived many incarnations. With each revision it got better. In his youth, Chief Executive Hayes had worked on major improvements to it and come up with his famous "Tricky Dick" formula. He was loved for his efforts. Both male and female children were often named "Hayes."

For some reason no one remembered, graphic art work had been banned. It mattered little. If you desired visual stimulation, you could admire a wide variety of temperate and semitropical plants everywhere around you. Or you could gape at the crowds on the walkways and sooner or later see everyone in the dome. At night, if you were coupled in the right direction (and you would be coupled), you could stare at your lover's face. A pleasant time was possible just counting pores or hairs or respiration or pulse beats.

You could even admire the way the three- and four-story cliff-dwellings, which is what they called the apartments, had over the centuries been stacked and squeezed into every nook and cranny.

If looking around at the marvels of a self-contained society wasn't enough and you wanted

WILLIAM BORNEFELD

to exercise your ears, you could take note of the instrumental music that constantly flowed out of the speakers in every living room and public place. But this was unlikely. Nobody paid much attention to that bland nonsense, or even to the message now and then from Hayes or someone else in the Central Committee. It was background noise. It beat time to the old in-out. Only if it stopped would it have been missed.

Mostly The Family of Man entertained itself. It had made an art of the world's most ancient activity. "At night we fuck each other's brains out or our socks off, whichever comes first, so to speak," Hayes liked to say.

As a result of the sexual imperative and the limited population, everyone was related to everyone else. No one called it inbreeding. You did not seek out sexual relationships with close relatives. But it was not always possible to know your partner's bloodlines. Sometimes you found out only when a defective child was born. You did not worry. The child disappeared at once. You were told you could not have children again. There was no stigma. It was just one of those things.

Still, a certain selectivity was evident. Three distinct major groups of people had evolved. One group was short and stocky and had swarthy skin, dark brown eyes, and black hair. These people did much of the hard work. Another group was not as short, but still not very tall; it had lighter skin, brown eyes, and brown hair. This was the largest group; its constituents were noted for their cleverness and their ability to talk and acquire supervisory positions. The smallest group was tall and fair with blue eyes and blond hair. Its members were widely admired. They tended to be aloof and overbearing and often had important professional jobs. Dr. Noreen belonged to this group.

On several occasions Noreen had been on the Executive Committee to determine if the drug should be added to the central water supply.

It had been decided each time not to. How could you control the dosage that way? everyone asked, quite alarmed at a possible threat to his or her own well-being. One of the great things about living in the dome was being able to manage your own intake. That was freedom.

"If you can figure out how to deliver the right amount by adding it to the water, certainly," Hayes had said. "We would, of course, be sure then of the minimum dosage. But we could not guarantee any Quality of Life. I for one would not want to ingest the number of glasses of water it would take to get the occasionally-necessary killer high. Why, we'd be peeing all over the place and getting up to go to the bathroom all night. Besides, I can't imagine anyone willingly forgoing the pill, though I can see them forgetting to drink the water."

Dr. Noreen remembered this as he stared at the small round white pill sitting in the middle of his galley table.

It was about 6mm in diameter, 2mm high, and scored on one side. It contained 25mg of a compressed powder. The normal dosage was one tablet a day. A larger amount would not hurt. Taking three or more at one time would result in a massive, unyielding erection. A man would stay home from work such days.

He had not taken the pill in several weeks. He wondered now if he had done the right thing.

At first he had experienced a slight nausea. This was rapidly followed by an acceleration of his vital signs and a tendency to emotional flare-ups that had not gone away. Something had also happened to his eyes; though he had never been aware of any problem with his vision, it seemed to him he could now see more clearly.

He wasn't sure why he had stopped taking the pill. But going outside the dome had changed him. Not taking the pill had changed him more.

"Yes, why would anyone not want to take the pill?" he said to himself, and he picked up the pill and let it drop back into its bottle.

BOOK ONE

THE
PERSISTENCE
OF
VISION

CHAPTER 1

Beyond the radioactive cemeteries lay the
Forbidden Zone, the rubble of ancient cities.

Doctor Noreen aimed his remote rad detector,
and early morning sun glinted off its chromium-
plated baffle. The sun's rays warmed his chest even
through the white barrieralls, and he could feel
heat building up uncomfortably next to his skin,
especially in his armpits and crotch. Sweat had
begun to run in itchy narrow rivulets along the
sides of his rib cage and down the soft inner flesh
of his thighs.

He didn't mind.

Somehow it was comforting to know that the
barrieralls protected him from the enemy rays, and

at the same time he was enjoying an early spring in the open spaces beyond the cramped dome.

"But—" he said to no one in particular, not even to himself, half out loud.

He was pointing the instrument directly at the bumpy plain thirty miles east of the dome. According to his map, here fulminated the most deadly concentration of the penetrating gamma rays. Yet the audio indicator barely purred, and the liquid crystal readout cycled peacefully in the neighborhood of innocuous background radiation.

The reading, in fact, was less than he would get in his own dwelling.

He shook the instrument gently in a futile and primitive gesture. He got some pleasure out of doing so.

Once more he raised the device and this time peered very carefully through the viewfinder. The cross hairs overlapped what looked like an ancient tree. But it was a tree he didn't recognize, a species beyond his knowledge of taxonomy. This gnarled, spindly outcropping resembled an upright rodent. In the dome, where such graphic representations were not allowed, a zealous gardener would have chopped, pruned and whacked it into a non-objective shape long ago.

He let the cross hairs settle on the "rodent's" chest, pulled the trigger.

His sketchy map said the pleading rat-like figure

stood in the *exact* center of an immense concentration of radioactive substances.

He expected the speaker to yip and the numbers to shuttle crazily.

But he got the same low reading.

He suddenly snapped open his visor and let the sun's rays and the mild matinal air brush directly against his face.

It was something he had looked forward to for a long time. To escape the confines of the cloying barrieralls.

The sudden rush of the outside over his skin felt very exciting and pleasurable. It was like the other side of sex. Sex was everything. A two-headed coin: sex was on one side and everything else that felt good that was not sex was on the other.

Then he started to *think* about what he had just done. He flipped down the visor.

He walked back to his airbike with his head down. As if that would help him.

He was surrounded now by sadness, which seemed to fit him suddenly tighter than his custom-made anti-radiation suit.

He leaned on the handlebar.

This moment of regret, this letdown, this beginning of deep depression was the kind that comes with the first realization that you have just shortened your life. Which he was sure he had just done.

It was as if his body had turned to molten lead and was seeping into the ground.

Why had he opened his visor? He had betrayed himself by relying on the instrument. He could not believe the stupidity of his impulse. He tried now to find excuses, rather than face the truth of his mistake. Yet he knew this was stupid too.

The rad detector could be defective. Perhaps, when he dropped it earlier—

He sat with one leg thrown over the saddle, the other still touching ground. He looked up at the distant mountains. The sun had thrown their backsides into deep shadow. But their fronts gleamed almost white.

He felt no pain.

And the air *was* bracing.

And now he was all right again. He was no longer melting into the ground.

He felt lighter, as if he could fly. Not worried about anything.

He felt that something had changed when he lifted the visor. Perhaps he was going to die. But if he was going to die from radiation he would not die that morning. He had at least a few hours, maybe days.

And that limpid air! Unlike anything he'd ever experienced in the dome.

He snapped up his visor again and looked around.

He didn't want anyone from Fullerton to see him with his face exposed. They would think him crazy;

they would have him sent to Twelve-Nine for evaluation; in spite of his medical ranking they would withdraw his clearance to search for botanicals.

He could see empty landscape in every direction. The mountains in the east under the sun. The shimmering clear western sky behind which the dome had slid out of sight and from which it would reappear when he drove back. No sign of anyone. He had traveled so far that morning, the dome had been out of sight for a long time.

In the dome someone was always watching; it was unbelievable they weren't watching out here. He knew patrols existed though he had not seen any during the three weeks he'd been making his daily forays outside of Fullerton.

He snapped his visor shut, and began to breathe the filtered but now stale-feeling air inside his suit.

For appearance's sake, he bent over and examined a small green shoot pushing through a rock fissure, removed it carefully with tweezers, and rested it in a plastic compartment in his specimen bag.

He'd collected dozens of similar plants during the time he'd been allowed outside. He didn't need more. This one was his excuse for stopping at that spot.

He gave them an excuse for everything he did.

He straddled his airbike, revved its idling motor. For a moment he thought about returning to his office; and then he drove smoothly forward, away from the dome.

The airbike's motor hugged the land with a steady throbbing sound. Everything, including the noise, struck him as puny and futile under the vast sky. His mind began to drift and ride along the top of the motor hum. He had no thoughts. After a while, he seemed to feel himself leave his body and he was high above, looking down at himself. The part of himself that remained below and the airbike looked small and very far away. Then he was no longer looking down. He was hunched into the wind, and paying attention. The bike sound now roared around him.

Suddenly, he yanked the handlebar sharply to the right. He didn't know why. The airbike veered off the comforting ruts of the ancient road. It was a crazy impulse. But he kept going. From then on he didn't look back again.

He was headed toward the forbidden rubble. Toward the east and the morning sun.

CHAPTER

2

He drove over the nearby hill and then down into a slight valley, out of sight of the roadway. The bike floated on a column of air about a foot over the rocks, jiggling only now and then to avoid the bigger projections, without effort, barely putt-putting.

The rocks got larger, and more dense, and the scarred mountains loomed ahead. He decided to hover in place and take another reading.

He snapped open his visor again, sure no one could see him in the valley. What difference could it make now, anyway? If you die, you die. With radiation, you die sooner.

This reading was somewhat higher than the last one, but well within guidelines. Higher but still safe. He told himself the machine was working.

The sun was rising quickly and it was much warmer. He had never felt it directly against his face. When he got back home, he would smother himself with E-Lo oil, just for good measure.

Without the plastic lens in front of his eyes, the blotches of color—red, yellow, and purple—that he'd noticed near the base of the nearest mountain were incredibly bright and pure in the sunlight. A little chill had crept into his suit with the wind and was drying him off, and he felt himself shiver. Or was he trembling? He made a mental note that he would later write down in his journal: "Years of the monotonous blues and grays in the dome have not prepared me for pure color." The most intense colors he'd ever seen had come from inside human bodies, but even the color of fresh blood viewed under tube light lacked the intensity of the hues in the field ahead.

The motor's pitch rose slightly but was still low and throaty. It felt good.

He drove up the incline, and when he crossed the ridge he saw that the bright colors were a field of flowers.

He squeezed the brake lever built into the handle grip and stopped abruptly, jerking forward and then back. Still rocking slightly, he hovered for a moment above a flat outcropping of volcanic rock, then allowed the bike to set down, and he let his feet rest on the hard mineral floor. Even flat on the ground he still had a good view of the dense patch of flowers thriving near the mountain's base.

The plants, which he could see now waving gently from side to side, looked mysterious and overwhelming and, perhaps, threatening, though he was not sure why he felt that way.

He had seen pressed and faded specimens of flowers in the Organo Institute's research files, but they had dried and shrunk from years of storage, and one could hardly be distinguished from another. Even from that brief exposure to floral taxonomy he could recognize some of the species now growing in front of him.

"Marigolds... hyacinths... and... jonquils... azaleas, and... rhododendrons...?" He dragged names from his memory.

But he saw none of the species that lived today in the dome, none of those pale, dwarfed pariahs or clingers; all of the flowers in front of him fulminated in intense color such as he had never experienced, and these flowers were monumental in size with luscious orange, red, pink and other blood-and-flesh hues including the color of venous blood, with voluptuous petals and sinuous green stems.

Did flowers exist like this a long time ago, were they from the beginning supposed to be this way, or could radiation have mutated them so much that, starting over now, they grew out of hand? Did this gaudy appearance cover some more sinister purpose than the sexual impulse that encouraged living things to look good? How long had they been there? Had anyone else from the dome noticed them? Surely, he would have heard some report of their existence if they had been discovered earlier. The desultory collection of new botanicals had just started a few years before, when the first outside plant life had been detected. Each year the plants had become more numerous. It was possible this was the first year flowers had bloomed and he was the first to find them. How had they remained hidden for an eternity? What nourished them, what did they eat? Did something in the soil at the base of the mountain lead to their unusual fertility? They were no doubt harmless, though the extravagance of visual beauty unnerved him. He assured himself he had nothing to fear in this place except the radiation, which so far, if he could trust the instrument, seemed to have been overstated. To put it mildly. *Yes yes yes, let it be so.*

Yet he had truly entered the Forbidden Zone. Any discoveries he made now were undertaken at his own risk and might not be rewarded. His curiosity could easily be considered insubordination and the reward would be punishment. He would have to think about that.

As a collector of botanicals he had a duty to remove samples from this field, but the flowering area was so dense and widespread, it would take days to catalog, require a number of workers, more vehicles. He was sure he had made an unusual discovery that, if announced properly, would be rewarded, not with punishment but perhaps a larger apartment and complete responsibility for an organized expedition. He looked forward to busy days ahead. Days outside the dome.

Whatever, it didn't sound bad. He was ready for a change in his life. He had felt change imminent ever since he started leaving the dome. Why? Was it a real impulse for transition or a premonition? Of his own death perhaps?

When a slight dry breeze came up carrying the perfume of the flowers, he became wary, and again considered the possibility the meter was defective. Could the scent be poisonous? He snapped his visor shut, and turned up the positive air flow in his suit.

All these morbid thoughts! I'm adrift, and all this beginning does is make me think of endings.

He decided the correct first step would be to cruise along the base of the mountain just out of reach of the plants and see how far the flower field extended, following it around to the other side of the mountain if necessary.

He had never gone that far before, he had never come close to the mountain or even approached it, nor had he ever heard of anyone from the dome straying that far from the main road; but he knew the airbike was manufactured to extreme tolerances and could be relied on for rough travel.

He glanced at his wrist time.

He had not been authorized to go this far. But he

had not been specifically told not to. And now that he was here, it seemed like a good idea to check things out. He had at least ten hours until dark, when he would be expected back in the dome. He could just about complete his survey of this forbidden area if he got started right away. He could resume his investigation in earnest on his next visit. And then he would know where to begin, and he would start early.

He was authorizing himself.

He assumed it would be a simple trip over land such as he had just traversed and be no strain to his vehicle.

He twisted the airbike's throttle handle to rev up the motor and strained to hear any sign of its faltering. He detected nothing but a cool, steady, admirable throbbing that urged him on.

"*Andale!*" he said out loud to himself and to the machine, invoking one of the dome's ancient expressions for ambitious occasions.

He let out the altitude clutch. The racing motor jerked the airframe up about four feet above the terrain and held it there.

You were never supposed to travel more than a few feet above the ground, but he knew that the bikes were designed to reach twelve or even fifteen feet for short periods before overheating, though at that height they were undependable and easily thrown off balance by rocks or debris.

He was a doctor and a level-five manager, and

had always been a model of prudence and responsibility. But he had lately wondered what it would be like to ride the airbike at full speed.

Since his experiments with his dosage of the pill, he had picked up a noticeable edginess. At first this seemed to have an advantage, but now it occurred to him that the medicine may have quite simply always masked a basic character flaw, and such infantile urges as the one involving his speculation about the airbike could be a warning symptom. His unscientific recklessness today regarding the radiation was perhaps another sign of personal weakness, even identity deterioration, something to be watched.

He decided not to think about such things until he could do so in a quiet room, perhaps this coming weekend. Certainly he could not tell anyone in authority about his apprehension about himself because they would have to know about his illegal adjustment of his medicine. That could result in embarrassing retaliation. He would watch himself carefully for the rest of the day and be especially cautious in pursuing his investigation of the flower field.

You can't be too careful, he told himself, remembering an old saying that summed up his life so far. And then he let the words tumble out of reach into the back of his brain like a mathematical equation he no longer understood.

His mouth had an unusual bitter dryness. He

attributed that to a change in body chemistry as a result of stopping the pill. It would go away in time, he told himself.

Would his sex drive go away too? That's what the pill was for, wasn't it? Supposed to make you horny and keep you calm at the same time.

And he was still horny? But with differences? Thinking more about sex than doing it?

Giving up the National Pastime?

So early?

No way! And I can always be a good boy and take the leadership's pill and step back down into my old self any time I want.

But you really can't be too careful. For a second he remembered the old motto, then—

What is careful?

His Mach-Nine was idling comfortably in hover mode. He let out the clutch.

The bike dropped off the volcanic ledge and skimmed a few inches above mesquite underbrush. Its motor made a little trilling putt-putt that again seemed very small in the vastness of the open spaces. He too felt very small in the midst of all that desert brush with the mountain getting bigger and darker in front of him. He had attached his meter to his waist and turned up the audible signal as far as it would go, but it made no noise.

He locked his visor open and breathed in the fresh moist air of the valley, and it quelled the dryness in his mouth, and he smelled the perfume of the flowers blowing over him, and he found the scent invigorating. It seemed to remind him of something, but whatever it was he couldn't remember, and he was busy now navigating over rough ground. The bike swayed from side to side, sometimes dipping as much as twenty degrees from upright and occasionally fishtailing with a disturbing lurch.

And all the time he was thinking he didn't care. He was perhaps the first warm-blooded creature to occupy this space in what? A million years? Whatever, a long time.

It occurred to him he was now directly over the so-called worst part of the Forbidden Zone. The knowledge gave him a little bubbling charge of excitement. He looked down, and, rushing below his feet, in the spaces between the mesquite, he could already see signs of strange debris: rusting iron pipe, charred plastic, moldering primeval ashes, and layabout monolithic concrete slabs with weathered planes that glowed white. He stayed clear of another large field of flowers, these intensely blue, away to the right, and soon he was in the shadow of the mountain.

The mountain rose up sharply from the plateau and he was very close to its squatty base now; soon he could see a foundation of black rock that had cracked and shifted into a rugged pile of large flat boulders with sharp jagged edges. The angular boulders were spread around haphazardly and touching each other at odd angles and squeezed one on top of another, so that they would be impossible to traverse on foot. The flowers did not grow here, but as he drove closer to the mountain he could still get a faint whiff of their incense, flowing now against his back. Without the sun directly on him, the rushing air chilled him. And he could feel little droplets of condensed mist pinging against his cheeks. Suddenly cold like pin pricks, and then gone.

He let up on the throttle and idled just along an edge of a heavy black granite outcrop.

From a distance it had appeared to be one large mountain, but up close here on the talus he could see it was really two mountains with a narrow crevice between them. He was now approaching this interstice, which was maybe three hundred feet wide and angled back to the left out of sight and explained why in silhouette the two mountains merged. The barren rocky portion of the mountain on his left went on up along the chasm's side and then out of sight around the back of the mountain, and formed a steep precipice that at the top fell sharply down to the gully between the mountains. At the base of the draw, the rocks were smaller, more regular, and flattened out as if a river had once flowed over them. The rocks did not go up the steeper wall of the mountain on his right, just along its base in the crevice, and then came out and

35

continued toward him and to his right and into the valley. The face of the mountain on his right rose straight up from the rock river as a vertical igneous slab and didn't stop until it reached intense blue sky.

He wondered if he should turn into the fissure and go across along the rock bed, between the two peaks, which would be easy on the bike, and perhaps quickly come out into sunlight on the other side of the mountains. But he would be below the rocky precipice that way—and he didn't know for how long, and the rocks didn't look very stable, and he worried that the motor noise might cause an avalanche over him, so he abandoned that notion.

It would be better to follow the rocky slope up the steep trail alongside the near mountain, and even if the noise and the air pressure caused the rocks to shift, he would at least be above them.

As he turned inward across the rock bed and up the jagged incline, he realized it was dangerous, whichever way he went, but it would not be as risky as actually trying to fly twelve or fifteen feet above ground level—which he had also been thinking about doing.

Now he could see the sharp edges of the boulders passing under his feet and they were bigger than they had seemed from a distance, and the crevices were steeper and deeper, and the engine made a new noise, a high pitched whine as it exerted the

T
I
M
E

A
N
D

L
I
G
H
T

effort necessary to begin the climb, and the bike itself twisted vertically from side to side as its forced air met the constantly changing uneven surfaces and tried to compensate.

He was leaning back almost forty-five degrees and holding on over the bumps. He had climbed very high now and he looked down along the precipice's wall of stacked rock and at the bottom saw the rock river, and the rocks looked very small. He wondered if he had made a wrong decision; instead of concentrating on just climbing the rocks he was now trying to figure out what he would have to do to turn around in the diminishing channel of rock path beneath and ahead of him and go back down.

"I'm a doctor," he said, "and I should not be doing this reckless thing," but he went on anyway, because there was really no room to turn around and nothing else to be done.

He could not even stop the bike and rest for a moment because the way underneath was too steep and the rocks too sharp and irregular.

Then he had reached the apex of the rocks and the narrow ledge flattened out, with fewer and smaller rocks, and stretched ahead of him for several hundred feet. The motor had lost its whine and had reverted to the gently reassuring putt-putting.

He had almost reached the end of the path when

he noticed that he could not see where it went back down the other side of the mountain.

He braked, and switched into hover mode, just in time to look over the place where a deep gap appeared in the path, much deeper than the twelve or fifteen feet that he knew the machine would handle, even if he were prepared to take the risk and could pull the altitude lever all the way back in time.

He backed up a few feet, let the bike lower itself to the ground, dismounted, and pulled the bike close to the side of the mountain. The patch of ledge here was only about five feet wide, but dark crumbly dirt covered the rock and was somehow comforting. He took a deep breath.

He refused to look directly over the side of the precipice. He could feel a little panic and cold sweat starting again and he knew he might go to pieces if he thought too long about where he was.

Oh, Doctor Noreen, you have gone too far away from the dome! You are much too high!

Don't, don't look down. You can feel vertigo rising.

He kept one hand on the bike and pulled it a few inches closer to the mountain's inboard side, then he sat down and leaned his back against the mountain and rested.

He would have to do something soon, but what that was he didn't have a clue.

CHAPTER

3

He removed the meter from his waistband and checked the readout, pointing the barrel in different directions, looking at the side of the other mountain, the rock river below, all somewhat magnified by the optical system of the instrument, and got almost the same low level response he had observed down below, which was really no reading at all.

He took a drink from his water bottle, felt calmer, and wondered if he should take a pill. But it was really all right up here, the air had a very thin refreshing feel in his lungs and against his face, and he would be able to turn the bike around now and go back down the way he had come up. It was still before noon and there was plenty of time. Though the sun had disappeared somewhere behind the mountain.

He decided that it was better not to think about the trip back down, because of the frightening steep angle of rock, and how high up he was, or to wonder if the bike could grab hold in the short space he had to take off. He would squint his eyes and rev the throttle and hope it would all work out fine.

His eyes were adjusted to the mountain shade now and he was breathing easily. He lowered the rad meter and looked around, avoiding the space directly in front of him.

The sky straight up, which was all he could see, had even more depth and hue than he had ever observed below. The color was some form of blue, he supposed. Blue was the color of venous blood, and water in some light, and he tried to remember other things of that exact blue, without traces of red or green, but he couldn't recall any.

Then he turned his neck to the left, and squinted straight over the gap in the ledge that he had narrowly missed tumbling over, and he saw something on the other side of the dropoff that he had missed earlier because it had merged with the shade, an opening the size of a large door in the side of the mountain, and covered halfway up with rock. It looked like the entrance to a cave or a doorway. He stared over the precipice and he wanted to go over there.

But the gap in the path was too wide to jump over, even with the bike, and the depression was too steep and rocky to climb down and then over; even if he had the courage, which he doubted; and, besides, the rocks could easily shift and bury him or slip with him over the side of the mountain. He could feel the sweat forming on his forehead even though it was quite cool at that elevation in the shade.

But across the way in the cave something was fluttering just on the other side of the opening.

He wondered what it was.

If he hovered at seven or eight feet, then throttled forward, he might have enough momentum for the thrust outward and over and he would have enough room for his trajectory to drop so that he could easily cross the gap and land on the path that continued at a lower level on the other side. The shelf was about ten feet wide there, giving him a little leeway for his landing.

It did not occur to him that he should think now about how he would get back.

He wiped sweat from his exposed face, could feel the beading start again.

This was a little strange for him, to be thinking this way. But he was sure he could make it and it was all a scientific experiment anyway and he had no wife or children and he had already accomplished any permanent contribution he was going to make to Fullerton, so he got on the bike again, aware that not taking the pill had jerked his mind to some new place. He did not think ahead. He turned on the ignition, revved the motor until it felt good, then pulled back on the hover lever and rose until the bike was seven feet above the path, and held it there in power-draining levitation mode. He could look over the gap, and down onto the path where it resumed again, and it looked narrow now, and far below, as in an optical illusion. He grabbed the forward lever, pulled it all the way, back back back, held on so he could shove it forward into neutral just before he landed, and he shot forward now like one of the birds that flew around the top of the dome. Right away he could feel the downward push of the jet catch the edge of the path he was leaving, then nothing as it searched for the too-deep bottom of the draw. The motorbike descended heavily in a helpless steep arc, now balanced in air only by his own guiding, and he wondered what he was doing.

But even in midair he did not think about how he would return. All he thought about was holding on tight.

It took the jet only a second to catch the ground, and push up, and then it overcompensated because it was already all the way out and it bucked up the front of machine. He had already pulled back the lever, and he held on for the counter jerk, and then it all hovered nicely on the other side of the precipice.

He let out a little laugh, shut off the engine, got off, turned the bike around so it would be facing the right direction, because he was going back the way he had come, no surprises, because he knew now you could not count on a gentle uneventful trip around the mountain. He didn't want to think about the return trip now, because he might already have used up his luck getting this far. He climbed up the gentle slope of rocks to the opening in the wall of the mountain.

What was fluttering was a stiff sheet of paper, a rectangle about eight by ten inches, like nothing he had ever seen.

He laughed out loud to himself. He had crossed over to the Forbidden Zone and he was really in it now, maybe in it forever, and it somehow all seemed worthwhile.

As if he had been bidden.

No, that was not possible. No one else to blame. Had done it himself.

And he was no longer sweating. The flight across the void had dried his face. In fact, he felt quite cool now; he could feel the chill seeping out of the mountain's shade and the cave, but he was not chilled.

He grabbed the paper, stared.

He had never seen a photograph before, or

anything like it, because all strictly visual stimuli, all graphics, had been banned in Fullerton for many generations. You could listen to music and poetry or radio dramas or instructional disks but you couldn't look at pictures. There were no pictures, drawings or paintings. Even graphics that would have simplified the use of electronic equipment were prohibited. During his medical training Doctor Noreen had been allowed to study disks that contained skeletal outlines of body parts, but access to this material was closely guarded. It was told that at one time in its early history the dome society had been excessively visual with a great emphasis on looking at things including pictures in printed books; but it was decided a long time ago that a visual society was in a constant state of imbalance and agitation due to stress on the optic nerve, and produced discord, especially harmful in the small controlled dome atmosphere; therefore, visual paraphernalia was phased out and then totally eliminated. The idea of blinding every citizen was at one time considered, turning the dome residents into a kind of mole people, but that radical notion was after lengthy debate among the elders discarded as unworkable and regressive.

Doctor Noreen had never even imagined what a photograph would be like, because it had never occurred to him that such a thing was possible, but now that he was holding a photograph in his hand he knew at once what it was and what it was for, and he accepted it for itself completely. Its presence struck him in the same way the world would affect a blind person who had just acquired the ability to see.

An object that was obviously a pepper was rendered in smooth continuous black and gray tones on the surface of an exceptionally white sheet of paper. The smooth surface of the paper, mounted on a stiff board, had a lustrous glow and the image of the pepper lay just below the sheen.

Doctor Noreen sat down on the upper edge of the rocks blocking the cave entrance. He felt his legs grow weak as he stared at this object he held in his hand; he could almost hear himself hyperventilating. He closed his visor to diffuse somewhat his perspective and switch his suit over to pure oxygen. His breathing became slow, regular and easy. He couldn't stop looking at this image. He could not tell if it was red or green but knew it was a pepper and most likely green and something rare and lovely, and he marveled at the depth and particularly the subtle tint of the deepest black tones. Somehow he felt he was looking in on another world, and this world was so inviting he wished to be able to crawl into it and look around at what was hidden by the edge of the frame. If nothing else, he wanted to reach in and remove the pepper, and he had to restrain his hand from submitting to such an obviously stupid notion. After a while he turned the picture over and inspected a smudged ink stamp that had a name in old style letters that he could not decipher.

Holding the print carefully by the edge with two fingers, he scooted up the rocks and stuck his head into the opening in the side of the mountain.

He was staring into the ruined concrete hallway of an underground room. He could now also see the rusting remains of a thick steel door that had once covered the opening in the mountainside and had collapsed and fallen away and now was partially buried under rocks.

The floor of the room was covered with sagging corrugated boxes, some of which had split open, letting stacks of uniformly shaped sheets of paper fall out. In the light that came in from the opening he could see that all the paper sheets were covered with some kind of black and white images.

He stuck one leg through the opening and let his shoe find a place to stand and then he pulled the rest of his body through and slid and then dropped into the room.

He was standing on a loose stack of paper, but didn't think he had damaged anything. He stood for a moment and let his eyes adjust to the light that came in overhead from the slit he had just traversed.

It occurred to him he was completely out of reach of the dome and he could die in this chamber and no one would know where to find him.

But he stayed and looked around anyway. He felt

the presence of ancient peoples but he was completely alone.

He could see now that the objects spread about on the floor were also black and white photographs.

Someone a long time ago had obviously gone to a great effort to create an archival storage vault for photographs, and now he saw, and could only guess how long, sometime after the twentieth century, before the cataclysm, as indicated by the still-intact dates on the dark green filing cabinets which lined the walls and went back deep into the darkness of the mountain. The latest date he could make out was 2525.

The dry air of the high plateau and until relatively recently the hermetically sealed chamber had been good for the preservation of paper. A few of the black solanders near the door had crumbled into flakes and powder. Most everything else, especially the boxes concealed in the metal cabinets, had survived remarkably intact. He could not imagine the individual sheets of paper ever looking much better, though many had small yellow flecks.

The ancients of the twentieth century had mastered the art of manufacturing one-hundred-percent rag paper and Noreen's discovery seemed to justify their use of it. No one used paper very often in the dome, but Noreen recalled with pleasure the time he had run his thumb over the edge of a ream of paper in the Organo Institute's artifacts wing.

He activated his flashlight, walked back, and on his right found a door leading to a large room. Opening the door stirred up dust but not as much as he expected.

The room was filled with rows of floor-to-ceiling green cabinets. So many they went on into the mountain beyond the reach of his light.

This is my place now, he told himself. *Some day I will open every drawer. I will know everything about this place.*

Then he went back to the cave entrance, began picking up the stacks of paper directly in front of the fallen door, squared up the edges, and piled them carefully on the exposed tops of file cabinets. When he left he would not have to trample them again. Then he sat down, leaned against the wall, and in a beam of skylight that came in through the cave's opening looked at pictures.

CHAPTER

4

Receding behind his back, lay the mountain range and the brush-covered steppes leading to them. The flower fields, which he had not yet searched, lay far behind too. But it seemed to him, although perhaps he just imagined it, their perfume still lingered in the air.

He braced himself. The road bank loomed just ahead. He pulled back on the throttle and leaped effortlessly onto the road. He landed neatly with the airbike pointed in the direction of the dome.

Here the ruts blasted into the dirt by air jets were barely visible. But as the miles passed they got deeper and wider. None of the tracks was fresh. Patrols had been this way, but not lately and not often. The world outside the dome held little interest for the dome residents. He could imagine the troops killing time, taking a nap as soon as they found a place to hide.

The sun was setting. If he hurried he could make the dome just before dark. He twisted the accelerator grip and the bike shot forward, easily now, over the old ruts.

He had concealed a thick packet of flush-cardboard-mounted photographs in the deep inner flapped pocket of his barrieralls and he hoped it did not bulge. He also had a desperate urge to chatter. This was odd. Small talk was not consistent with his status or his nature or even with the prescribed etiquette of dome life. It was an impulse he would withstand. Besides, he didn't know anyone he could really talk to about himself.

And that included his girlfriend, Beta.

You spent all your free time with some people and you made love to and with them, and yet you never really talked to them. They didn't know who you were and you really didn't care who they were. What you cared about was what felt good at the time and it was usually Beta.

He did not care much to recall what had happened a little earlier. How he had at first stared across the gap and felt forever lost, and how he had projected himself and the airbike across the precipice, and how, just when he was about to slam into the other side, and could feel himself staring into the ravine and knew it would be the last image ever to fill his retinas, he yanked the bike around ninety degrees, leaned out over the void until the air pressure caught the rock projections, just that second it took, and then leaped up from level to level, coaxing the vehicle and twisting with it until he and the air jet became a single snorting animal, and he was back on the upper path again, each time he had jumped thinking it was his last, and dying, though yet not dying, dying each time, dying so many times that he would never die again.

His heart pumping so wildly now, and knowing that he could never do what he had done if he had been on the pill and that then his heart would not be thumping now, resolving to take the pill again, if only to stop his heart's wild thrashing about, knowing that whatever happened he would live forever, something that had never occurred to him, and which now seemed a delicious prospect.

"Worried about you. Thought you got lost. You have any trouble with the airbike?"

"Not at all. The bike was fine. I was so wrapped up in my work, I forgot what time it was."

"How's the radiation out there?"

"About the same as always, I presume."

The guard nodded, took the bike, set it on a mobile charging station and gave it a shove toward the regeneration area.

"I'd like to reserve that one for tomorrow," the

doctor said, watching the bike, which he now considered an old friend, move away.

"They're all the same."

"I know, but I'm used to that one now."

"See what I can do, Doc. Good evening."

"Good evening."

CHAPTER

5

In the locker room he removed his barrieralls, and hung them in his narrow locker, arranging the folds so that the pocket containing the photographs was underneath. He put his climbing shoes on the bottom shelf next to his briefcase. A note inside the door said, "See me when you return. Brack."

He would transfer the photographs from his radiation suit to his briefcase just before he was ready to leave the building.

He closed the door, which did not have a lock, nothing in the dome had a lock except personal quarters and high level offices. Everyone was supposed to be honest and leave things alone; but he knew that lower level employees were nosy and out of boredom searched things. He had already placed the sample valise with his brief notes and the specimens collected in the conveyor that went up to the lab where they would be catalogued and filed in the morning.

He wondered if he should transfer the photos to his briefcase before he took his shower, but he decided that any curious underling would more likely check his briefcase than a suit that had been worn beyond the dome. Since his briefcase had been there all day, it had probably already been looked into if anyone with that nature had been on duty.

But it was time for a new shift to come on. It would be a small crew, with little to do except sweep up, check gauges and listen to records until morning, and they might begin by checking the lockers. It was not supposed to be like that in dome life, but not everything went according to regulations. Everyone had a job but not everyone had to work hard. Citizens came to work but they had time to kill. They would rather be at home. Night was the best time for most people in the dome. Then they were in their apartments and they could pass the time by fucking each other. The favorite game among the lower classes was counting the number of times an orgasm could be reached. During the day, or whenever their work shift was, many tended to be listless. They often passed the time with gossip or snooping. They were resting up for the evening.

His own behavior today was a good example of waywardness; he was probably having some kind of reaction to the drug withdrawal. He was sure nobody else had that problem.

Only a crazy wayward doctor of the upper class would be nutty enough to even think of going off the pill.

He was getting paranoid. That was from not taking the pill. So maybe the pill was a good thing after all. He would start taking it again soon, and that would manage the paranoia. But then he would lose something that had allowed him to do what he had done today, and he wasn't sure now he wanted to send that new part of himself away.

He acknowledged that a certain recklessness had crept into his personality and once again with a frown he recognized a symptom of this as he closed the locker door and told himself it didn't make any difference, if someone found him out, whatever would be would be, and he was a doctor and would have an excuse and be given another chance anyway.

He removed his one-piece underwear, tossed it in the laundry chute and entered the shower, let the needle spray wash over him for a long time.

He wondered if he had received a massive dose

of radiation that had not been picked up by the instrument, and how soon he would start the uncontrollable vomiting and when his hair would fall out.

"Where have you been all this time? I had that note put up early this morning."

The voice behind him had a crisp resonance and was used to telling people what to do, looking down rather than up, but it was not at the moment unfriendly.

Dr. Noreen stood up and turned around.

He saw Brack standing by the door. Brack was short and stocky and his boss.

"I just got back from the outside," Noreen said. "There are so many new specimens, I kept collecting and collecting."

He felt self-conscious about lying.

"My god, man, you can't do it all in one day. Pace yourself."

Brack had an amazed, somewhat contemptuous look.

"That's what I kept telling myself, but I went on anyway and before I knew it, it was evening."

The little lies slipped out of his mouth as easily as the shower water rolled over his head.

Brack shook his head as if he pitied Noreen.

"Well, I'm glad you're back. I want to go home."

"You waited for me?"

Brack nodded.

"I'm sorry you had to stay late on my account," Noreen said.

"Didn't *have* to. Oh, don't worry about it, it wasn't strictly on your account. I had some work to do myself and my new secretary stayed late with me. I don't mind staying late when she's around. You've seen my new secretary, of course?"

"No."

"You must stop by and take a look. But that's all, just a look."

"Right. I'll be sure and do that. What'd you want with me?"

Noreen was certain it had something to with his expeditions outside, that they were pulling him in. He was too high-ranking for that job in the first place; but he had always been interested in botany, had an advanced degree in the subject, one of many, and was glad that Hayes had chosen him. He did not want to be pulled in.

"I'd like you to come to dinner," Brack said.

Noreen hadn't expected that and felt awkward trying to figure out something to reply.

"Tonight?" he said.

Brack laughed a little friendly laugh.

Noreen wondered if Brack's wife knew about the secretary. It didn't matter, of course. Everyone in upper leadership had a "secretary."

But Brack-type wives liked pretending they were

the only one, and when they got older sometimes caused trouble. Noreen knew. He'd often treated them, when he saw patients. *Double dose, ma'am, that's all. Be a good girl and take your medicine.*

"No, not tonight. Don't be silly. It's too late tonight anyway. A real dinner invitation, at my house, later this week."

"I'm flattered. Of course, I'd be delighted."

He had to say that, what else could he say, but he didn't really want to go. He was tired in the evenings after his trips outside, and now he had something he wanted to do. He wanted to look at his photographs. Beyond that, all he could think about was going back out and getting some more. It was as if the pictures had been placed there, thousands of years ago, and were just waiting all that time for him to come out and find them. He was the inevitable viewer.

Besides, he didn't understand Brack's invitation. Perhaps they weren't going to bring him in. Perhaps they were going to promote him or give him a surprise service award. Either way, it would mean the end of his trips outside. He wasn't sure he could stand life in the dome after being outside. After today.

It was as if the photographs were already speaking to him. As if they were some kind of multiple recording medium and they had an imbedded aural message in addition to the two-dimensional world of the images and he was starting to pick up on these messages as if they were some until-now futile radio signal from outer space.

He wasn't sure a handful of photographs was enough. His brain could absorb hundreds, thousands. What was he missing that he would find in his ancient archive? He had to know.

But Brack said, "I have to warn you—we're not going to talk about business. This will be a strictly social evening. You'll get to meet my beautiful wife for the first time."

"I'd like that."

"And my sister will be there. Do you remember my sister?"

Noreen forced himself to think a moment, then recalled.

"Yes, of course. A lovely child. I remember treating her for something—"

"She's not a child anymore. If fact, she asked me to set this thing up in the first place. She remembers *you* quite well. Of course, it was inevitable that you and I get together socially sooner or later, but Martine made it sooner."

Noreen felt distinctly apprehensive. He was thirty-three years old and so far had escaped marriage and women who were determined to have a certain kind of spouse. He had heard stories of influential men being chased by marriage-obsessed young women, and he could not be bothered by that now that he had been outside the dome, now that his outside investigations were still unfinished.

And he could hardly bear to have this conversation and would not under other circumstances, for instance, with someone other than Brack. He couldn't risk showing lack of interest or boredom, but all he wanted to do was rush home and look at his pictures. They were waiting for him in the locker on the other side of the room. He knew it was true but he could hardly believe it and couldn't wait until he could check and make sure they were still there. It was somewhat exciting to think that his precious cache was just a few feet away from Brack.

If Brack knew they were there and how they got there, he wouldn't be able to resist doing some great harm to Noreen, because keeping others in line was Brack's greatest skill and satisfaction. Brack was a few years younger than Noreen, but already he was much higher in the organization, and he was expected to continue a meteoric rise, perhaps someday becoming President himself. It was wise to be on Brack's good side and ordinarily Noreen's situation now would be wonderful, except for his present extraordinary distraction, and all he could think of to say was, "You know, I already have a steady woman. We've almost made a commitment to each other."

Brack sneered.

"I know about your 'steady woman.' That fat pig from research. I don't know exactly how old you are because I haven't looked at your file in a while, but I suspect you are older than you look. Even so, that woman looks old enough to be your mother."

Noreen hadn't thought of it that way, he just liked being with Beta and they had a wonderful life in bed.

Noreen shrugged.

"Let's make it Thursday," Brack said suddenly. "About eight. My god!"

He was staring at Noreen's naked body, focused on his genitals.

Noreen had turned off the water and stepped out of the stall. He was reaching for one of the thick, executive towels.

Noreen had an athletic frame, slender but rugged, over six feet, with very fair white skin and blond hair and eyebrows, and the lightest shade of blue eyes, the most desirable kind. Brack had blue eyes but they were grayish and flinty and lacked the impression of depth that Noreen's had. Under the pale, almost invisible eyebrows, Noreen's had a three dimensional luminosity like pure skylight.

Brack looked up, embarrassed by the length of time he had spent checking out Noreen's equipment.

"Now I know why Martine's interested. You are amazingly well-hung. Has Martine ever seen you like this?"

Noreen tried not to show his embarrassment.

He shook his head. Then he toweled off while sitting on one of the ceramic benches in the changing room.

"Women have an instinct about these things," Brack said. "Have you had any children?"

"No," Noreen said. "None that I know of."

"Well, you should have. *You and Martine* could have fantastically marvelous children. Have you seen Martine lately?"

"No."

"Well, just wait. You won't believe your eyes."

Brack, having done what he had come for, glanced up at the ceiling for some new inspiration and to change the subject, and then stared across the room at the lockers.

Noreen saw Brack focus in on the open locker door and the barrier suit hanging there.

"Are those your barrieralls?"

"Yes," Noreen said, and he watched Brack walk toward the wall of lockers with his right arm outstretched, as if he intended to remove Noreen's suit. He would wonder at once and ask questions if he saw the bulging storage pocket. But he stopped his hand just short of the suit, as if he had looked at its soiled condition and thought better about touching it.

"My god! This suit is filthy. You can't go around in that. Especially now that we're getting close. Get this thing cleaned. Better still, throw this away and requisition a new one."

Getting close?

Once more he made a gesture as if to grab the suit, then changed his mind, and simply flipped his hand as if turning the whole matter over to Noreen, and, finished with that subject, he glanced at his wrist time.

"Okay," he said, impatient to leave now. "Thursday night then. And get rid of the suit."

He gave Noreen a limp handshake and his hand felt cold and dry.

"I'll take care of it," Noreen said.

He watched Brack open the door and go out into the hall. Before the door closed he heard Brack greeting someone and he caught a glimpse of Brack's secretary waiting there.

Getting close with her too?

CHAPTER

6

He'd been wondering for a long time how to break it off with Beta, but because she was so comfortable to be with and they had fucked so long without getting tired of each other, he never got around to it.

She was sitting on one of the benches under an acacia tree near the front of the Organo Institute, and when he came out she looked up and saw him. As usual, she smiled.

He was glad to see her, but with her wide hips, harlequin glasses, short-cropped practical hairdo and low heeled shoes, she looked dumpy. She was very brainy but you couldn't really tell that just by looking at her, especially with the dinky glasses. It had never bothered him until now, the way she looked on the street. He remembered the smooth skin of her body. There was nothing wrong with her naked and he was glad that maybe only he knew about that. And being very smart was a plus and maybe why they had stayed together so long.

"I saw you come in with your airbike and decided to wait for you," she said, "but it took an awfully long time. Is anything wrong?"

"No, I just had to talk to Brack."

"I'll ask again then. Is anything wrong?"

"No. In fact, everything is quite nice."

"You look tired. What did Brack want? To give you a promotion?" She said it with a little sneer at Brack.

"Something like that. Nothing serious and nothing definite."

"You deserve something, recognition and a promotion," she said. She was always looking out for him, sticking up for him.

"I know," he said.

She was not a fat pig.

They walked across the street, empty at that time of day. The street lamps had already come on. They stepped onto the old gently thumping moving sidewalk that connected the busiest parts of the city.

Noreen felt the familiar old walkway shuffling and groaning under his feet and held Beta's hand, and they both leaned against the railing. Noreen looked up. He could not see the top of the dome which was lost somewhere in the midst of deep night, and a few drops of rain fell against his face. Moisture from the city rose up during the daylight hours and condensed on the hot dome ceiling, then at night cooled and fell back down as rain. Beta took out the umbrella she always carried in her shoulder bag and held it over them.

The air in the dome tonight seemed thick and lacking in oxygen.

"What shall we do tonight?" she said and looked up into his eyes, and it was a joke that she always asked every night.

"Tonight I'm going to bed early," he said. "We'll do *that* this weekend. I'm tired from my work now and I have to get up early in the morning. Very early."

"We'll see," she said. And smiled.

He gave her one quick fuck as soon as they got to his apartment, because he knew he couldn't get out of it, and it felt especially good after the day in the sun, but he knew he had to get rid of her in order to look at his pictures. She of course wanted to spend the night, but he said he couldn't get any sleep that way. As it was, he got rid of her right away, and he didn't get any sleep anyway.

Just before she left she gave him a quick kiss, then held him pressed to her a little longer than necessary, then he kissed her tightly and pulled away with his lips making a familiar smack.

"I think you're working too hard," she said.

"No problem."

"Then what is it?"

"What is what?"

"You're acting different lately."

"Maybe I've stopped taking the drug. Maybe I'm taking it but the dosage is too small."

"Don't be silly. I think you've grown tired of me."

"Ridiculous."

"That's all it could be. I don't think you're pleased with me anymore, anything about me."

"Don't you be silly. What about just now?"

"That's different too. When we first started going together and I forget how long ago that was, we said that if we got tired of it we'd tell each other right away. I remember saying that but I bet you don't."

"I remember."

"No, you don't. But I'm reminding you now. If you're tired of it, for god's sake tell me. Do you want to tell me that now?"

"No. Let's just stop this. Everything's fine. Let's just stop talking things to death. I don't want to have anything to do with this crazy conversation. Everything's the same as it always was."

"I don't think so. You've lost interest in me. It's just that simple. Well, there's a young man at the lab who thinks I'm wonderful and would like to prove something to me and if you drop me I guess I'll let him try, but right now I'm not encouraging him, not encouraging anyone."

He had always told her he would not stop her in

anything she wanted to do and she was always free
(they both were free) to do anything she wanted.
And he wondered if she was trying to tell him she
was getting ready to fool around. Or, worse, already
had, and liked it. But he wasn't ready to break off
with her right now, and he didn't like the idea of
anyone else having her. He was tired of her, maybe,
or just tired of himself, changing inside anyway, and
he needed time to think things out, especially after
today. In some way, he loved her, had always loved
her, and perhaps he should have told her, but he
had always found it difficult to express emotions in
words. It had something to do with being a tight-
lipped, high-level doctor, he told himself.

"What are you saying? No, don't talk like that. I
don't want you seeing anyone else."

He could see her settle down.

"I was hoping you'd say that," she said. "I'm
hoping you mean it. I was always hoping you liked
me enough to get married sometime and have a
child, and I always told myself I would only say
something like that if you brought up the subject,
but now I've said it and you haven't said anything
nice like that yourself, I mean about getting
married and having a baby, certainly not about the
baby part," she said, and he could see small tears in
the corners of her eyes.

"That would be nice," he said, "very nice,"
holding her. "We'll talk about it soon."

"We just did. Talk about it."

"I told you I'm very tired."

"All right, love, I believe you." She pecked him on the cheek, wiped her eyes, and left. He sighed.

He locked the door and got out the pictures and set them down carefully on his dinette table and went through them one by one, then looked at them again. He wanted more. Needed them.

He was too excited to sleep.

There was a picture of a mountain with large boulders in the foreground, that reminded him of the mountain he had climbed today, but this mountain was more distant and larger, and the boulders that filled the foreground were smooth and round, and reminded him of Beta. Except he knew that these boulders were definitely hard and impenetrable, like the rocks he had traversed today whose jagged and sharp edges made him shiver now, and Beta was firm yet cushiony and contained interesting openings he could crawl into and feel the mysteries of flesh and night and the warm wetness of the human body, while the odor of night prowled around him, and he did not want to lose Beta or the photographs. Someday he would have to tell her about the pictures. He would see then how much she loved him. Would she turn him in to the authorities or would she understand—and keep—and enjoy his secret with him?

Or not understand, and yet keep his secret anyway?

These were the twelve photographs that had been waiting for centuries for his eyes to discover. These were the visions that his eyes had never known existed but had always wanted to find.

CHAPTER

7

W
I
L
L
I
A
M

B
O
R
N
E
F
E
L
D

As if taken under duress, the picture is blurred, shaken.

The man is suspended in midair, slammed by a bullet, ready now to fall, already falling. But the arms are extended and the feet still running, in their last human act, like a dog dreaming. The rifle, which this man will never fire again, will drop soon from his left hand.

Whether contrived for effect or captured in some futile real battle, the man in this picture is dead. This is the instant of his sudden death. The moment of death, though not unexpected, has come as a surprise. Consciousness has lasted long enough in a millisecond to realize that youth has ended and there will be no second chance. The light-colored costume will not dance again on this young body.

You can still hear the rifle shot ringing in your ears.

This must be a scene from a small war somewhere. Was it the one that wiped out all living things all those years ago, except the privileged survivors of Fullerton? This is how it ended for some people in those days.

Blessed be Fullerton. Blessed be the protective dome.

CHAPTER

In the morning he was up before daylight because he hadn't slept at all that night, and he knew he would not sleep again soon, especially without the pills. At the dome exit he put on new barrieralls and checked out a different rad detector and the same airbike he had used the day before. The sun was just coming up as he nodded in a friendly way to the guard who had been on duty yesterday, and the guard nodded back in the blunt manner that was typical of his intelligence level. Noreen pushed the idling airbike through the interlock and then outside.

The new suit was pumping fresher oxygen than the one he had worn yesterday. He wondered if the air tank contained anything else they hadn't told him about, some mind altering stimulant, because he felt rested and fit and enthusiastic even though he had not slept or taken the pill. It all might simply be his anticipation at returning to the cave where more photographs waited for him.

In the lifeless open space outside the dome he heard no sound except the putt-putting of the airbike which, recharged, ran smoothly over the rutted path. In the distance somewhat to his left the sun was just rising, like an inflamed eye, and he tried to imagine the dawn of time when small birds awoke at this time of day and began twittering in the few gnarled trees scattered here and there.

He planned to check the cave first, spend only a few hours there, conceal the entrance, and then come back and allot several hours to collecting specimens along the road. In order to have as much time as possible at the cave, he turned the airbike accelerator handle all the way over until it hit the stop, and drove dangerously fast straight ahead. He was skimming the road just a few inches above the dirt and small rocks in order to conserve power and was bouncing roughly around. Soon he saw the top of the mountain rising up and when he looked back the dome had dropped below the curve of the earth.

For a moment it made him happy not to see the dome, where he had always lived, the only place one could live, one was told, the only inhabited place on the planet, and as far as it went he had always been happy, so to speak, or at least not wanting anything, not knowing that he wanted anything.

He thought about flipping up his visor, letting the dry mysterious air blow against his face. Daring it now to do him harm.

But two dark spots had appeared at the end of the road behind him as far away as he could see. They looked like a pair of airbike riders.

As far as he knew, no one was supposed be outside the dome at this time, except an occasional patrol and himself, and he wondered what was going on. He would soon reach the point where yesterday he had turned off the road and gone on to the base of the mountain. He couldn't do that if someone was watching. In fact, he didn't want to draw attention even to the flower fields, which were his own discovery for the time being, and anyone else interested enough to approach him might also decide to search the mountain the way he had done.

The archival vault in the cave belonged to him, who had never owned anything before except what belonged to the dome, and he wanted to keep his new ownership—his new property—a secret until he figured out what to do about it. The cave and the absence of radioactivity reminded him of something he could do now to allay suspicion and

he stopped the airbike and got off and aimed the
rad detector. A quite natural gesture at that point.

From the corner of his eye he watched the distant
airbikes and it seemed to him they weren't moving
now. When they saw him get off and take the
reading, they stopped and were just waiting. But
they were still too far away for him to tell who they
were.

Were they lazy oafs putting in a boring day of
dome watch? Or special police assigned to follow
him?

He couldn't think about that now.

The rad detector had an alarming message. The
readout was juggling numbers in a frenzy and the
audio signal was whistling in the presence of heavy
radiation.

Radiation couldn't jump like that in one day.
Either this detector or yesterday's was defective. If
it was the one yesterday, he had received a lethal
dose, and he would die soon.

He hadn't taken a pill now for several days, and
blood pressure rising and pulse throbbing, he felt
panicky at the concept of his own death, and he
was sweating within the suit, not from the sun.
When he was taking the pill he could think about
anything and it wouldn't bother him.

In the dome, you weren't supposed to think about
your own death or any other aspect of mortality.
The old poet Kafahvey who was supposed to have

lived to be over 130 was extolled, but Noreen knew from his own research that most residents didn't make it that far. The small dark people who did most of the work didn't make it half that far. Noreen suspected the pill affected mortality in direct proportion to the pleasure it gave.

It didn't do anything for radiation sickness.

He got back on the motor bike and drove abruptly off the side of the road away from the mountain into a forest of mesquite higher than his head. It seemed to him that just as he looked back, the other airbikes started up again.

He felt a vague lumpiness in the center of his chest, which was a symptom of what happened to you when you didn't take your medicine. Some kind of stress-related high blood pressure, erratic heartbeat, and breathtaking tachycardia.

He drove about a half mile, stopped, and knelt down by what looked like a small plot of moss. He got out his trowel and was carefully digging around the moss with his back to the roadway, now and then looking over his shoulder, when he saw the airbikes come up and stop at the point on the road he had just left. The two drivers sat on their bikes and watched him. They were short and squat and dark in silhouette, with thick round heads and clumpy black hair. The road bed was higher and they could look down and see everything he was doing. He could hear their airbikes idling. After a while, he separated enough moss, wrapped it in plastic film, and put the wad into his case.

He stood up, wiped his hands on his knees, and looked around.

He waved at the airbike drivers as if he had just seen them. They waved back. He got down on his knees again with the trowel and rooted like a pig. He decided he would take as long doing his job as was necessary to convince them he was a dedicated expert at retrieving botanicals. If they were security people and were just watching him, if they had no order to bring him back, they would watch and get bored and go on.

After about five minutes, he heard the motors rev again and he looked up and he could see they had turned their bikes around and he could hear their engines dying out in the direction of the dome.

He didn't like it. Being watched. They had followed him and might come back. Now he had to be careful.

He couldn't proceed to the cave.

Some other time.

Suddenly, he began to feel tired. Was the final illness starting?

He spent the rest of the day as if it were a normal search for plant life, and he felt all right. He speeded up his collecting and found twice as many plants as he would ordinarily. He put some in his pouch, but he hid most of them near a rock that he could find on his next trip out. That way he could pick up the already-collected plants and spend all day at the cave.

If by then he had not died from radiation poisoning.

He leaned against the rock. In the shade of an ancient mesquite, he got out his micro repair kit and removed the rad detector's back. He studied the circuit diagram on the opened case, then compared it to the circuit board. Almost everyone in the dome was required to take courses in solid state electronics, and in his childhood the subject had obsessed him. It did not take long for him to find and be puzzled by a resistor on the board that did not show on the drawing. This was not unusual because new models often came out with improvements that were not added to the schematic. It was part of the general laziness of a society that had everything worked out. But this resistor offered no improvement; it simply changed the nature of the readout. He clipped one end of the resistor near the board, then pushed it down so the break would not easily be noticed but still would not connect with the board.

He pushed the case back on, looked through the view finder and let the cross hairs rest on the base of a nearby saguaro. He pulled the trigger that ran the instrument's self-check mode. The inertia-speaker gave out a steady chirping sound and the LED read "Okay reference standard." Then he pulled the trigger all the way back. After a low whine the numbers settled quickly into a firm reading with just the last digit shuttling back and forth through three numbers.

He flipped open his visor, and let his back slide along the rock he had been leaning against until he was lying on the ground, laughing and rolling a bit from side to side.

He could feel his vital signs shifting into low gear. Heart pump no longer thrashing, forehead cool.

He had once again quite simply detected normal background radiation, about what you would get in the dome, nothing higher. Whatever the half life of the radiation here was, it had died a long time ago.

Yes!

The detector had been rigged to give incorrectly high readings.

Why?

To discourage interest in the outside world? To maintain the status quo? Yes.

He tore into the back of the meter again and soldered the resistor back in place.

The cave was more important to him than ever now, because whoever had placed the pictures there had done so a long time ago, longer than he could even imagine, before the time of radiation. And now the radiation was gone. He had not only found the pictures, he had learned that it was safe to live without barrieralls outside the dome. And it was also obvious someone did not want to change the status of the dome. Someone did not want any of the dome inhabitants to leave.

He wondered whether he would have known this, whether it would have been important to him, if he had not stopped taking the pills. But then he would also not have the nervous, almost burdensome feeling that had started up again.

It occurred to him that as long as the people of the dome were taking the pill, they probably wouldn't want to leave anyway, so what difference did it make?

He straddled his bike again and drove toward the dome. The sun was on the other side of the mountain now but it was still early afternoon. No one would wonder why a doctor of his rank would be returning at that time of day. No one expected a doctor to do a full day's work.

He felt depressed and frustrated because he had not reached the cave. But it had not been a wasted day. He would return to the cave tomorrow.

The dome was rising up in front of him.

He would look at his pictures tonight. Nothing would stop him from looking at his pictures again.

He turned the throttle all the way over and the bike jerked forward.

He held on.

He would not sleep that night, but it didn't matter, there were things within the frames of the pictures that he hadn't yet noticed, and he would spend all the time it required to decipher them, to find and memorize all their details.

When he looked at the pictures he was traveling to a different time and place. It was a privilege he was sure no one had had in an unimaginable length of time.

"Back a little earlier today?" the guard said, and Noreen detected some kind of impolite insinuation but nothing he could prove.

"Yes," he said, "but a doctor's work is never done." He emphasized the word *doctor* and the guard drew back a little, and probably decided it would be dangerous to be that familiar in the future.

BOOK TWO

A
VAILABLE
LIGHT

CHAPTER

9

He holds this picture in his hands and reads it with his eyes. He never finishes the story it tells, and it asks more questions than it answers. It's a relic, and in the end he can only marvel at its precise and mysterious beauty: geometry, texture, and elusive narrative of lost and humble human life.

In an 8 x 10 contact print, sharp as broken glass, the frame of a door cuts the picture almost in half and is stopped by a horizontal board that butts against the top border.

All this exposed timber is rough-hewn and weathered, its soft parts dissolved by damp air, cold night, and blistering summer, and the swirls that are left move among the saw marks like fingerprints.

Near frame top, a limp white cloth hangs like a narrow wraith from a nail on the upright board. Triangular and washed thin, with one main fold through its center, this communal towel balloons out with a soft tumescence in the form its own nature or inertia dictates, yet is barely as wide as the board.

The overall verticality of the cloth repeats the upright line of the door frame, but has its own overtones in unruly triangles formed by the point of its dangling corner.

His eye rubs against the rough unironed surface of the cloth, but the wraith is too white, as if towels in this poor place had been exchanged in honor of photography.

A series of seventeen overlapping clapboards go from picture top to picture bottom. These boards are not as weathered as the door frame, but they too are unpainted and streaked with rough saw marks.

Along the wall an enameled washpan sits on a shelf on a squared-off but still-jagged piece of worn linoleum, with a pattern imitating small interlocking marble tiles. The pan's surface appears to be covered with one-dimensional gravel and he suspects its overall mid-gray tone represents pale blue.

Inside the room, three table legs jut down below an oilcloth. Because of diminishing perspective each leg has a different length on the paper, although his mind tells him they are all the same. The oilcloth covering the table has a checkered pattern of small, dark and light gray squares that recall the piece of linoleum.

On the table sits a narrow upright object with three transparent parts: a round, opalescent, fluted base, an onion-shaped globe, filled with a clear liquid, and a narrow tube of thin glass bulging near its base and flared at the top. Soot has blackened part of the glass inside the tube, leaving a black accent near the photograph's left edge. Beyond the table, an upright kitchen cabinet seems to shrink from the burned-out glare of an out-of view window.

On its white bench rests a tall fat ceramic jug with a graceful little handle.

The window light scoots across the room, hits the cabinet and the jug, and slides under the table, and out the left hand corner of the picture.

If he continues to stare, other lines and tones appear.

He records, memorizes, and files.

Light emerging from shadow behind the cabinet makes a jagged stairstep design like a saw with seven points. This cuts like an improvised blade into his flesh by way of his eyes.

Lines, tones, shapes, lights, shadows, surfaces— everything locked into place as if for protection, not to be changed or moved or altered in any way by anyone for any reason. Forever, as it were, or a million years, whichever comes first. Like a computer program in an operating system known only to a single human mind.

He studies the design the way he would read a book. Cataloguing and losing track and then starting over. Straining for the secret message.

It's important to memorize all the details. Find the code that proves meaning.

Please—I don't want to guess anymore. I am obsessed and I want to know now.

CHAPTER

10

"What'll we do tonight?" Beta asked, her voice wan and uncertain over the phone.

"Nothing. I have to go to Brack's house," Noreen said. He resented having to explain. He resented his resentment, as if he'd been forced to apologize for something. "For dinner."

"Alone?"

"Yes."

She became very quiet.

She was not happy. She was itching for something.

Well, let her.

He was tired of explaining everything to Beta. That's what happened when you spent all your time with the same person. It'd be good to let it cool off, then come back together later. Maybe it could all be new again.

He'd put her in her place. She needed that. She was acting like a wife. His only secrets from her were the cave and forgoing the medicine, and he felt hemmed in by her. He found himself wanting to hurt her a little just because she was so loyal.

"If we were married, I'd probably be invited," she said.

"Probably. But we're not married."

"Just as well. You're going up in the world and will leave me behind. You'll forget about me."

He knew she wanted him to reassure her, so he just said, "Sure, whatever you say."

He set down the phone and cut off something she hadn't finished saying.

Her damned whining.

He had just dressed in a new white jumpsuit with the eight black stripes of his rank when the tone rang on the door; he got worried now thinking about the photographs spread out on the dining room table.

He was not used to anyone at his door without an appointment and if it was the police, although he had done nothing to arouse suspicions, they would search the house and be proud of themselves when they ran across the photos.

But it was just an aircab Brack had sent over for him, and he told the driver to wait outside until he finished dressing.

He carefully stacked the photographs and placed them deep under his king-size bed.

He checked his appearance in the mirror. For his age he looked pretty good. His height and his fair skin had always conferred special privileges. He had taken his looks for granted. The privilege too. But lately he'd been thinking about how lucky he was, and he even wondered whether his parents, if they were real, whoever they might be, were still alive. It was a casual idea, nothing important, something that had just slipped into his consciousness, and was maybe part of the recent general disorganizing of his personality.

He looked around the living room. He had to find a real hiding place. The cleaning lady was coming tomorrow for her weekly visit. If he didn't think of something tonight he would have to call and delay her. Postponing the visit of a cleaning lady was a risky act and the most obvious way to arouse suspicion and the arrival of a correction squad, because in the dome, where there was no other god, cleanliness and orderliness *were* godliness.

The tiny apartment had no crannies that would be hidden from the maid, but there was one possibility. He stared at the blank wall in the living room across from the couch. It was where he would have liked to hang the photographs so he could gaze at them all the time. But, of course, that was pure fantasy; looking at the photos would always be dirty and secret the way they taught you sex had once been, not something he would ever be able to share with anyone, not even Beta. He remembered Beta with affection now and was sorry he had been mean to her.

But he should have told her: "Remember there are no commitments forever. There are no strings in a relationship when there are no children."

He would tell her that sometime when he wanted to be cruel. He did not know when that would be.

He switched off the lights, locked the door, and squeezed into the aircab. He noticed the velour seats and the smooth ride of the Class Nine motor, and watched the pedestrians on the moving walkway, crowded at first, then none at all near the point where the walkway ended, as they drove quickly to the northern suburbs.

Noreen did not know much about the area. He lived a block or two from the South End in the old crowded cubicles that were stacked like cliff dwellings and he did not often go farther north than the busy central city.

Rarely had he ever entered the wide gate at the high brick wall denoting the exclusive North End. He was always surprised by the open spaces and the moist and fresher-smelling air tinged with the scent of newly mowed grass.

He saw no guards, no other persons.

The small clique of Fullerton's rich and powerful wanted to be left alone and to maintain a low profile. There had to be some punishment for bothering them but no one knew what that was, and no one was about to find out by straying somewhere they didn't belong.

"Do you come this way often?" he asked the driver.

"As much as I can," the dark-haired driver said, at first warily, as if uncertain about talking to a member of dome upper society. "But I've never been lucky enough to go into one of the homes. I'm not in that league."

What he noticed about Brack's apartment was its size, the many rooms, all large, so large you could count paces to go from one end to the other, and the blank rectangles that were the walls. He kept thinking what a wonderful gallery it would make. You could hang hundreds of pictures on those empty walls.

Somehow he had expected the rich and powerful to have an exemption with regard to the prohibition against visual art. He had been wrong.

In spite of his rank it was the first time he had been in a house at that end of town and he realized now that some people lived on a grand scale even in the confinement of the dome. A high brick wall separated the grounds from an elegant curving street that meandered before the banks of apartments with thick green grass and an underwater sprinkler system that meant they did not rely on the daily cycles of artificial rain. *Recycling of condensate and controlled precipitation*, it was called in *The Manual of Dome Life*.

No one who did not belong was allowed here. He was not surprised.

As soon as Noreen arrived, Brack and his wife, Betty, introduced him to Brack's sister Martine, who bowed shyly and didn't say much. Betty seemed even older than he had expected, though you couldn't be sure about anyone's age, because you couldn't be sure how many times face and body parts had been lifted and polished. He had done his share of nip and tuck.

All through dinner Martine stared shamelessly at Noreen.

And he could hardly keep his eyes off her. She was wearing a two-piece undergarment short in all directions, tight enough to exaggerate her cleavage, all covered by a gossamer slip with a thin silk belt at her narrow waist. She was not particularly tall, but she was so slender and had such long straight legs that she looked tall enough. She had deep brown eyes set in a perfect oval face and her long, brown hair was so dark it almost looked black when it was in shadow. Her skin was pure and smooth with a soft olive glow, and she was very young with red pouty lips. Everything about her seemed fresh and new. No part of *her* body had been repaired, everything about her was state-of-the-art, factory fresh.

He had not seen such perfect skin since his days as a resident. Then he had dissected the body of a young woman so recently dead she was almost still warm. She was so perfect and had such beautiful skin that he at once fell in love with her, or with what she had been, and felt such a pang at the thought of her death that he wasn't sure he could go on without a larger dose of tranquilizer.

Now it was as if the dead girl had not died, and time had stopped, and he was looking at her.

When they had finished the main course and the dessert with the most banal chitchat led by Mrs. Brack, the dark-skinned maid came in and placed a round gold foil-wrapped disc by each coffee cup and left the room.

"A dinner mint," Brack said in a tone of voice deliberately low-key.

Noreen knew it was no ordinary mint, and he wondered how he could politely avoid eating it. He did not want anything to change his state of mind or alter his plans for the morning. Then he said, "If it's all right, I'd like to save mine and have it later," and he reached for it and placed it in his upper right breast pocket, carefully, as if it were a treasure, and thoughtfully smoothed out the flap.

"Why, of course," Brack said. Noreen detected a slight double-take.

"Are those doctor's orders?" Mrs. Brack said, smirking, and she picked up her mint and let it disappear somewhere in her gown.

Martine spoke up suddenly then, and her voice was strong and clear and forthright, and Noreen liked its melody, although there was a little hint of the tyrant in its overtones.

"I think that's a wonderful idea. I'll have mine later too. Perhaps Dr. Noreen and I can have ours together." She snickered then and Noreen wondered about her age. Nineteen or twenty at the most.

Brack nodded, got up and glanced at his wife, and she got up too.

"Perhaps you'd like to see the house, Noreen," he said.

"I'll be glad to show him," Martine said, and she got up and shooed her brother and sister-in-law away.

They acted surprised, then put on a show of slinking away.

Noreen could hear Brack say, "We know when we're not wanted. All right, Noreen, you're on your own."

Noreen was always disgusted by cute behavior. It didn't seem to belong to dome life. But he said nothing.

Who was he now to bother with proprieties?

Martine came around the table and stopped in front of Noreen. Her hips were at his eye level.

W
I
L
L
I
A
M

B
O
R
N
E
F
E
L
D

He looked up.

She stared for a long time into his eyes. It was a young person's idea of an important gesture.

Then she grabbed his hand, said, "Come with me," and led him into the adjoining parlor. "I'll show you the house later, if you like, but first let's get acquainted."

CHAPTER

11

WILLIAM BORNEFELD

The room had several ethereal-looking chairs and a matching couch, and a red brick floor with a low fountain in the center. The fountain was not high enough to count as a graphic symbol, though it was picturesque, and it flowed constantly with a gurgling, almost living sound.

She pushed Noreen down on one end of the couch and sat in the nearby chair and leaned forward, perhaps so that he had to look down on her breasts.

"Do you remember when we first met?" she asked. "I mean the exact moment?"

He didn't remember anything like that exactly.

"I remember meeting you. You must've been thirteen years old," he said.

"Shame! I was more like eleven."

"I treated you for—what—a cold?"

"I had a sore throat."

"Aw, yes, now I remember—" He didn't, but he wanted her to enjoy whatever it was she was getting at. And he was looking at the soft pushed-out curve of her breasts, and remembering the ease with which a sharp scalpel had cut through similar flesh, and the pus oozing slightly from the wound.

"I was sitting in your examining chair, and you turned around to get something, a mirror or one of those tongue depressors—and when you turned back you brushed my leg with the side of your trousers. Even though I wasn't feeling well I was admiring your face—you were very handsome in those days. Then you made me stick out my tongue and you grabbed it with a cloth and then stuck something warm and metallic into my mouth and you leaned very close so I smelled your skin and your breath. You were very antiseptic but underneath I got a whiff of—what was it—sweat— your identity. You must have thought I was just a kid squirming around in the chair, but all that touching and so forth was causing me to have my first orgasm in spite of my sore throat and I was having it right then and there in front of you and you never knew."

"What makes you think I didn't know? And that it was an accident?"

She sat back. Her jaw dropped a little. She hadn't expected him to say that. Then she decided he was kidding her and she laughed and lightly brushed the side of his face with a mock slap.

"You didn't," she said. "You didn't even guess."

"Are you sure?"

"Did you?"

"No, but I wish I had."

"Oh? Why?"

He was looking at her so hard, he almost didn't hear the question. It was not just the corpse she reminded him of, it was the woman in the picture. She was the woman who was nude in the picture he had found in the side of the mountain. It was as if he had actually crawled into the picture and she had put on some clothes and they had gone into another room to talk.

"What was the question?"

"I said why?"

"Oh, I would have prescribed some medicine for you to slow down your obvious sexual maturity."

"How horrible! Why do that?"

"So you could finish your schooling without being nervous."

"You mean without being nervous around you."

"Whatever."

"You mean so you could save me for yourself?"

"That isn't what I had in mind but there are

worse notions. I was worried about you." He was lying and he couldn't help it. He was letting her pull him into whatever it was *she* had in mind.

"Don't worry. I was saving myself for you. Are you impressed?" she said.

He was now tired of waiting for her to get to the point, tired of her reminding him of the girl he had loved too late. He wanted to return to his apartment, where he had things to do, to look at, where he would not have to worry about the swelling between his legs that looking at and talking to her had started.

"Very. So what happens now?"

He glanced around the room, wondered about Brack and his wife.

"Not what you think," she said. "Certainly nothing here."

"Good," he said, "I guess now we forget about our strange but brief past and go about our business."

For a moment he considered grabbing her and shoving himself into her on the couch, then rolling her over the floor into the fountain, because that's what she wanted, and she was being coy about it, every boy in her school must have had her at least once, and now she was teasing an elder. But he had better sense than that, maybe there was something more to this than he was seeing, maybe Brack was testing him, and in that case caution was the only way to go.

"I hear you've been leaving the dome," she said.

"Yes," he said, glad to change the subject. But not sure that was the subject he wanted to talk about.

"Isn't that dangerous?"

"Not really."

"But with all that radiation—aren't you afraid of doing something harmful—I mean to yourself, to your reproductive organs?"

The subject hadn't changed at all.

"No," he said. "Not in any way. Our protective gear is thoroughly reliable. I rely completely on our equipment."

He was thinking now of the airbike.

"I can't agree," she said. "I think it's very brave of you to risk yourself like that. And reckless. But if I were your wife I wouldn't let you do it."

"Let's change the subject."

He could see her start to pout at his abruptness, then let the pose drop.

"All right, tell me something else about yourself. Where do you live?" she said.

"In a small old apartment on the other side of town."

"How interesting."

"Not really. I'm sure you would find it disgusting. After what you're used to." He waved his arm slightly at the room, the apartment.

"I doubt it. Places don't matter. It's what you do in them that matters."

She paused so he would be sure she had intended a double meaning.

"My place is so small there's not much you can do in it."

"I doubt that. I'd like to see your apartment some time. Is that where you'll have your after-dinner mint?"

"Probably."

"And will you be alone?"

"Yes."

"Shouldn't we have the mints together, meeting like this again after all those years?"

"Is this another dinner invitation?"

"No."

"So?"

"Whenever you decide to have the mint call me and I'll come right over and you can show me your apartment and then we'll have them together."

"All right. Whatever you say. Now I have to get some sleep. I have to be ready to leave the dome by sunrise."

Suddenly she leaned over and lightly kissed him on the cheek. She was wearing a perfume that reminded him of the flower field and for a moment he felt that she had surrounded him with her body warmth.

"Of course," she said, and she smiled a little smile to herself.

CHAPTER 1²

W
I
L
L
I
A
M

B
O
R
N
E
F
E
L
D

She's a muscular white woman with small hairs on her legs. It's high noon and she's lying on a long black cloth spread on the ground and the sun falls straight down on her nude body.

Her back is arched, somewhat uncomfortably, as in an exercise, and her arms are raised so she can cover her eyes with her left forearm, to protect her vision from the glare, or to half-conceal her identity.

The muscular upward thrust of her back has accentuated the cleft between her breasts, and this muscular separation continues down below her rib cage to just above her belly button. The breasts are wide and full with large broad dark spots around the nipples and, even in that pose, push up from her body like upturned champagne goblets. A fold of skin has produced a crease where her left leg, which has been pulled up to the rump, meets her wide triangle of brushy pubic hair. The belly lies flat and low and dips down under the hip bone. Barely visible under the protective forearm, the slightly parted thin lips and dimpled chin and the general ruggedness suggest a masculinity, but even in this clinical light and artificial pose her crotch has an inviting, definitely female architecture. Her right underarm, which he can almost reach out and touch, has not been shaved, and the pubic hair and this grassy patch and the black stretch of cloth that separates her from the ground are the only notable black areas in the sunlit photo except for one other spot and that is the shadow that fills a dome-shaped opening near the top of the picture. White ashes spill out from it.

The entire effect is three-dimensional, palpable, and alive, even though no obvious pictorial framing exists within the borders, and very little overlapping suggests depth.

He yearns to penetrate her, to feel the soft expanse of that abdomen against his, to feel the rough edges of the hair brush against his skin, to slip inside. He can almost feel himself now, trying not to touch anything but now and then feeling the inevitable excruciating tip of something.

Now this was too much.

Maybe he should start taking the pill again. Fill up the gaps that seemed to have appeared in his brain. The pill, not pictures, oiled life in the dome. Let you accept the long stretches of what now seemed like tedium and that you relieved only by putting your prick into a vagina as often as possible.

But isn't that what he was thinking about when he looked at this picture? He wanted to fuck this woman, because she was there, exposed to him for that purpose, and because she looked like the girl he'd fallen in love with during the autopsy and he could never have, because she was dead, and not only was dead, he had dissected her.

Yet, she was this same woman, and she had survived; she was like this, alive somewhere, now and forever, and waiting for him. It was inconceivable that something so palpable, someone so definite, could not still be alive.

After the moment—the taking of the picture—she had sat up and placed her feet so she could raise herself up, and then brush the dust off her rear, and, now that the picture was over, for a moment get lost within her self, and bend over and pick up the black cloth and shake it out in the high clear air, and then wrap it around herself so she could turn to whoever was on this side of the picture, the photographer's side, which is the same side as the viewer's side, and she would say something about the sun, or ask if it had looked all right.

And he would look up from what he was doing and back at her and say yes, everything was fine, yes, yes yes yes yes yes.

CHAPTER

1³

The cab drove away behind him and he staggered up the front steps like a drunkard. He glanced at wrist time. After midnight. He felt like flopping on the bed. He wasn't awake enough for anything else.

But he found a screwdriver and started removing paint-covered screws he had noticed under the large wall panel across from his couch. When the bottom screws were out, he could lift one corner of the panel away from the wall and stick his hand underneath far enough to know that he could hide the pictures there. The surface of the wall underneath his hand surprised him with its smoothness; it felt like glass or marble. But it was in shadow and the panel had not been pulled out far enough for him to see what was underneath. He wanted to take a good look at it, and he would do so soon but he was too tired now. He placed the photographs in a large envelope and slipped the envelope behind the panel and then he reinserted the screws and twisted them down tight. The heads of the screws had been painted over with the white wall paint and he had barely scratched into the paint with his screwdriver. He gently brushed the paint over the screws with his fingers and decided it looked like they had never been touched.

Now try and get some sleep. He was going outside the dome again at first light, and this time nothing was going to stop him from returning to the cave. He needed more pictures. The cave was filled with photographs and they were all his and he wanted them now.

CHAPTER 1⁴

But the next morning another guard was on duty and when he saw Noreen moving toward the exit, he called out, shaking his head:

"Not today!"

"What?"

"I'm instructed to tell you not to leave the dome today."

"That's ridiculous. I have a job to do. Whose instructions?"

"I don't know. Just higher-ups. Here's the memo."

He held up an official-looking paper.

Noreen felt his face get red. He turned his back to the guard. He didn't want the guard to see him like that. No one got angry in public in the dome.

He left the bike in the center of the aisle and walked away.

"Hey," the guard called to him. "You're supposed to put your airbike back in the storage room."

"Put it back yourself!" Noreen said without looking back. He was a doctor and he was pulling rank.

CHAPTER

1⁵

But in the basement hallway he leaned against a post, unable to control his anger. He was shaking and his face felt about to burst. He knew that was his blood pressing against his arteries and that it didn't know what it was supposed to do without the pill.

A young doctor from Noreen's floor passed by and had a frightened look and came over cautiously.

"Are you all right, Doctor Noreen?"

"I'm all right. Just a touch of radiation sickness. Please continue on your business."

The young man was glad to go on.

Trembling, Noreen straightened up. A shower would help. He entered the locker room, removed his barrieralls and let hot shower needles shoot at his body. He didn't know anything could bother him this much. He was still shaking. He had to calm down so he would be fit to talk to Brack. They had no right to deny him the chance to do his work. Brack would know what was going on. Whatever it was it had to do with Brack.

He should have taken a sedative, but he grabbed a mild holo drink from a dispenser and let it cool and numb his insides. The effect was helpful; he didn't feel like he was exploding anymore, and it would last about a half hour, long enough to see Brack.

Brack's office was on the upper floor. It had a picture window and a balcony. You could look out over the green-plant and twisted-iron vista of the city and almost touch the bare electrodes used for the stormy light displays.

"I've been expecting you," Brack said without getting up from his desk. "Sit down."

"Then tell me what's going on."

Noreen sat down and the outside glare bounced into his eyes, so that Brack was a hazy silhouette.

"You're too important to risk your butt outside," Brack said. "I want you to work inside for a while. I'm thinking about your future, even if you aren't."

"What?"

"Yes."

"Why?"

"Guess. I'm a nice guy."

"That's very kind of you. But it's embarrassing to be stopped at the gate by a guard. Isn't it important for a man to be able to finish work he's started?"

"I agree—and you'll be able to finish—I too think a man's dignity of purpose, or whatever, is extremely important. And I'm sorry about not telling you first myself, but I knew you'd leave early, perhaps before I got here, and I had a little hangover, I'm sure you can imagine why, so I just sent word to the guard station. But for the moment—and under the circumstances—Martine's very worried about your going outside and I told her that I'd look out for you."

"Martine?"

"Yes—Martine. She's taken, shall we say, an interest in you. I think it's your nicely muscled physique and your truly remarkable blue eyes, which she chatters about all the time. There aren't any *really* blue-eyed children, well, not that blue-eyed, in the Brack family, and I'm not sure you're exactly who I would pick for a brother-in-law, but as long as you're what Martine wants, I'm a hundred percent behind her—and you—of course. You don't mind being Martine's protégé, do you?"

"Martine wants—?"

Brack nodded.

Noreen stood up and paced back and forth, shaking his head in disbelief.

"I'm not marrying your sister. I just met her. And I'm not interested in getting married. My work is too important, and, oh yes, I appreciate the dinner invitation, thank you. I had a very nice time and your sister is lovely, but—"

"What Martine wants she usually gets."

"With your help, of course."

"Of course. Well, think about it. I'm sure you'll be hearing from my sister. In the meantime, I've got some new assignments for you. In the event you do come into the family you'll want to have some good social connections so you won't embarrass us—or I should say so we can all be proud of you. I believe that can best be accomplished if you start seeing patients again."

"I don't believe this. No."

"Oh yes."

"But I haven't seen patients on a regular basis in years. I'm strictly a researcher now. And I like it that way. Besides, seeing patients at my rank now would be a step backward."

"Doesn't matter. May be a plus. Nice to have a little intellectual background. And these won't be ordinary patients. No, *au contraire*, you'll be stepping up in the dome world. I want you to become personal physician to some of the dome leaders. I'm setting you up with social connections. In case, somehow, you enter the family. You should be flattered. Only the most trusted and responsible and best-connected physicians ever get this opportunity."

"I'll think about it."

"Good. There. You've had time to think about it. Now I'll tell you about your first house call."

"I accept only if I'm allowed to finish my work outside. Soon."

"Oh, you'll be allowed. Soon. After you've had sex with Martine a few times I'm sure she'll let you do anything you want. And after you're married, well, I'd keep an eye on her if I were you. Although maybe not, I've seen you in the shower and I think you'll do all right even with someone as nubile as my sister. Now the first thing I'm going to want you to do is visit Kafahvey in his home and make him feel comfortable with whatever elixir you've got."

"I have no—elixirs. Kafahvey—the poet?"

"The one. I knew you'd be impressed."

"But I thought he was dead. He must be a hundred and ninety years old."

"More or less. And very much alive. But you can judge for yourself. One of the dirty secrets of the upper class. You'll be finding out a lot of things like that and as one of us you'll be expected to keep the secrets. Can I count on you? To keep the secrets? Of course I can. You will keep the secrets, won't you?"

"I didn't know there were any secrets."

"Come now—surely you aren't that naïve. This is the real world."

"I've always been open and aboveboard," Noreen said, "but I think I can learn to keep secrets for some higher good."

An image of the cave in the rocky mountainside flashed into his brain. It had taken on a mythic quality of a dream in his mind. It was a real secret, a monumental one, the only secret he had ever had, and he was going to keep it to himself, no matter what happened.

Brack smiled at him and said, "Congratulations!"

CHAPTER

16

The cleaning woman had already come and gone. He flopped down on the made-up bed without taking off his clothes. When he awoke it was almost dark. He was sweating and had a fever.

Beta was leaning over him taking his pulse. He was startled at the sight of her so suddenly close and he was frightened that anyone could come in at any time and surprise him.

"I'm going to take your blood pressure now," she said and she snapped a cuff around his right arm. "Oh my! What's going on? You're two hundred over a hundred and ten."

He mumbled something, didn't care.

She looked then for his pillbox in the bedside table and couldn't find it.

"Where are your pills?"

"Don't know."

"Don't know!"

She looked some more.

"What dosage have you been taking?"

He didn't answer.

"How much did you take today?"

She stopped searching and faced him.

"You did take one today?"

He shook his head.

"None. I've stopped taking them."

"That's crazy!"

"I felt wonderful."

"Well, you're not feeling so wonderful now."

She stared at him for a moment with mixed fear and pity, then reached into her belt pouch and removed a pill bottle. She took out one tablet, set it on the table, and went away. She came back with a glass of water and shoved it and the pill toward him.

"Sit up. Take one of mine."

She had such a concerned look and he was so worried about himself that he sat up and swallowed the pill and downed all the water.

"I'll leave the bottle. You'd better have another one in a little while and then take it easy. I'll sit with you."

He nodded; already he could feel the drug seeping into the corners of his body, and a little fog

covering his thoughts. He was very sleepy and he
lay back down.

When he awoke Beta was sitting there, watching
him, and he had stopped sweating. Under his back
the mattress was still wet, and when he sat up he
could feel the dampness evaporating. The cool spot
felt good.

He felt better, but not as good as he'd felt the last
few days. It was as if he'd lost himself. After a while
he thought again about the photographs, as if for
the first time. He wondered if, like the fever, he had
lost them too, if they had ever been real, or if he
had just dreamed them.

He got up and staggered around looking for his
screwdriver, and Beta got up and tried to steady
him.

"What are you doing now? Get back in bed."

"I'm looking for my screwdriver."

"You're delirious. Take another pill."

"No, really, I'm all right," he said and he found
his screwdriver and carried it into the living room
and squatted in a lump on the floor in front of the
large wall panel.

As he bent forward over the baseboard, Beta said,
"Really. Please get in bed."

"No, I'm all right. Look at this," he said and he
began to remove the screws from below the panel.

As he worked, she could only see his back, and
he was alert enough to know that what he was

doing looked crazy. He could feel her being patient behind and over him and wondering what he was doing. But he removed the screws just as he had done the night before and pulled the corner of the panel outward. He saw the edge of the envelope drop down to the floor but most of it was still hidden behind the panel. He inserted his hand, noting once again the exceptional smoothness of the wall under the panel, and withdrew the envelope. It occurred to him that if someone had searched his house, they could have found the envelope, removed the pictures and simply replaced the empty envelope. Quickly he lifted the flap and looked in. They were all there. He turned, swiveling around on his rump, and faced Beta.

"Can you keep a secret?" he said. He felt drunk.

"That depends. What are we talking about?"

He got up and carried the envelope into the kitchen and placed it on the table.

"I mean a really big secret. Something that would have me in your wretched power forever."

He was telling her about the pictures now because he had to see them. The pill had done something to his mind and he couldn't wait until she was gone. At least that's what he was thinking. He knew it was a crazy thought. Under ordinary circumstances he would never have acted that way. Perhaps there really was radiation outside the dome, a kind that was not detectable by the rad machine, and he was now succumbing to its first symptoms.

"I don't want to have you in my power. I love you. I just want to be with you forever."

"Speaking of forever then look at this. This is about as much forever as we'll ever get."

With a flourish he slid the pictures quickly out of the envelope and spread them face up on the table.

She didn't move. She stared at them from the other side of the table.

A lamp with a wide round shade hung down from a cord over the table. It was as if the lamp had been put there to shine on the photographs.

"I wish you hadn't done that," she said.

"No, just look at this. Can you believe your eyes?"

"I see nothing," she said. "Put them away."

"Come around. So you can look into the frame. What do you see?"

"I see the flat surface of the table with sheets of paper on it. There is nothing on the paper."

"No, look."

At first he got what she was trying to do. Then he didn't get it. He could see the pictures and for a second he wondered if she was telling the truth. Maybe the pictures weren't there and he was simply hallucinating. But then he really got it. He knew she was just trying to protect him and that she would go on protecting him as long as she thought she loved him. It was too bad that at the moment he liked the pictures more than he liked her.

"Really, I don't see anything. I'll testify in court to that."

"But there's another world here. You can almost touch it. Don't you feel like climbing inside and exploring a different world, going back in time? This *is* time, Beta, stopped for a millennium, just waiting for us to go back to it."

She stepped back, away from the table, and she was looking just at his face.

He could see she felt compelled to give a speech. To go on record.

"You can count on me not to turn you in, to deny that this ever happened. But based on your agitated condition lately, I can see why our forefathers were wise in not wanting us to use our eyes in ways that would irritate us. You're in bad shape and, now I know the reason, I don't feel guilty about it. It wasn't my fault at all. You brought it all on yourself. You've done something, I don't know what, and I don't want to know, that had nothing to do with me—with us. And I think I'd better go—you need rest—you're better now but you need to sleep some more and get over whatever's been bothering you, and then rethink what you're doing. And when I'm gone, I think you should tear that stuff up, whatever it is, and then burn and forget about it.

If you can't think about us, think about your own future."

"I am—thinking—" he said, reluctantly looking up, "and I'm rested and relaxed now and I know exactly what I'm doing and what I have to do and I'm getting a big erection for you and you know what that means we have to do."

She hesitated, then she shook her head, and started to gather up her things.

"No. That wouldn't be right tonight. I'm not sure I can handle all this, but if you insist I'll jack you off and call it therapy. I'm a doctor too, you know."

His upper lip curled higher, and he could see her recoil slightly at his obvious contempt.

"Forget it then. Maybe I do just need some time alone."

"I'm leaving," she said. She had a sad face that seemed rounder than usual and she had slumped over a bit. He had never seen her look like this before. She looked old, older than she was. He had offered to fuck her for charity's sake, and to protect himself, and because something about revealing the secret had made him tumid, and now he just felt sorry for her. For turning him down, and the pictures.

"If you like, I'll take that stuff and get rid of it for you. I'll do that for you," she said.

He shook his head.

"I offered."

"You don't know what it means to me."

"Never will."

"An impasse."

"Then take another pill. Get yourself back where you were. I'll call you in the morning."

He watched her back as she went into the living room, past the loosened panel and then out the door.

"Not a bad idea," he said to himself, and he went into the bedroom and took another pill.

CHAPTER

1⁷

He noticed the dinner mint lying on the table next to the glass, and wondered what Beta had thought about that. If she had asked he would have told her he planned to share it with her. Then he looked down and saw that he not only had a large erection from the sudden ingestion of the drug but he had a truly priapic condition that wouldn't easily go away.

He took off his pants so that he could move around more easily and waddled back into the living room and flopped on the couch with his legs spread apart and stared dumbly at his large projection, which was framed nicely by the panel, out of focus, on the opposite wall.

He wondered what Martine was doing.

As he stared across the room, he couldn't decide

whether to submit to the ignominy of masturbating or removing all the screws from the panel and he knew vaguely that he wasn't quite himself or thinking clearly, when the phone rang.

He was trying to decide whether to answer it when it stopped. It was probably Beta checking up on him and he wondered if she would turn him in. He didn't care right now.

Right away the phone began to ring again, and he decided to hell with her, he wasn't going to answer, but after a while he got tired of listening to its harsh electronic trill and he picked it up.

"I said I would call," she said, and it wasn't Beta. It was Martine.

He mumbled something.

"What are you doing?"

"Just sitting around. Being very unhappy with you. I had planned to go outside the dome today, but thanks to you I didn't get the chance."

"I'm sorry."

He could tell from her tone she didn't give a damn, that she had just learned to say things like that to get something for herself.

"You should be," he said.

"Perhaps I should come over. Make it up to you."

She sounded worried. That didn't seem like her. But maybe he'd misjudged her. Maybe she really was sorry. No, she wasn't sorry. He just wanted to believe her because he had a big erection.

"No."

"Why not?"

"I'm indisposed."

"Even more reason."

He could feel her starting to hang up. Getting ready to leave her house. He didn't want her showing up at his door. Not tonight. In spite of the erection.

"No, I mean that. You wouldn't like it here. Besides, you don't know where I live and I'm not giving you my address."

"Don't be silly. Hidalgo Street. I'm leaving now."

She had hung up.

He rose, put on a loose-fitting robe, and turned out the lights in the kitchen. If she showed up, he'd give her something to think about. He pressed down on his erection to push it out of the way, but it wouldn't stay down. He loosened the robe so more cloth draped down from his waist.

She understood his problem the instant he opened the door. For a moment she pretended not to notice.

Then she grabbed his shoulders and pressed her firm young body so hard against him that the pressure on his unyielding penis hurt. She felt very warm and supple and she thrashed around against his chest, and then she grabbed his hand and she said, "I'll bet the bedroom's in here."

As he followed her he looked down, and saw the screws lying on the floor near the baseboard.

CHAPTER

18

The first thing she did was set him down on the edge of the bed and kneel between his legs. When she was finished she didn't swallow, she just glanced at him as if to make sure he was still there, then she spit it out in her cupped hand and lay down on her back in the middle of the bed, pulled up her legs and began rubbing the stuff in her hands into her crotch.

"I don't want to lose any of it," she said, then she wiggled her butt and pulled him onto herself and guided him in. It was like slipping into an endless pool of motor oil. He felt himself shiver as if his own body were going to turn inside out and then he touched bottom.

He was hard and stiff, exactly what she wanted. He had never been fucked this way before. Her slender body was in constant motion, now under him, then on top, constantly slipping around trying to find some more gratifying angle and stopping now and then at just the right moment for an excruciating pause. Then, when he thought he was going to wear out, she pulled away and rolled over and let out a big sigh.

"It's more than I could have asked for. More than I ever dreamed," she said.

And she fell asleep. He sat and looked at her. He had never seen a more beautiful woman. She looked exactly like the shadowy picture of the naked woman in the photo. He almost believed he had crawled through the picture plane and was in the photo now. He wanted to go into the kitchen and get the picture and hold it in his hand while he sat on the bed and looked at her and the picture at the same time.

When she awoke she smiled and he was touched by the childish look of happiness and contentment on her face. When she rolled over and saw the dinner mint her smile broadened and she said, "I almost forgot. I brought my mint too. Shall we have them now?"

She removed another gold-foil wrapped mint from her waist belt lying with her gown on the floor and placed the wafer next to the one on the night stand.

"I don't think so. I'm almost worn out now."

She rolled over and kissed the tip of his penis. He could feel her warmth and her long hair against his waist.

"No way," she said. "You're remarkable, and now I'm really looking at you for the first time." She wiggled against him a little and he could feel a twitchy hardening start up all over again. "I'm counting on you."

"The next time you come over."

"Tomorrow you mean?"

"The next time whenever that is."

"Tomorrow," she said. "But I should go now. I don't want you to get too used to me, to take me for granted."

"No way."

"But I can't go without one more time."

"You're insatiable," he said.

"And you're not. I'll bet you've done this a lot."

"Not really."

"How many?"

"We'll discuss that some other time. And what about yourself?"

"I'm a virgin."

"True? No, of course not. I would have known."

"Tomorrow. I'll tell you for sure. Now—send me home properly."

She sat up, grabbed him and, kissing, they rolled over until he was on top of her.

When they had finished this time she clamped her legs around his back and pushed her pelvis tight as she could against him. He could feel himself deflating and ready to slip out but she wouldn't let go.

"I'm going to hold you tight like this until I'm sure none of it will ooze out of me," she said. "I don't want to lose a drop. I want to make sure you've impregnated me."

He shook his head, and waited.

CHAPTER

19

WILLIAM

BORNEFELD

When the cab arrived, he ran with Martine down the steep front steps and could feel the warm rain against his face falling from the dome ceiling. And saw the first flash of artificial lightning from that night's summer storm simulation. In the glare he thought he noticed someone standing in the doorway across the street, but they had reached the open door of the cab and instead of jumping in Martine turned and grabbed him and gave him a lingering kiss.

"Darling, you've made me very happy. More than you know. Aren't you glad I'm not a little girl anymore? You do love me, don't you?"

"Yes."

"You're the love of my life. My one and only love. My first real love."

"Good," he said and pushed her into the back seat because he was getting wet. "Amsterdam 65," he told the driver, and closed the door. He could see her looking back at him through the rain-beaded back window as the cab drove off.

The lightning display had started in earnest now, hissing and sparking, and then the flash igniting, and fulminating, and in the distance mock thunder like boards dropping. Already the giant sparks had attempted to light themselves enough that he could smell the freshly generated ions, and he knew then it was midnight. He felt remarkably well and fit and amazed by this young woman.

He should have turned and gone back in out of the rain but he just stood still gaping at the empty street where her cab had been.

"Is this what you mean when you said you'd be all right?" he heard someone say.

Beta was crossing the street now from her hiding place in the doorway and in her light-colored raincoat cinched in at the waist she was a startling apparition. *Strange, she was not carrying her umbrella.* His brain had gone numb and all he wanted to do was run back in and crawl into bed alone, start over in the morning.

He could hear himself stuttering as if someone else were talking for him.

"Beta...Beta...what are you doing here?"

From a distance he marveled at the stupidity of his clichéd speech. But there was nothing else to say in that situation. It was a cliché anyway. His once tightly controlled life had become a pointless, stupid joke in a few days, and he had no control over it.

Beta said, "I felt bad about leaving that way. I decided I should come back and keep an eye on you. I was wrong. Who is she?"

"Brack's sister."

"Oh, so that's what it was all along?"

"No. It's not like that at all," he said.

"You should have told me right away. You really were tired of me and you wanted someone younger. You didn't have the guts to play it straight."

"Not like that at all."

"To hell with you, Noreen." She gave him a final look that was mostly all sneer and turned and marched away. He saw her climb the escalier that led up to the moving walkway and step onto it with a little surge forward; then after she had planted her feet squarely on the platform he watched her back move away, alone and small, swallowed up by night

Interesting—that would make a good photograph. He was beginning to think of life now in terms of photographs that he might find or photographs that he might make. He wondered what it would be like. Swallowing the pill again hadn't changed his ability to think at all, had just lowered his blood pressure and raised his prick and pasted a little dullness overall, but he could deal with it.

Too bad about Beta. He always liked Beta. It would have been better if she hadn't seen Martine. Beta was really mad now and he had stupidly revealed his secret to her. He wondered if and when she would turn him in.

It had almost stopped raining, just a few drops here and there, and the light show was running down, sputtering out. The air was as refreshed as it was going to get that night. In the distance there was just a little muffled clattering of dropped boards.

CHAPTER

2º

A dim light from a man-made device was flickering in the room Noreen had just entered and gray daylight seeped in from the gauze-curtained window.

The honored, most-revered poet Kafahvey, who was sometimes referred to as the father of the dome, squatted in the middle of a large rumpled bed with his legs out of sight. He looked like a wrinkled hard-boiled egg that had been peeled and the broken shell parts scattered around on the bed. In this case, the pieces of shell were wavy sheets of paper smeared with watercolor paint, something Noreen had never seen before. He had also never seen anyone this old or this pale and white. Kafahvey seemed to merge with the sheet that had been loosely thrown around his shoulders and gathered in front. He looked dead.

Two hard but attractive young women dressed in nurses' costumes, oddly, with spiked heels, huddled nervously near the window, and nodded for Noreen to approach the bed.

The old man's eyes were closed and if he was breathing Noreen couldn't see it; there was no obvious rise and fall of the chest.

"I'm your new doctor," Noreen said softly, and waited beside the bed.

After a while the patient's right eye slowly opened and Noreen saw that it was covered with a thick cataract, adding to the overall white effect.

The hulking figure mumbled something that Noreen couldn't make out, so he leaned closer to the mound of flesh's puffy porcelain-like face, and he was revolted by a faint acrid stink.

He reminded himself that he was a doctor and when you dealt with patients this was sometimes part of the job.

The left eyelid opened then, revealing something in the socket that was no longer an eye—the remains of an eyeball, just a scarified dark and worthless lump of tissue. It looked like something had been poked into the cornea, destroying it and most of the surrounding tissue. The damaged lump had been left in place to heal. It could still twitch and flick and it did so now, the movement relating to nothing that Noreen could fathom. He wondered how much vision was left in the other eye. In what he could not quite refer to as the other organ of sight, the one "good" eye.

"I'm going to check your vital signs," Noreen said and he did it as if he assumed the man had normal hearing, calmly and matter-of-factly as if it were normal for him to talk to historical personages every day.

The poet mumbled something incomprehensible and tried to clear his throat.

Noreen reached for the wrist and let his forefinger search for a pulse, while he stared at wrist time. He expected a wispy rapid beat and got ready to count. He had no difficulty finding the pulse, but he had to wait for the beats. Kafahvey had a strong heart and an exceedingly low pulse, about twenty beats per minute. Noreen was surprised. Did it indicate a morbid condition? No, the beat was too strong for that. Or did it simply explain why he had lived so long? Very curious now, he was anxious to get to the blood pressure. He let one of the "nurses" pull up a chair and sat next to the bed. He removed a symfomanometer from his little black bag and strapped a cuff around the blob's flabby right arm.

As he inflated the instrument, he glanced around the room. The flickering light was still pulsing from the illuminated panel that covered the inner wall. Behind the rapidly changing colored lights he could see a hard surface sheen that was the substratum for the reflected light display. Around the perimeter he made out what looked like painted-over screw holes that could be used to hold an outer panel if one wanted to conceal the screen that gave off the light. The constantly changing color and the variations in luminosity almost hypnotized him for a moment. He forgot what he was doing and he ran the cuff pressure up too high. Quickly he released the valve, let the needle drop down to one forty, then listened as he let out more air, slowly now, and watched the needle drop down under red green blue yellow light brushing the crystal, the needle slipping below one hundred. Only at eighty did the Korottkoff sounds start. He could still get a beat at twenty and then the sounds cut out.

"I'll just take your temperature."

Noreen stuck a mercury thermometer into the puckered aperture where the mouth was supposed to be and the organism let it slide in and allowed it to rest under its tongue.

Ninety-five. When he removed the thermometer and had read it, the voice had found itself and now said clearly, "I shall live forever, doctor, with or without you."

Noreen jerked back slightly. He was still thinking about the abnormally low blood pressure. Eighty over twenty.

"Ah, very good, sir, I wasn't sure we were going to be able to talk to each other."

"My hearing is excellent, if that's what you mean."

"Good. I was also wondering about your vision."

"I have always been renowned for my visionary skill."

"I know. It's the visual acuity in your right eye that interests me."

"I can still make out things, if they're very close. Lean forward."

The eye opened and Noreen leaned forward and waited, smelling the acrid smell.

The patient moved his eye in a narrow irregular circle as if it were drawing Noreen's face.

Then the blob leaned back and the near-mouth opened a little and Noreen could see one or two stubby teeth, and the old man was laughing, that is, he was aspirating a little wheezy trill that tried to break into a real laugh but couldn't quite make it.

"Ho, ho—a relative. They usually stick me with one of the little dark people who seem to have overrun the premises, probably because they don't take up much space. Now that the end is near I finally get one of my own kind."

"I thought you said you would live forever."

"That was a figure of speech. Since it looks like I'm getting special treatment, I'll ask again. Where is my daughter?"

"I don't understand."

"They didn't explain?"

"No."

"They promised to bring my daughter to see me. I believe it's some kind of privilege in exchange for the opportunity to poke my orifices. If you wish to continue to treat me, I'll insist that you follow through on their promises."

"Where is your daughter?"

"You mean which daughter, don't you. I have many."

"All right then. Which one?"

"The fair one with blond hair and blue eyes and tall like yourself."

Noreen glanced helplessly at the "nurses" and all they could do was nod.

"I'm going to give you some new medicine. A tonic."

"Don't change the subject. Just tell me you'll bring her to me. Soon."

The nurses were shaking their heads *yes*.

"All right, anything you say. Where will I find her?"

"Check your file. I'm sure you have the exact coordinates."

"I'll do what I can," Noreen said. "Now let me continue my examination."

He got out his stethoscope and removed the towel from the patient's body, revealing the entire pyramid of naked flesh. Resting on his legs which were crossed under his buttocks in some ancient configuration, Kafahvey's testicles sagged blue and swollen under a massive erection, like Priapus himself.

"Before you ask," the poet said. "It never goes away."

The laugh started again, but now it was deep in the chest, like a death rattle. Rattling like death but the white eye continued to blink at him.

After the exam and the parley, the patient slumped back and fell asleep. Noreen couldn't tell if fatigue or boredom had got to him. The blob took on a different crumpled shape, with its old man's head on pillows, but it was still a blob. Right away it started snoring. Kafahvey's wheezing and epiglottal pauses had a definite musical lilt. But it was not Noreen's kind of music.

On his way out now, he inspected a cluster of bottles, vials and pill boxes on the night stand.

"Gather these up, put them in a box, and follow me," he told the women.

The bathroom cabinet was even more loaded down with medications, some in faded quaint packages. They had all expired, some before Noreen was born.

The nurses came in carrying a large box, and stood at attention.

Noreen had memorized Kafahvey's medical history. He knew what his current regimen was supposed to be.

"What are you giving him?" Noreen said.

They pointed to four bottles. Noreen set them aside.

"Remove the rest of this stuff. Put it all in the box and have it sent to my office. Continue giving him the currently prescribed drugs, but in withdrawal dosages. I want him off all this stuff in a week. You understand withdrawal dosages?"

"Yes. But—"

"No buts. I'll send you some new medicine, megavitamins, and tonics, and a pro-biotic. Who arranges his diet?"

The skinnier "nurse" raised her hand, cringing as if she expected punishment.

"Order your meal shipments through my office. No place else. Give him as much as he wants to eat as long as it's garlic, anything else only in my prescribed amounts."

"But—"

"The old man's going on a diet. I can't stand that blubber. Things are going to be different around here, if I have to look at him."

"But—he's Kafahvey."

"I don't give damn who he is. *I'm* a doctor. Which one of you fucks him?"

Each one raised her hand. Noreen couldn't hold back a little sneer.

"Okay, I guess you know what you're doing in that department. No point in changing that."

"What about the daughter?" they said.

"What about her?"

"You're going to find her?"

"So he can fuck her too?"

"Yes."

"Not my problem," he said. "If she wants to see him I'm sure she knows how to get here."

The monstrous snoring which they could hear through the door subsided for a moment, rose on a gasping stumbling crescendo, then settled down into silence.

Noreen listened for the upbeat, heard nothing. He got ready to flee on tiptoes.

CHAPTER

2¹

Noreen sat in Hayes' visitor's chair and stared across the wide desk at the dome's most important person. Noreen wondered if he could ever be like President Hayes.

Armand Hayes had once been a leading scientist, but you couldn't tell by looking at him now. He had settled comfortably into his role of Director of Organo Institute—Fullerton's major scientific and political entity—and become the genial administrator and level-headed father figure for the entire dome. He wore a dark two-piece suit and had let his white hair grow out in a wavy halo-like brush that reminded Noreen of the mesquite bushes. They had been friends ever since Noreen was his student, and had kept in touch, and now

TIME AND LIGHT

Noreen worked for him. Noreen had always wondered if Hayes' interest in him had something to do with the light skin, blue eyes, and blond hair they had in common. Hayes' genetic configuration did not come off as striking as Noreen's but they shared similar genes.

Hayes had been staring at the ceiling for a long time, as if waiting for a cosmic revelation.

Slowly, he looked back at Noreen.

"You know he's asked every doctor for twenty years to fetch his daughter—he even asked me when I had him as a patient—but I don't think anyone's ever done anything about it."

"Why not? It doesn't seem unreasonable."

"Well, for one thing it's damned inconvenient to try and arrange—the daughter's 'down below,' and I don't think she really wants to come up. He certainly isn't going down there. He isn't going anywhere. You saw him."

"Down below?"

"Yes. You know about 'down below,' don't you? You've been down there, I mean at least once, haven't you? I thought every student got a whiff of it at some time or another. Or—is it possible—you haven't been down there yet? Ever?"

"You mean down in the infrastructure?"

"Yes. I used to assign all my students a little reconnoiter in the lower depths. At least once. Good for them, made them appreciate up here. But maybe that didn't get started until after you'd gone through the course. Now you're getting up in the world, you really owe it to yourself to check everything out. Including 'down there.' Although a little bit of 'down below' goes a long way."

"I've spent a lot of time outside the dome lately. I'm in my exploratory phase it seems. I suppose 'down below' would be an interesting supplement. And couldn't be much worse. Than outside, I mean. But I really would rather go outside."

"Well, you won't find any—radiation—down there." He paused at the word radiation and stared at Noreen pointedly as if expecting Noreen to comment. But Noreen didn't say anything.

"You certainly won't need a rad meter," he added, as if finishing the subject or further giving Noreen a chance to say something about radiation.

But Noreen said, "Why is it so important for him to see his daughter?"

"Well, he can't live much longer, don't you agree?"

"I don't know. I don't know why he's alive now. But why *this* daughter? Doesn't he have several? At least that's what he said and it seems I've heard that about him."

"Yes, lots, we've lost count, and probably so has he—but this one, she's the youngest that we know of, and she ran away. And—"

"And what?"

"He wants to fuck her, man."

"I find it hard to imagine him fucking anyone."

Hayes slowly raised his right hand. He looked like he was blessing something.

"Don't rule it out. Remember he's Kafahvey. His brain doesn't work like everyone else's. We can only guess what goes on in there. I dare say we all owe something to that brain. And that prick. And he's fucked all his other daughters. He might as well fuck this one. Or fuck her again. Whichever."

"Well, let him."

"You mean that?"

"I'll bring her up and watch."

Hayes had a good gentlemanly laugh, and Noreen joined him by squeezing out a little smile.

"Good chap," Hayes said. "And speaking of fucking, if I may be so crude, your fiancée is a toothsome dish. Really! What a remarkable coup! You moving up in the world and getting laid in luxurious style at the same time. Congrats, old boy. Brack will look out for you. Already has."

Hayes let himself indulge in a little bout of extended chuckling. His old man's body shook like jelly.

CHAPTER

2^2

In a vertical photograph with glistening blacks and pearly whites, with just a trace of amber overall and an elusive warmth in the extra black blacks, a soft surface sheen asks to be touched like fur or velvet.

The silhouette of a young woman rises in the center of the picture, and stops almost midway, under a wooden plank she's balancing on her head.

She's moving across and out of the frame and has just paused to enter a door and will be gone soon.

Her right leg is stretched out and slightly raised, the foot itself invisible behind the door frame, as if she is kicking open the door. Not kicking, pushing more likely, rather than upset her balance with any abrupt gesture.

She wears a loose-fitting dark dress, cinched at the waist, somewhat full in the back.

The small black silhouette of a dog waits top center in an open sunlit space framed by the right foreground building's wall, the plank below, the stonework enclosure on the left, and, on the top, the shadow of a distant building. The dog is standing on its own shadow, its body slightly curved so that only the right rear leg is clearly visible and the front legs almost look like one.

It's high noon in this village. The walkway, once paved with rocks, has worn away to hard-packed dirt.

The pointy edges of the walkway's remaining original stonework catch small shadows.

He peers into the large shadow that is the girl, trying to identify the person, but he comes up with nothing except he thinks she is young because she is short and has a certain vigor suggested by the ease with which she handles her burden, the slight frizz of her neck-length hair, and a youthfulness about the shoulders.

There's no sign of any other human; the girl could be entirely alone in this village, the last person in her time; but if she is carrying bread, as suggested by the lumps resting on the plank, there is enough for her to eat for many days or to supply a large gathering at once.

He searches the photograph for some other sign of life or movement. He wants the right foot to come down and the girl and her burden to move into the building. He wants to see the left foot pick itself up and follow the girl. The dog should flick itself, and then move out of view, and someone should come around the corner, perhaps then talk to the girl.

He strains all his senses expecting something to

happen; after staring at this photograph for hours, he knows he's just on the edge of the frozen moment that will melt into life, if he gives it enough time.

But nothing happens. He will have to stare again, maybe many times, before he elicits the transcendent experience.

He swoons at the special blackness of oxidized silver and catches up with his stomach as if he has just dropped suddenly in an elevator.

CHAPTER

2^3

At the entrance to the underground stairway, which had an airy cast-iron fence around it— filigreed grapes, pears and vines, and a word that looked like "Metropolitaine" almost rubbed away in the casting—he felt the same pounding in his chest, a charge of excitement in his blood; he'd had it every time he'd left the dome. In a way he was leaving the dome now by going "down below."

A warmish and at the same time rimy breeze drifted up from the shaft.

He was wearing a black suit with slouchy coat and trousers on which he had pinned his new Organo Institute badge, upper-level blue now instead of the administrative-assistant yellow one he'd had for years. He nodded to the guard and without hesitating went down the steps into a world of steam and smoke and sweating concrete walls on which bare bulbs reflected. Soon he began to see shadowy figures shuffling along on errands that had to do with the secret underpinnings of the magnificent dome and its perfect citizens.

He had brought a map and an address given him by Central Census and now and then he stopped beneath one of the lights on the string that seemed to run into infinity and checked his location.

At Tullahoma and Coventry he turned right and could hear the thumping of a piston that shook the concrete under his feet and the space-occupying hum of giant dynamos. Open fires were being stoked with fossil fuels at that level, and he smelled the smoke and the steam. He was beginning to sweat. Overhead, he heard the lumbering and clicking of narrow gauge tracks. He realized that he had been descending at a narrow angle and was now in a sub-basement, because no trains of that type ran in the dome itself.

He stopped in front of a door with the numbers 1223 on it, folded his map, and went in.

He had entered a large, bare concrete-block room with smoke-streaked walls and a bank of furnace doors on the far side. Short, dirty men in shabby trousers and undershirts shoveled coal. On the other side of the room, far from the furnaces as possible, a worker was slumped over a table and was sleeping face down.

When he heard the door open and close, the sleeping man sat up and stared at Noreen.

"I'm looking for a woman named Kafahvey," Noreen said.

"Never heard of her," the man said. "I'll get the supervisor."

He went into another room and closed the door. When the door opened in a few minutes, he was followed by a tall woman dressed in similar shabby pants and undershirt. Black grime covered her skin and had caked in her hair, but Noreen believed she was blond under all that dirt, and in the circles that had been rubbed around her eyes her flesh was paper white and she had deep, pale, gray-blue eyes like the ones Noreen saw in the mirror every day.

"I'm Nora Kafahvey," she said. "What you want?"

She glanced over her shoulder, yelled something technical to the men near the furnaces and they started running around like little dogs. She pointed to a chair at a long table and sat down and Noreen sat down across from her.

"I bring glad tidings from your father," Noreen said, and hated himself for the stupid way it sounded. He was already getting like Hayes. He would be Hayes in another ten years. Would probably have Hayes' job.

"Bullshit. I know what you want."

She found a cigarette in her pants pocket, lighted it, and whistled at one of the men. She took a deep drag, let the smoke roll around in the bottom of her lungs, and then let it out in a long plume.

The man she had called came over with two grimy tumblers and a whiskey bottle and poured into the glass he set in front of her. After a while, she said, "Enough!" She picked up the glass, swallowed half its contents, and pointed for the man to fill the other glass.

Noreen stuck out his hand and held it over the mouth of the glass, not quite touching the scummy rim.

The man set the bottle down and joined the other stokers at the furnaces.

"Busy place," Noreen said.

"Fuckin' A."

The whiskey had hit bottom now, and she got a red, wet-eyed look, as if she had found something she had lost and hadn't expected again.

In the distance, now and then, the busy men stopped and took swigs from flasks that each seemed to have in his hip pocket. Some of them were sticking cigarettes into their mouths and lighting up by leaning into the furnace. No one had eyebrows.

On the walls farthest from the furnaces he noticed sheets of paper had been stuck up. The paper was yellowed all over and some had been scorched along the edges. The paper seemed to have small pictures—photos?—placed in different locations on the page. It was the first example he had ever seen of any kind of wall hanging and he wondered why these people were allowed to enjoy something that had been denied to the upright citizens of the dome.

He had little interest in continuing his conversation with this outlaw woman. He was just going through the motions. All he could think of was the photographs, and he kept glancing in their direction, no longer aware much of the woman. They were illustrations of some sort on mass-produced printed pages, not magnificent prints like his own, but real lens-formed images nonetheless.

The woman was dirty and needed a bath and he did not like filthy people, but he went on anyway, forcing himself to remember why he had come all this way.

"Your father's dying," he said, looking at her but squinting now and then at the wall. Yes, they were small, faded color photographs.

"Again? Good."

"It would do him some good, be nice if he could see you one last time."

"I'll bet. Good. I ain't going."

She was staring at him now. She had a puzzled look.

"Are you my brother?"

It was an absurd question.

"No," he said.

She was about thirty, had probably been an attractive young woman. But life in the infrastructure was doing her in.

He had a strong urge to help her, to see her get cleaned up and save her life.

It was presumptuous of her, and insulting, to think he might be her brother.

"I'm offering you a chance to get out of here, improve yourself," he said. He realized he sounded like a doctor talking now and he was coming off as stuffy; he didn't care. He was keeping her at a distance, just getting the parley over, so he could walk over to the wall.

"You gotta be kidding," she said. "I don't wanna improve my fucking life if it means going up there. This is real life, man, this is where it's at. We got everything we need down below." She emptied the glass.

Noreen slid the bottle over and filled it again for her. He noticed a flicker of gratitude under the black dirt.

"You could just go up for *one* day, come right back down again. I'll even accompany you and see you home."

She got crafty and low-lidded.

"And what'd be in it for you? I guess you'd expect to get fucked."

The way she said the ordinary word jolted him.

Not on your life, he said to himself, but he didn't say it to her.

"I'm a doctor. Your father's my patient. A very important man. I make house calls. It would make me look good. Besides, call it a service to poetry."

She seemed to accept that, was maybe a little disappointed.

Then she got a puzzled look and laughed.

"You call that old fart a poet. He ain't no poet. His stuff's shit. This is poetry. Hey, Dingo, bring the book over. Show this guy some poetry."

A short, wiry man with black bushy hair like the others but skinnier came running over with what Noreen identified as a book.

"Read something," she said.

The man opened the book and began flipping the pages. The book was very old, had worn round edges and a cracked flexible cover. The pages were yellow and crumbling. Finally he found what he was looking for and started to read. After he got started he looked up away from the page but his lips continued with the words he had found on the page.

Noreen didn't understand what it meant but the sound was strangely alluring and he forced himself to appear indifferent; he felt exhilarated now the way he felt when he looked at the photographs.

"Horloge! Dieu sinistre, effrayent, impassable,

Dont le doigt nous menace et nous dit: 'Souviens-toi!'

Les vibrantes Douleurs dans ton coeur plein d'effroi

Se plainteront bientôt comme dans une cible," read the man.

But the woman stopped the reader suddenly and sent him and his book back across the room.

"That's poetry," she said.

"Right. We were talking about your father."

"What's in it for me?"

"I don't know," he said. "What do you want?"

"Have the shit-heads upstairs send down a vat of good whiskey and a truckload of cigarettes."

"I'm not sure they're available." He had never heard of anyone drinking whiskey or smoking cigarettes in the dome.

"Trust me, take my word," she said. "It's available."

"Then I'll see what I can do."

"You drink whiskey? I mean when you get clean glasses?"

"No."

"You ever drink whiskey?"

"No."

"Bet you take the shittin' pill, don't you?"

He didn't answer.

"Whiskey's what keeps us going down here," she said. "We keep you warm up there. Whiskey keeps us warm down here. I want the kind with the black label. That's got the old guy's name on it."

She got up suddenly and raised a clinched fist and she looked tall and huge.

She bellowed over to the men: "Hey, guys, I'm going up to see my old man, the fucking poet."

They let out a group yell.

Noreen had already eased over to the wall to inspect the sheets of paper. They were what he deduced were pages torn from ancient books of some kind. He wanted to ask how they had got there, but she'd already disappeared into the back room.

She came out right away carrying a square bottle of whisky. And he was glad to see her again, because they had not really said good-bye then, and he would have a chance now to talk about the pictures.

The whiskey bottle had a blue paper seal covering the cap. She held the bottle out to Noreen and said, "Here, take this. A souvenir of your trip in the lower depths. Bet you don't get down *here* often. Drink some of this and you'll know what you're missing."

Noreen said thanks and put the bottle into a deep coat pocket, steadying it with a hand on the outside.

"Just one more thing—" he said and started to ask her about the wall coverings. But then one of the men called over and he sounded irritated.

"Gotta go," she said. "We're ten degrees below normal. That fucking dome can't keep itself warm. Somebody's got to do it for them."

And at the same time she pulled off her tank top and threw it on the table.

"But—the arrangements—"

"I'll be in touch."

Noreen looked at her. She had a fine strong chest and shoulders. The coal dust had seeped through her top piece and her torso was just as black as her arms, except for small circles in the center of her tight globular breasts. That part of her had remained clean and white and he could even see the pink of her nipples.

She let him stare straight on for a minute as if she was getting back at him for some affront he couldn't remember, or daring him something, and he could feel a slight urge suddenly mounting between his legs. But he looked at the dirty rest of her to quell his reflex and besides she had already started to move away.

He watched her join the group of men, pick up a shovel and push it into the coal bin. She swung around with a heavy shovel full of coal and tossed it into the furnace.

For a moment she was facing the blazing red light and her entire front was lit up and so washed out he couldn't see her dirt anymore. She looked pretty good. Then she turned away from the fire and joined the men shoveling coal now as fast as they could, sweat gleaming now and then, and for the most part they were all in silhouette and he couldn't tell one from the other, except she was taller.

When Noreen stepped back into the corridor sweat was pouring down his face and the damp fetid air rolling over the water that ran in the gutters chilled him.

Armand Hayes said, "I'll begin right now arranging for the shipment. It'll be ready when you say the word. By the way, you ever tried whiskey?"

"No."

"Good. But just take a little sip sometime. Not much, of course, I wouldn't want to see you end up down there."

He chuckled and Noreen put on a show of laughing with him.

CHAPTER

2^4

It was dark night out and he was staring at the bottle sitting on the galley table.

He had bathed and eaten and had looked at the secret pictures two or three times and in spite of them he still couldn't get the image of the girl with the dirty face "down below" out of his mind.

The pictures had started somewhat to lose their enchantment. They were so still and sad and everything in them had been dead for centuries. It was stupid to think that another world existed beneath the picture plane.

What he needed was a woman and a steady supply of new pictures, but mostly a woman tonight. As for the pictures, you needed a large number so that you could look at a batch each night and do that for a long time before you started over again. By then you would have forgotten the first ones and they would seem new once more.

Certainly he didn't want to fuck a woman who didn't take a bath, that would be stupid as well as unhealthy. But—

Going down below had increased his restlessness. It had made him realize that even the highly organized and simplified dome life was more complicated than he had dreamed. It was time once again for humans to explore and observe the world and he was sure a new category of man was about to arrive who would take up that chore soon. Perhaps he was one of them, though now he was unsure.

He had stopped taking the pills again and he knew that his restlessness was in part caused by that.

Perhaps this would be a good time to find out about whiskey.

He let his hand caress the cool glass bottle the girl had touched, and his thumb fooled with the loose edge of the paper stamp. Archaic lettering covered the square black and white label on the bottle's face. He wondered what Beta was doing tonight. He was afraid to drink whiskey alone. Besides, he missed Beta. Martine was all right, and very beautiful, but he and Beta had something he knew he would never have with Martine. A familiarity. A fitting-through-use. He wondered what Beta would do when she found out he was getting married to Martine.

Was anyone ever more fucked up? Did the people who took the pictures have such problems?

Maybe Beta would turn him in to the authorities because he had contraband and tried to force her to look at it, but somehow he didn't think she would do that, because she loved him too much, and she wasn't that kind of person. In a way, he didn't care, didn't care what happened to him, because he felt now that whatever he was supposed to do with his life had been shortcut and shortchanged, and he wasn't sure he would ever be satisfied with anything again.

After a while, he screwed the pictures down under the panel again and went into the bedroom and saw the gold foil-wrapped disk on the night stand and he called Martine.

"Have you eaten any candy lately?"

"That depends. What you mean by candy?"

"Come over. It's time to open the foil wrapping," he said. He didn't have to explain.

He should have felt contempt for himself, but as usual he didn't feel anything.

CHAPTER

2⁵

He turned out the overheads and lighted a large red candle, which was very pictorial, he imagined. He wondered why candles hadn't been banned, and assumed they would be soon, when the word of how lovely they were got out. Martine looked beautiful in the flickering light.

She was lying on her back on her side of the bed with her head propped up on the pillow, her feet pulled up and her knees crossed, now and then swinging her leg.

They hadn't done anything carnal yet that night and he couldn't understand how he could wait with this beautiful woman lying next to him. He had a huge erection which had started earlier in the sub-sub-basement and whenever he twisted over to her she would grab it with one hand and giggle and use it gently like an excruciatingly sensitive handle to push him to the side.

"Silly. You'll just have to wait until I'm fed."

"Did you bring yours?"

"No, I'm saving *that*. For our wedding night."

He couldn't be sure if she was telling the truth. Perhaps she had already eaten her foil-wrapped wafer. Perhaps she had already had a fling with someone else, some younger person, man or woman, who knows, she was so highly sexed.

Only people like Brack had a seemingly endless supply of the little tastees, and it was unlikely he gave them out except on an important occasion, even to his little sister.

"Quick now, and afterward, I'll tell you something."

He removed the wrapper, broke the chocolatey disk in half, and let her choose a piece.

She took the larger piece and began to rub it lightly across her lips.

He rolled over and on top of her and for an instant touched her face, and her eyes, nose and lips filled his entire field of view, but she pushed him back.

"I can't stand this," he said.

"That's all right," she said. "That's the way it's supposed to be, the way it's going to be. Once it gets going, you'll be glad. I'll do everything you need, over and over again, you won't be able to stand it.

Now just lick your candy a little, lie back, and I'll do the same, and we'll wait and see what happens."

"I'll go crazy, mean," he said.

"No, silly." She gave him a gentle push in the ribs with her elbow.

"I'll have to have a sip of whiskey after this," he said.

"What?"

"Nothing. We're talking too much."

"Bite off a piece now," she said. "And I will too, and we'll chew together."

And he did, and he could hear her little soft tongue wiping itself across her lips. And then they both stuffed the rest of their wafer into their mouths and swallowed and licked their fingers and she had little traces of chocolate on her fingers and by then she was dreamy and she stretched out with a little groan and let him over and on to her and he could feel her smooth warm skin all along his skin, and she let him slide down and slip-slide into her and then something in his mind clicked off and he let himself get lost in the darkness of their mutual desire.

CHAPTER

2⁶

It seemed like a long time had gone by but it was still dark. The candle had burned out and left just a waxy smell, yet there was a light in the room, and the walls were covered with pictures. It did not seem strange to him to find the pictures, but he didn't remember how they got there and he wondered why he had never looked at them before. They didn't seem to hang on the walls so much as they glowed like neon a few inches from the walls.

He got up to go look, walking over Martine's face, and he could feel her septum bend in and then crunch with a dry ripping noise under his foot but it didn't seem important, and when he stepped off the bed which became a steep gorge with rocks below and scratchy branches overhead so he had to duck his head and he was dizzy and his legs gave out and he fell and hit his forehead on the floor. She was still asleep with a pillow between her legs. She didn't know he had just broken her nose which was funny and from where he sat he couldn't really see how bad it was and he decided that since she didn't know yet and it wasn't bothering her he could wait on the floor until later to check the damage. But he knew that something was wrong and he managed to get up and drag himself to the wall but he couldn't stand up and he stared up now at the pictures which were directly above him.

They were foreshortened of course but more than he imagined possible, almost into a triangle which indicated that the keystoning ended somewhere in infinity. Directly above him protruded a mushy jumble of trembling and sputtering neon that had formed itself in a murky tableau and looked like it was supposed to be a mountain scene with boulders in the foreground and lush jungle after that very green and then a path went up the side of the mountain. At the top a black dot was moving down the hill getting larger growing bigger until halfway down he could see it had become a motorcycle that was coming toward him.

Now he could hear the sound of the motor and it began to hurt his ears. This was not an airbike. This vehicle had two wheels one in front and one in back and it was coming so quickly he knew it would completely fill the picture soon and if it

didn't stop it would roll out into the room and over
him, and he assumed it would crush him the same
way he had destroyed Martine's nose. But the
damage would be much worse. He knew the smart
thing to do would be to get up and move away but
he felt that he had abdicated all movement in his
skeletal structure and had been fixed in concrete
that covered him all white from head to toe,
reminding him of Kafahvey. He waited for the
engine roar to go away which would take the
motorcycle with it but the sound kept increasing
along with the expanding pictures and it was
shredding his eardrums. He had to clasp his hands
over his ears but he could still hear the noise and
he pressed so hard he could feel his skull giving way
inward but he could still hear it and then he knew
the bike was coming out of the picture and he
began to scream but he couldn't hear himself. As
it left the frame and leaped up trying to rise above
him he felt and saw the little chrome-plated lever
under the masked hunched-over driver's foot tear
into his forehead and then he felt it slicing through
his cranium, his head separating and held together
at the bottom by his larynx which could now
breathe the air directly without going through his
mouth and the motorcycle gone and taking the
sound with it and then that was all he heard or saw
because his now-separated eyes closed and
whatever there was about him that felt and saw
went to sleep somewhere.

When she found him he was lying on the floor muttering something that she couldn't understand, he trying to remember what it was he wasn't supposed to forget.

CHAPTER

2⁷

The photograph disturbs him. He can't figure out what's going on.

Why isn't it clearer?

Is it a fault of the taker or the viewer?

Here there's just a shimmering, forms that move up from the shadows, and he has to label the objects, to find his way around the frame, not sure he's getting the words right.

He looks awhile and decides he's in an inner room. Two figures are entwined on a flowered bedspread. He's very close, looking down, but all he can make out are three plump legs glistening in dim light, the legs of one person underneath, spread-eagled, and the leg of another person on top, outstretched, pressed against the other's crotch.

The body on top has a thin white undergarment covering its buttocks but pulled down at the waist to reveal the curve of hips and the indented part of the lower back. A white chemise floats above that, a blur of arm, everything tremulous, as if in motion, nothing definite, no faces or hands, all the rest lost in coverlets and shadow, or beyond the frame.

He strains to see into the blur, can almost make out details, then gives up, as whatever he thought he had slips away from his eyes. He squirms.

What you have here is pure sex, he tells himself, lower bodies copulating, with the movement and the blur and the dimness and the secrecy of a bedroom.

He can feel that, and he can feel himself almost drawn in, wanting to touch the flowered cloth and the thin silk material and to caress the glowing back.

But he feels left out, not wanted: this is sex real but symbolized, the actual moment of sex, sex floating and sex detached, like two disembodied cartoon figures, and both participants appear to be women.

CHAPTER

2

He woke up thinking, if he just had a drink of whiskey everything would be all right.

He opened his eyes, and he wasn't exactly dizzy anymore and he felt his head and it had been put back together again. But when he tried to stand up his knees got rubbery and he let Martine help him set himself down on the edge of the bed.

He could see sweat on her upper lip and her forehead and when he started to ask her about her nose, he saw that it was all right, lovely and straight and fine, and he didn't say anything. He looked around. Someone had taken down the pictures. That was all right. You had to be in the right frame of mind for pictures. Otherwise, they could get you in trouble. Right now, all he wanted to do was lie back down.

"What happened?" she said.

"I don't know," he said.

"It's just a reaction. Haven't you ever done this before?"

"No."

"Silly, you really have to work up to it. I'm glad you didn't take a whole one. If I'd known I would have just let you have a sixth."

She sat down, put his head in her lap, and stroked his forehead. Her hand was warm but it seemed to cool him.

She helped him back in the bed and they were lying down side by side.

"Are you all right now?" she said.

"Better."

"Is it all right then if I tell you what I said I wanted to talk about?"

It wasn't all right, but he didn't want to be alone and he thought he had to be nice to her. He nodded, and squeezed her hand.

"I'm pregnant," she said.

But he had fallen asleep and he heard it through a mist and he felt her wrap a leg around him and hold him while he slept.

In the mid-conscious space between awake and deep sleep he was surprised by her kindness and wondered if he had misjudged her.

When he awoke the next time, it was getting light. The only window in the apartment was next to the front door. The window was covered with very fine venetian blinds so no one could look in from outside, but he could now see a little rectangle of light coming in around the edges.

She was still sound asleep. As he watched her he had tender feelings for her, that he had not anticipated. He had never had really tender feelings for anyone, not even Beta, though it was hard to tell about his feelings for Beta; perhaps he had forgotten how he really felt about Beta.

The feeling now for Martine surprised him. It was even a bit repulsive, and he had a skull-busting headache and a dry mouth, but he wanted to do something for her.

First he wanted her to get as much sleep as she could and in order not to wake her he went into the kitchen and sat down at the table. Perhaps they should take a sip of the whiskey together, he thought as he stared at the bottle which was still in the center of the table. He decided to open it and try it first before offering it to her. He poured about two inches in a water glass, raised the glass, and let the contents drip down into his throat.

At first it felt like he was trying to cauterize his insides and then it was burning in his stomach, and then he got used to it and he leaned back and let it begin to seep diluted outward into the other parts of his body. Aware of choking fumes that rose up from his gut and flowed from his pharynx into his nasal cavities, he felt his sickness and the fatigue going away. He liked that, and he was also getting revved up, surprisingly clearheaded as if the fog were blowing out of his brain and at the same time fuzzy again in a pleasant mild way.

At first he wondered if they had put the wrong contents in the bottle, perhaps some cauterizing agent or antiseptic or solvent, but then he began to feel so good he poured himself another serving and drank that. He was ready for the burn and braced for it but nevertheless it burned down the inside of his chest and into his gut. He shivered and shook. It was all right, all right. He didn't want to drink it all up before she had a chance at it, and he also wasn't sure about the correct dosage. In the catacombs they seemed to swill it down ad lib, but of course they were habituated to it.

He still wanted to do something for her, to share something with her, now that she was going to be the mother of his child, a preposterous situation, and he was about to accept through her the responsibility of getting married. He figured this was as good a time as any to show her the photographs. They would share the photographs, man and wife, share an unusual intimacy for the dome.

He got his screwdriver and went into the living room. So much light was coming in around the blinds he didn't have to switch on the overheads. In the nacreous morning gloom that had started as bright sunlight outside Fullerton and then seeped down through the opalescent dome skin and then through his crystalline one-way window around the blinds, he squatted on the floor in front of the panel and began removing screws. The envelope containing the photographs slipped into view and he removed it, glanced in, and caught a glimpse of the photograph of the nude woman who reminded him of Martine, whom he was sure he was falling in love with, though he felt no one could ever take the place of Beta. He had known Beta longer than any other person, and he felt a sharp stab of regret at the possibility of not being able to see her again and he wondered if mutual love was a commodity that Martine understood.

He carried the envelope into the galley and set it in the middle of the table next to the bottle. Then he picked the bottle up and placed it on the sink where there was no chance of it falling over and ruining the prints. Then he removed the photographs and spread them out, all twelve of them, in the sequence of two rows of six each he had come to feel was proper for these particular images, at least in the way he wanted her to see them for the first time.

Then he had a sudden brilliant idea and he

carried his screwdriver back into the living room and, standing up for the most part, removed all the screws surrounding the panel. Except for the end that he had loosened, the panel stayed in place, held by the thin bead of paint that covered its edges and the wall.

Starting at the lower right-hand corner, he inserted the shaft of the screwdriver and began forcing it up the panel's side, breaking loose the paint holding the edge. Then he ran the tool along the top and when it had almost reached the left-hand side, the panel dropped down and forward and he caught it with his other hand. He grabbed the left-hand edge with both hands and dragged the floor-to-ceiling panel to the front of the room and leaned it against the window opening. It was heavier than he expected and he was a little out of breath from the unexpected exertion. The panel now covered almost the entire front wall and blocked out the light coming in around the window so that once again the room was dark except for the light seeping in from the kitchen.

Even so he could make out the glassy panel that had been hidden by the wall covering. Its perfectly smooth face had an opalescent off-white tint that reminded him of Kafahvey's glaucous eye. It looked exactly like the liquid crystal material used for the display in the remote rad meter, but much larger, of course. Below, near where he had first removed the screws, a plate had been affixed containing a row of switch buttons, all black except for a single red button on the right end.

What he had just done—removing the panel—reminded him of the first time he had lifted his visor outside the dome.

He ran the flat of his hand over the smooth cold surface of the panel, then bent down and pressed the red button.

He jumped back, as a charge of static electricity cracked and shivered over the entire wall and the panel began to emit an irregular and frantic sequence of moving patches of light. The lights crackled and jumped around and appeared momentarily in different seemingly random sections of the screen.

Then its electronic convulsing stabilized, and a series of narrow horizontal bars appeared and began to roll in a regular rhythm up the wall. Now colorful designs slipped into the interstices the way they had at the poet's apartment. He found the design and the bars fascinating, and the rolling rods put out so much light he didn't need the overheads.

He backed up suddenly without turning around and when he felt the couch touching the back of his knees he let himself flop down and sat there staring at the screen.

CHAPTER

2⁹

He must have dozed off a little, because the next thing he knew Martine was shaking his shoulders. And he saw the outline of her body in front of the screen and the bars that were still rolling now around and behind her.

"Explain," she said, and there was none of the tenderness left that he thought he had seen in her earlier. It had been used up, if it had ever been there, and was overdrawn. The currency now was Martine's anger—willful, selfish and mindless— Martine angry at something.

"What are you looking at?"

"You," he said, and he felt a little careless and mindless himself, and he was making a joke that she didn't find funny, perhaps it was not his style to be amusing, and he knew then that he had to try and wake up and focus and concentrate.

She started to raise and swiftly lower her arm in a trajectory that would hit him across the face with her flattened hand, but he jerked his fist up, caught her wrist, and shoved her away and stood up.

"I wanted to surprise you," he said. And he felt it was just like she had caught him in bed with another woman. Or had discovered his most shameful secret.

"You know that thing is against the law," she said. She backed away, cringing and rubbing her arm where he had touched it.

"It's all right," he said, "Kafahvey has one and his shows pictures."

"Pictures are not allowed. Even the name is not permitted. I'm a law-abiding citizen of the dome and my family has an example to set. I have to think of the baby and you should too. We don't need pictures and we don't look at them. They should not exist. I'm sorry, pictures do not exist."

"C'mon now," he said, and he gently grabbed her wrist where he had hurt her and rubbed it and she let him. "It's not so bad. There's a screen like this in your brother's house."

She hesitated, then thought of something.

"But he doesn't look at it. It remains hidden."

"Are you entirely sure?"

"Yes."

"But you've seen the panel?"

184

"Not really."

He held her close to him and she let him, sobbing, and he rubbed her back, up and down, and pressed his hand hard against the small of her back and over her buttocks. She squeezed against him.

"Don't worry. It's not so bad," he said.

"But you'll cover it up?"

"Whatever you say."

"And we'll never speak of it again?"

"Of course."

"You know I'm really supposed to report you to the authorities now. And I should start by talking to my brother. If I were really a good Fullertoner I would. But I can't do that to my fiancé and the father of my child."

"I wouldn't think so."

"See—how much I love you."

"I'm a lucky man," he said, and decided that he could never trust her.

"Yes, lucky for you." She maneuvered her face into a mock pout.

"You discovered my little secret," he said. "I have a devilishly inquiring mind, you know. No, you don't know—but you're learning. I'll try and do better in the future."

"All right, I am learning—your secret is safe with me as long as you keep that thing shut off—and covered."

"And what else can I do for you, my sweet?"

W
I
L
L
I
A
M

B
O
R
N
E
F
L
D

"You know what. But I'm going to leave now. I think I'm a little shaky after last night. And this."

"I have just the medicine for you."

"What?"

"It's called whiskey."

But after he explained what it was she looked disgusted and stared at him for a long time.

"You don't know when to quit, do you?" she said, and started to gather up her clothes. She straightened herself up a bit and he called a cab and she gave him a peck on the check and he felt her warmth moving out to him and it seemed her hips and breast were fuller already now than they had been when they first met. She dressed and ran out, slipping through the door so the screen couldn't be seen outside. After she had left he wasn't sure they had really made up, and a little worm of trouble began wriggling in the back of his mind.

He pressed the red button again and the lights on the screen shrank into a little point before disappearing, and then he replaced the panel and the screws. He called in to the office and said he was going to work at home that day.

He drank the shot of whiskey he had intended for her and it didn't burn so much. Then he went back to bed.

CHAPTER 30

W
I
L
L
I
A
M

B
O
R
N
E
F
E
L
D

He didn't hear from Martine for three days. Each day he went in to work and tried to catch up on the data shuffling he had neglected in his days outside the dome and down below. The sun was almost overhead at noon now, that is, its diffuse image was, because you couldn't really see through the opalescent tissue of the ancient and still growing skin that covered Fullerton's bio-metallic framework. He wondered what marvelous new species were budding in the open spaces outside the dome.

He didn't see or hear from Brack either, although he was sure he was in the building, and he wondered if that was an ominous sign.

Beta didn't call, and that was what he expected.

But he remembered her now and then, and it was not like thinking about Martine. It was like remembering a part of you that had been amputated and whose outline you could still feel.

It was strange that Martine didn't call. Perhaps she wasn't pregnant. Perhaps she was having second thoughts about the wedding. He didn't care. Perhaps she was going to turn him in as an enemy of the dome. Perhaps she had already told her brother, and Brack didn't intend to see him until the police brought him to his office. He cared about that. He wondered what would happen to his photographic prints after they arrested him. Perhaps they would never find them.

They would find them.

CHAPTER

3¹

On Friday Brack summoned him to his office. He could see right away Brack was angry—the cold eye, the pushed out mouth, the rigid neck. No trace of the genial brother-in-law-to-be.

"Noreen, you're insensitive."

"What?"

"I shouldn't have to do this."

"Do what?"

"Why haven't you called Martine?"

"I've been busy. She hasn't called me."

"That's no excuse. I think you've upset her. What happened?"

"Nothing. I saw her just the other night. Everything was fine then." He thought it best to exaggerate.

"Then why is she moping around the house and looking forlorn?"

"No idea."

"She says you won't agree with her on a wedding date."

"What—?"

"That's wrong, don't you think?"

"I'll call her. We'll talk about it."

"No, you and I will talk about it—in fact, we already are. Let's set a date now. I don't want to waste a lot of time on this. I have other things to do. What do you say?"

"Well—"

"How about two weeks from tonight? Is that all right? Don't bother to answer. Two weeks then."

"Fine. Anything you say, oh most certain successor to Hayes."

"Leave Hayes out of this context."

"As you wish, oh future brother-in-law. I'm sure we'll all have fun together. And in the meantime, I'll finish my work outside the dome."

"No! No way! I want you in one piece. Why, I don't know; I'd really like to see your privileged body squirm. After the wedding and the honeymoon, you can do what you want. I assume by then Martine will be pregnant."

"Of course."

He didn't know. Or was Martine lying?

"And we can expect a bunch of tall blond and blue-eyed eggheads running around the place?"

"Of course."

Brack had relaxed. His face assumed its natural puffiness.

"A personal question: have you stored extra samples of your seed in the sperm bank?"

"Naturally. It's standard procedure, especially for doctors."

"Good. You scientific types are something else. You're always thinking of possibilities and parameters that have been mined out years ago and you don't even know it. Or don't care. Instead of important real-life things. Somebody else has to be decisive for you. You're lucky you've got me around to think for you. And pretty soon you'll have Martine. I mean, really have her. Already she's looking out for your ass. That girl has a real head on her shoulders. You don't deserve her. As I've said before I don't know what she sees in a dreary type like you—but I must admit you have a good physique. I guess that's all it takes—being smart's okay, but what does your braininess get you? Okay, enough of that, we've covered everything we need to today. Get out of here, before you make me puke. Go back to your office and have lofty thoughts."

"Thanks, Brack."

"And one more thing."

"Yes—?"

"Monday go down and bring up the girl and take her to her father."

Noreen's heart skipped a beat. The thought of the whiskey? Or something else?

He'd make an effort to speak slowly from now on, to conceal his interest.

"As his doctor, I say that's not a good idea."

"Why?"

"He wants to fuck her."

"So?"

"It doesn't seem like something we should encourage or abet. I'm not sure the girl wants to be abused."

"Abused? Look, he's the national poet. A lot of— or maybe all—of his reputation is based on fucking. That's what those long stupid poems are all about. She doesn't have to go along with it if she doesn't want to. I'm sure that big-assed coal hauler can handle a one-ninety-year-old, or whatever, man. But maybe she'll want to. Isn't that after all what life is all about—I mean, fucking? And everything in between is just waiting. Say, man, he's not only the father of poetry he's the founder of the orgasmic principle. We ought to keep that in mind. And I don't want anyone to say that Brack led to the death of this living icon we all love because we have never really seen him and don't know what a disgusting shit he is—because he couldn't screw his daughter. We're not broadcasting everything we do like its a goddamn report on the composition of our water supply. But behind the scenes we're making everything as sweet as possible. And that means keeping our national heroes happy."

"All right. I'm not sure he can fuck anyone anymore. And if he tries, it might kill him. But consider it done. I can go down below but I can't go outside?"

"Not outside for a while. Like I said. Don't you listen? And down below—maybe you ought to get used to it. Maybe you belong down there yourself. You treat Martine badly, we'll find out. Good-bye now."

CHAPTER

3^2

That night Martine came over. She didn't call. When she came in she didn't even look at the panel that had been put back over the transmission screen.

She looked a little tentative and shy. She was carrying a small glass vial with a screw cap.

"The first thing we're going to do," she said, indicating the vial. "I don't care about the damn public sperm bank, I want to start my own. I worry about you. You're not like a normal dome man and you do unconventional things that we won't talk about except I want you to know I'm a very conventional person, I want to be like everyone else, except prettier and sexier and everything else like that that's better than anybody else, and I'm not sure what your children are going to be like but I want to find out. Maybe they'll be all right, better than all right, like I want, because they'll be *my* children too. Here!"

She handed him the vial.

She stayed around until after midnight and they went through the motions of being a newly-engaged pair and she made him couple with her once just for the form of it and afterward she pretended to be relaxed and pleased and she thanked him for setting the date, and she said, "That's perfect. When I get married I want to be able to feel a little dome pushing out from my belly but I don't want it to be big enough to be noticed by anyone else. I don't know why, I just want to know it's under my dress, and you and I can feel it under our palms and it will be our little secret, the only kind of secret people should have."

She let the last little point linger in the air with a pause that was a conditional threat.

It was at that point he decided she was crazy, and he wasn't, but he had got himself onto some kind of self-propelled vehicle and couldn't get off. He would have to figure out something.

Like maybe running away and living outside the dome. But he didn't know how to do that even if he had the chance. No one had lived outside the dome for a millennium which was a long time that had no real numerical explanation.

He wondered why, then wondered why he had

never bothered to ask. You just didn't live outside, that's why.

It was after midnight when she decided to leave. He was so sleepy he felt like a little child being forced to go to the bathroom so he wouldn't wet the bed in the night, but he got up and walked with her out to the cab.

She pecked him on the cheek and got in the cab and looked back at him through the glass with a tiny forced smile that he couldn't figure out.

Condensate was dripping down in mock rain and he was getting wet. But he saw a figure in a light-colored raincoat standing in the doorway across the street with a blue umbrella pulled down in front of the face.

He watched the cab go out of sight at the next corner and then he called over: "Beta!"

The figure didn't move and didn't answer. He started to walk over to it. The umbrella moved to one side and he glimpsed Beta's face, just as she started to walk away down the sidewalk and then cover her head again behind the umbrella. He walked behind her.

"Give it up, Beta," he said.

She stopped and turned around. Water was dripping from the ends of her harlequin glasses. In the dim yellow light of the street lamp he could see that she hated him and wasn't trying to hide it. He was sorry it had turned out this way.

"I understand now perfectly," she said.

"No, it's not that at all."

She turned and walked away from him. As she did she closed the umbrella so she could walk faster.

He stopped and watched her go. Then he started running after her.

He was losing Beta. He didn't want to lose her.

"Wait, Beta, we have to talk."

Still walking, she turned around.

"It's too late," she said, walking backward, away from him.

He stopped and watched her go down the street and out of sight around the same corner the cab had taken.

Then he walked back across the street and up the stairs that led to his apartment and he went inside and had a drink of whiskey.

CHAPTER

3³

The photograph is almost square, and has the overall cold brown of an albumin print or selenium toning carried too far on silver.

The camera has been placed on a dining room table. The flat surface of the table almost fills the lower half of the picture space, and is out of focus. The table cloth is light-colored, perhaps from overexposure, and has a regularly spaced floral pattern suggesting lacework.

The upper torso of a man in a suit sits in an out-of-sight chair behind the table's edge in the center of the picture.

On the table top rests a velvety black fedora with a wide band.

He can't quite see the man's face. His head, a small

blotchy white spot in the exact center of the frame, is bent back. It has a soft round chin, two dots that are nostrils, and a slightly larger half-moon-shaped shadow that is his mouth. A little left, almost near the top of the white circle that represents the upturned face, a small black dot rests, where the bullet entered his brain; from it, a dark line has trickled downward over a curved celluloid collar.

The camera is pointing slightly upward and part of the ceiling can be seen, framed with decorative molding. The ceiling has a cracked and irregular surface, and appears to be moving away from the man at the table.

A single light comes down from upper left—a burst of flash powder from the holder in the photographer's hand, a lamp of primitive incandescent light, or a time exposure of whatever available light existed then, and falls directly on the man's right side.

A lace curtain, pulled away from a window on the right wall and held by a nail, falls into pathetic triangular folds. The window has four glass planes separated by flimsy muntins. The lower right pane has a large hole with crusty edges. It's dark night outside.

Is this where the bullet entered that killed the man?

Was the man standing by the window when the shot was fired? Then he would have moved back into the room, pulled the chair out, sat down, and rolled his head back?

The expanse of the table, the empty wall, and the edge of the ceiling are raw and bare and the man seems small in the center of the room. The room appears to be going away and leaving the man behind.

This is not a picture of the man, after all. This is a picture of emptiness. Almost nothing. Near nothingness. The room is exploding, running away from the victim.

This is the way everything ends. Everything including the picture about to turn white. The man will soon disappear. He will turn white and be the last to go.

In the silence the viewer hears the sound of the wind and the wolves outside and the rustling of rats on paper, and he wishes to go no farther; he turns around and shoves the picture beneath the stack.

CHAPTER

3⁴

The police didn't knock on the door. They let themselves in with their passkey and surrounded his bed and shined flashlights in his eyes and waited silently for him to wake up.

"We don't have to explain, but just for the record you're under arrest for violation of ancient and sacred rules of the dome and possessing contraband detrimental to the welfare of dome society. You have no rights now, because you never had rights. Your life was given you in trust by the dome and it's always been the dome leaders' right to do with it as they wished—to allow you to live and flourish in comfort and satisfaction and orgasmic peace or to snuff you out and dispose of you in any manner the dome management sees fit. Apparently the latter is the end you prefer. Get up."

He was awake, but they didn't wait for him to respond. They yanked him, almost pulled his arm from its socket, and at once he could feel his shoulder beginning to swell.

He had not expected this and his mind was numb.

They had already removed the bottom screws from the panel. Noreen saw one of cops pick up the envelope that fell down. He held it away from his body with the tips of his gloved fingers. As if afraid of contamination. He did not check the contents. He dropped the envelope into a thin black portfolio and closed the flap.

"You bastard," the cop said, when they dragged Noreen into the living room, as if he had some personal complaint, and he stood up and hit Noreen twice, as hard as he could with his fist. Noreen felt knuckle-bone under vinyl indenting his jaw and then his sternum and heard the breath push out of his mouth and a deep soreness start radiating in his ribcage.

So this is the way it ends. He'd always wondered. There were no old people in the dome.

Except Kafahvey.

A funny notion: Kafahvey would outlive him.

He assumed Beta had turned him in, but somehow he didn't hate her. He didn't hate anyone. He just had an awful premonition he'd never leave Fullerton again.

CHAPTER

3⁵

W
I
L
L
I
A
M

B
O
R
N
E
F
E
L
D

They threw him into a windowless room with padded walls, a cot, a washbasin, and just enough space to walk two and a half paces. The ceiling was a few inches above his head; if he stretched he could feel his hair brush against plaster. Not much call for cells in the crime-free dome. He lay down and waited. He stared at the ceiling as if looking for something to appear, he wasn't sure what, a neon Exit sign or next year's calendar, or a reprieve signed by Hayes, but he saw nothing.

They seemed to have forgotten him. He had already missed three meals. Then he heard someone at the door and he sat up. He wasn't hungry; if they were bringing food he wouldn't be able to eat. His ribs shot fire when he took deep breaths.

They took him to Brack's office. One guard on each side of him. Brack told the guards to leave the room and wait outside. They left, long-faced, as if they couldn't bear to be out of range of hitting him.

Noreen started to sit down, but Brack said, "No, you don't have that privilege anymore. You'll have to stand."

Noreen stood up, placed one wrist over the other with his arms hanging down, and waited. His shoulders slouched and made a slight hump in his back. He hoped he wouldn't get too upset. He was taking little short breaths and his ribs didn't hurt too bad. He wanted to keep it that way.

Brack looked at him. After a long while he cleared his throat and said, "I knew you were problematical, as I indicated in previous conversations, but I didn't think it would turn out like this. Or so soon. What happened to you?"

"Nothing."

"Am I correct in assuming you're not even ashamed of yourself?"

"I haven't done anything wrong. I haven't done anything that Kafahvey hasn't done."

"You compare yourself to Kafahvey?"

"No. But I was taught no one has special privilege in the dome."

"Good. Then you understand that you can't expect any."

"I don't want any. Any more than the ones I have already as a level-five and a doctor. So, what's the problem?"

Brack stood up, his eyes bulging with anger and blood pressure.

"Tell me where you put them?"

"What?"

"The contraband."

"You'll have to be more specific."

"You know, the graphic material you tried to share with another citizen."

"What?"

"Pictures, man, pictures. Don't play games with me."

Brack's voice kept rising and getting louder.

Noreen could feel his pulse speeding too fast to count, and his respiration rapid and shallow.

But he didn't mind the pain now.

They didn't have the pictures. The envelope must've been empty. He didn't know how or why. Brack was just fishing now.

Someone had turned him in, all right. But they had no evidence.

Beta? Martine? The cleaning lady?

If they had evidence, Brack would be cool and dry now. Brack liked to torture people. It relaxed him. If he'd found the pictures he'd be down to the real thing. Looking at Noreen's blood. No cat and mouse for Brack.

But where were the pictures?

Brack sat down with a sick look as though he didn't know what else to do.

He had a chance now. It was Noreen's word now against someone else's. He'd call Hayes, if necessary. Did Hayes know they were doing this to him?

Usually Hayes knew everything.

"I don't know what you're talking about," Noreen said. "Don't have a clue."

"Where'd you get them?"

"The same place you got them, wherever that might be, whatever it is we're talking about."

"Down below?"

"That what you want me to say?"

They didn't know they had come from outside. Keep it that way.

"Yes."

"All right, then, down below," Noreen said, smiling.

"The girl?"

"No, not the girl."

"But down below? You're sure?"

"Yes, if that's what you want me to say."

"Where down below?"

"In a heating duct. Or maybe a shoe box. No, in a corpses' vagina. You never know what you'll find in an autopsy. I'm trained to look everywhere."

"Cut the crap. Who helped you?"

"No one."

"Explain."

"I got lost. I saw some movement in a duct. The grill was loose. I presumed I was unblocking the airflow."

"Suitable work for a doctor?"

"It seemed right at the time."

"Why did you keep them?"

"I didn't know what else to do with them. Whatever they are. I assume we're talking about something cuddly."

"You *cherished* them."

"No! I don't even know what we're talking about, remember."

"You protest too much."

"I did nothing wrong."

"Who helped you?"

"No one."

"Explain."

"No one except Kafahvey."

"What does that mean?"

"He came along and egged me on."

"You're not repentant at all, are you?"

"I have nothing to be sorry for. Besides, it's my professional opinion you've carried this charade a little too far. What are you pulling? Some kind of prenuptial family joke?"

Noreen sat down and Brack didn't complain. He leaned forward, feeling he was in the driver's seat.

"If you're going to treat a level-five manager like this, you'd better have a reason. What is it? Who got me into this mess? I want to talk to Hayes."

"Don't be silly."

"Was it Kafahvey?"

"I'm not going to reply to that."

"Does Hayes know you've got me like this?"

Brack wouldn't answer.

Brack swiveled his chair away from Noreen. His fat neck was sweating. Something had gone wrong. They had heard about the pictures but they didn't have them. Without the pictures they looked silly. Brack was trying to figure out a way to get on top again, to hurt Noreen, and he wasn't coming up with anything. Hayes didn't know.

"If we let people get away with things, we'd destroy everything we stand for," Brack said, as if starting a lecture on civic responsibility. "This is a great place to live. This is the last outpost of the human race. We're safe from radiation in here and we have happy, satisfying lives. You're a bright guy, maybe too bright, the kind of guy who can throw things out of kilter. I worry about you and I've decided to keep an eye on you. Whatever it takes. Wherever it might lead. It's as simple as that."

Noreen stood up and leaned over the desk.

"There isn't any radiation."

"What?" Brack blinked, gasped.

"You heard me. The rad meters are jiggered," Noreen said. "There hasn't been any radiation for centuries."

Brack turned his back to Noreen and looked out

the window. He spent a long time clearing his throat. Then he swiveled back to face the front of his desk. He pointed to the chair and said, "Please sit down again."

Noreen sat down.

Then Brack indulged himself in a long spell of fitful nervous laughter, mostly to himself. As if he couldn't help it.

"You know?"

"Yes."

"My god! What on earth are we going to do with you?"

"I say let's forget all this and let me get back to my work. Does this have something to do with Martine?"

Brack looked away and started to sweat again. Noreen knew Brack was about to tell him a lie.

"Of course not. I wish it did. Say, if you were already married to Martine, I could do something for you. Maybe I could do something anyway. You say you could accept the knowledge of the radiation—and contraband, whatever—and keep everything confidential?"

Noreen didn't remember saying anything like that but he figured it was okay if Brack wanted to believe that and he nodded.

"My sole wish in the world is to make you proud of me," he said. At the moment, if it would get Noreen out of Brack's office, it seemed true.

"Yeah?"

"Yeah."

Brack looked pleased, as if he needed flattery to get back on track. He beamed, and when he mopped up the sweat it didn't come back.

"My, my. What *are* we going to do with you? Let me think, and come up with something. Have you told anyone else—about the—radiation?"

Noreen didn't answer.

"I think maybe we've had a false alarm," Brack said to himself.

Brack called the guards in and told them to take off Noreen's chains and to get him something to eat. When they walked him out, they weren't rough with him and he knew that something had changed. He wondered what it was.

He wondered what had happened to his pictures.

CHAPTER

3⁶

When he got back to his cell, he felt better, as if he'd passed a test, sneaked in without paying admission, or opened a locked door, and he was hungry.

Something had happened in Brack's office. Something good. They were going to let him go and holding him a bit longer was just Brack's way of scaring him and staying on top.

This was mild stuff for Brack, the essential sadist. Noreen was lucky. His only punishment would be marrying Martine and that wasn't half bad. He was thirty-three; it was time he got married anyway. He thought of deceitful, lubricious Martine, and he wanted to see her as soon as possible.

After a while they brought him a steaming tray of food from the first-class commissary, not the prisoners' mess. He ate every bite, even mopping up the corners of the indented compartments with the best croissant he'd ever met. Then he sat back down on the cot and slapped his knee and had a laugh at his good fortune. He lay down and quickly fell into deep sleep.

He would have liked a long night's sleep but he heard the door open and woke up and saw Brack coming in.

"It's all fixed now," Brack said, "Get your things and go home. Forget this ever happened. I'll have Martine call you."

What about his pictures?

Noreen wanted to ask questions.

But Brack said, "Like I told you, it's all forgotten. We'll talk some other time if you like. Right now I want to forget this. A little misunderstanding, nothing more. You're okay, and you forget it too. No harm done, right, old boy? Now I have work to do. It's not necessary to ask questions. Just keep moving."

Noreen wanted to know where the pictures were.

They're historical flora and fauna. I found them. I should get them back. My research. Brack didn't have them. Who did?

Who had turned him in? Noreen didn't want to let go.

"Who fingered me?" he said.

Brack shook his head. "No more. It's all over." He meant it.

Noreen could see Brack's secretary waiting in the hall just outside the door. She had on her raincoat.

Brack extended his hand and Noreen let him grip his hand and they shook.

"As I've said before, welcome to the organization," Brack said. "And the family. And—oh yes—we won't mention this to Hayes—the part about your arrest."

Noreen nodded.

Brack's smile almost cut his face in two. He had taken care of a problem without involving Hayes. It really was over.

Noreen watched Brack go out into the hall, take the secretary's arm, and go out of sight in the direction of the main entrance. Brack left the door standing open.

Noreen took a final glance at the cell. He didn't ever want to see it again.

CHAPTER

3⁷

He did not like answering the door. You really weren't supposed to have company in the dome, especially at his level. Residences were intimate and private, usually occupied by only one or two people.

If you wanted to create a social gathering you did it at an official cubicle in the central city near the arboretum. Doorbells of a sort were present at the front of apartments but were often out of order. If you wanted to visit someone, you called ahead, specified the time, and were met at the door. One of the things that annoyed him about Martine was her tendency to drop by. It was—had been—all right for Beta to do so, but they had an understanding. She had a key, and it was practically her place too. But Martine dropped by in the spirit of a superior. An expression of her contempt for everyone except herself. She was exercising her rights as a member of the ruling class. But he had rights too as a doctor, and a level-five at that.

Martine would not be given a key to his apartment, no matter how much she pleaded. After they were married he would keep the apartment; he was sure he now had that right. She wasn't going to take that or anything else away from him.

He was also looking for reasons to get back at Martine, because she was interfering too much. He knew what the score was. He was letting her lead him along because it would be helpful in returning to the outside. He reminded himself that he would not forget it was all part of a game; Brack was playing a game; Martine was playing a game; he was playing the biggest game of all, and making up the rules as he went along.

The doorbell was not a bell at all; it was a tiny electronic bug, an electron-conducting membrane that emitted an unpleasant shriek. Now it startled him. His mind was racing so fast these days he was often unaware of his surroundings and reluctant to be reminded of them. If it was Martine he would send her running and make a point of letting her see the anger on his face, let her know that it would not always go her way.

But when he saw the man standing there he regretted showing any emotion. He suddenly felt he was in his clinic office and had just been set upon by a new patient.

"My name is Walter," the man said in a hollow whisper that had trouble placing itself, as if he didn't often speak out loud. "They sent me to get you—to take you down below."

"Who sent you?"

Walter looked startled by the question as if Noreen were about to thwart his task. Already he appeared to be thinking about his escape from dome proper.

"Why, the people who run things up here."

"Why would I want to go down there?"

"To get the girl. They said you would know."

"Wait. I'll be right with you."

Noreen closed the door in Walter's face and turned to get his coat.

He glanced at the apartment. He had wanted to check things out. Everything was a little too neat. As if the whole place had been torn apart and put back together. The screws were back in place in the panel. But more paint had been rubbed off the heads. They glinted now.

What the hell, he'd check when he got back.

Where were his pictures?

Then he suddenly stopped thinking about himself. He was thinking about the tall blonde with the dirty face. He would see her soon.

Down below. It sounded dirty. So be it.

CHAPTER 3

Walter was of medium height but so skinny he looked taller. He was wearing a long, black cloth coat. Thin legs protruded, barely visible below the coat's frayed bottom hem, and above the plain, worn collar a thatch of stringy, grayish hair stuck out. In the bright, diffused dome light, Walter had a striking pallor, not from fairness but from long lack of light. In fact, what Noreen remembered now was the pallor of all the down-below residents, even the small dark ones.

Noreen watched Walter's back. The coat rose and fell and tilted to the right as Walter hobbled along. He had something badly wrong with his hip and legs. Noreen expected he would have to walk slowly, but, now that Walter had gone ahead, he was watching Walter's back getting smaller, and he had a hard time keeping up. Walter was not trying to lose him; every now and then he looked back and slowed a bit, but he kept to that fast pace as if to comply with instructions.

Two louts in the baggy jumpsuits of security functionaries lounged against the cast-iron filigree that decorated the subway entrance.

Walter had slowed down and was waiting, one frail hand on the railing, his body slanted over the darkness below. The guards didn't say anything when Walter and Noreen started down the steps.

The warm, moist air wafting up the stairway struck Noreen with familiar acrid scents. He walked faster.

Already Walter had moved ahead into the gloom. His footsteps echoed from the stone walkways and merged with the flowing slurp of the water that ran constantly in the gutters.

Noreen pulled up his collar to shield against the chilly dampness that now greeted them. It was not as warm down here as he had expected. Perhaps this trip to the infrastructure would not be as interesting as the last one.

He began to walk even faster, almost at a jog, trying to keep up with the hobbling man, who had just turned a corner. Noreen expected to find Walter had disappeared into the mist.

"I'll wait here for you."

Walter had stopped outside the dark niche that contained the door to the boiler room.

Noreen could hear no sound from the door's other side. The echoing gutter noise of the tunnels masked everything.

"No," Noreen said. "This is fine. Go on about your business."

"This is my business. You know your way up? Out?"

"Yes," Noreen said. He wasn't sure though.

Walter hesitated. Noreen wondered if he was supposed to give Walter something.

"What do I owe you?"

Walter stared at him blankly. "Oh, nothing. I have everything I need. Sure you'll be all right?"

"Yes, thank you."

Noreen watched Walter go out of sight around the corner. He heard his uneven footsteps for a moment and then they were eaten up by the general echo of the tunnels.

Noreen placed his hand on the doorpull. It was warm to the touch. He shivered and pulled the door open, entering a cocoon of damp warm air.

The boiler room had changed. Only one furnace glowed. No one was attending it. One man was reading a book at the wooden table. Another was slumped against the wall beyond the furnaces dozing. He did not see the girl.

He would take his time. He was looking forward to the girl, but he had really come to look at the pictures on the wall. He turned to his right.

He saw nothing but bare wall. Had he imagined the pictures? Or had the room undergone some ritual of purification? He was sure they had been there. He remembered they looked like they had existed on the wall for centuries, had become part of the wall, yellowed by time and effluent from the concrete, even singed at the edges as if from the overheating of the furnaces. Now they were all gone.

They've cheated me.

He was in no hurry. He had planned on spending a long time walking back and forth along the wall. He had looked forward to letting his eye movement retrace the lines in the pictures, then standing silently in front of each image, trying to decipher the original patches of color, letting it all wash onto his retina. He had planned on processing the images into his subconscious. But he had been thwarted. Perhaps someone had guessed that, if given the chance, he had decided to steal one of the pictures. In the light from the furnace he could see faint outlines where the pictures had protected the wall for so long.

He turned his back to the wall and stared for a long time at the room. No one looked up. No one cared if he was there.

He walked past the man reading the book at the table. The man didn't look up. He entered the hallway that led back to the room the girl had first appeared from. It was dark in the hallway. He stepped on something soft that didn't move. He kept walking.

Just as he was about to reach the door, it opened, and the girl ran into him. He got a whiff of cigarette smoke from her skin and a faint smell of harsh soap. She backed up.

He followed her into a high-ceilinged room. Way up above, a bank of fluorescent lights beamed down and it was brighter than in the boiler room. She backed up some more and sat down on the edge of the desk.

She looked different. She had on a clean, form-fitting jumpsuit. He could see her face. She had washed all the coal dirt off. Her hair had been washed too and combed, and he could see she was a natural blonde. She looked good, about thirty, with crows feet and little bags starting to show around the eyes. All in all, a bit rough from the hard work, the aging and the not caring. The jumpsuit was white and dramatically clean, a bit risky for a boiler room. Everything including the girl had been spiffed up as if awaiting inspection or an important visitor. He was sure it had not been done for him. He did not feel important today.

"What happened down here?" he said, withholding any comment about her appearance.

"What do you mean?"

"Where are the pictures?" He nodded over his shoulder.

"Oh, we cleaned up. I thought it was time. Those old pictures. You could hardly see them."

"I saw them."

"Too bad. Don't you know it's against the law to look at pictures? Maybe that's why we cleaned up. Against the law or something like that."

"Apparently not down here. All right, let's go."

He just wanted to get out of there, get it over.

"I'm not going anywhere," she said.

"What?"

"I've changed my mind."

"But you sent for me."

"I expected a shipment of whiskey. It didn't come."

"Oh, really?"

She shook her head.

"No whiskey, no go."

"Why is whiskey so important?"

"No point in explaining—you're a square geek from upstairs and wouldn't understand."

He didn't like the part about the geek, whatever that was, but he said, "They promised. You can trust them."

"I don't trust anyone, especially those bastards. Besides, I don't care if I ever see my father again. I have to have the stuff before I do anything. If you care, do something."

She stood up, unzipped her jumpsuit and started pulling it down around her shoulders as if he wasn't there. He got a glimpse of dark underwear and white skin. She had apparently bathed all over. She was muscled like a dancer. She was calling off the trip. She was getting ready to return to work, to get dirty again.

"Wait," he said, "I'll phone and see what happened."

She stopped taking off her clothes and waited with her upper body exposed. He could see her breasts in a black brassiere.

He had already pressed Brack's phone number on the pocket phone.

She sat down on the edge of the desk, holding up her jumpsuit, let her leg arc up and down as if counting time. He would have only so many bounces of the leg before she would call it all off and he would have to leave without her. And maybe never be allowed back. Maybe never see her again. If there were pictures down here, she knew where they were.

CHAPTER

3⁹

She had pulled the jumpsuit back on, buttoned it up, and sat down primly on the chair behind the desk. A faint black smudge covered her bottom from where she had sat on the desk top. The desk had been scrubbed recently, but centuries of coal dust had seeped into everything and wasn't letting go.

Small dark men dressed in suits like barrieralls had appeared with dollies of ancient cardboard containers marked "whiskey" and they were now pushing them past the desk into another room behind the office.

When they had finished they nodded and hurriedly pulled their carts away. You could not see their faces clearly through their tinted plastic face masks, but Noreen felt sure he could detect the dark skin and round heads of the working class. He wondered if they were breathing tube air inside the suits instead of the infrastructure atmosphere. It gave him the creeps. As if he were on a different planet and no one had told him.

Should he have worn barrieralls down here?

"Let's go," he said.

She had come out of the back carrying a key.

She was smiling.

"I keep the stuff locked in a room next to my bedroom. We'll take inventory when we get back."

"*We* won't be coming back. I'll see you to the entrance to the subway and that will be it."

"What if I told you there were more pictures down here?"

He had turned his back to her and started for the door. Now he stopped and faced her again.

He didn't answer but he could see she knew what he was thinking.

"So you'd rather come down and see more pictures than see me?" she said.

"I'm a doctor. I have a scientific curiosity about new things."

"And I'm not a new thing?"

"You're a patient's relative."

Suddenly she was trying to be considerate and friendly. He didn't mind. But it hadn't worked out the way he expected. He wanted to get things moving. Maybe he needed a pill.

What lovely breasts she has! Then: *Did they burn
the pictures?*

"What's your name?" Noreen said.

"Call me Nora," she said.

"Nora Kafahvey?"

"No. Just Nora."

She was wearing spiked shoes, but she walked
easily in them and her long strides kept up with
him. They walked side by side and saw no one in
the tunnels.

Two guards waited at the subway entrance but
they straightened up now to show they were on the
job. A jet-propelled police scooterbucket was
parked at the top of the steps. Noreen didn't like
seeing it there. He'd had enough of the police
lately.

When they came up into the dome, a short dark
man with a thin, very black mustache got out of the
vehicle.

"I'm Major Dork," he said gruffly with a voice
that sounded like rubber bands snapping. "I'll
escort you to your father's house." He spoke directly
to the girl and did not even look at Noreen, as if
he didn't exist. He was wearing the dark suit and
insignia of a high-ranking security officer. For some
reason, he considered this an important
assignment; otherwise he would not have been
here. In the dome organization chart, Noreen as a
doctor had always outranked such a person and
now, with his impending marriage to Martine and

T
I
M
E

A
N
D

L
I
G
H
T

226

consequent boost in status, he ranked even higher, but this did not seem to matter to Dork. It had something to do with Kafahvey, Noreen assumed. The poet's reputation preceded him. Yet Noreen had seen the poet's enlarged testicles and examined his stool and was not impressed.

Noreen and the girl climbed in and sat on the narrow back seat. Dork sat next to the driver and didn't look back.

It was almost noon; many of the workers were spending their lunch hour strolling through the Garden of Eden, the park in the flowery center of the city. Noreen watched Nora staring out the window, taking it all in. He assumed she hadn't been up in the dome in a long time. Perhaps he would ask her sometime why she left. He really didn't know why anyone ever left the dome for good.

The sun was burning down through the opalescent dome skin, filtering though tendrils of dwarf-tree branches, and it felt warm and good after the catacombs. The dome was large and livable and he was glad to be back up in it again.

The seasons were subtle within the confined ecosphere but this was spring all right and he wondered now what it was like outside on the empty roads and the rock-covered mountains.

The bucket moved swiftly through the downtown traffic, picked up more speed in the suburbs, then entered the gate that marked the neighborhood of very special people. When Kafahvey's apartment came in view, Dork began to squirm and make little clicking sounds in his throat.

As they got out, Dork said: "I'll come up with you and see that everything is all right."

"No," she said. "I know my way."

"I insist," Dork said. "My duty. I'm supposed to look out for you."

He started to follow. Noreen said, "Please. Wait here. I'll take care of the lady."

Dork could not conceal a look of profound disappointment or a layer of barely masked anger. But he nodded and watched them go into the building. For the first time he had glanced at Noreen and acknowledged his status. Noreen could see all of Dork's years of inferiority as a dark little person flooding his memory and weighing him down, and knew he'd made an enemy. It was not a good time for calling himself to the attention of a police chief. He thought about turning back and saying something to make Dork feel better. But he didn't know what to say and he decided it was too late anyway.

Kafahvey's wall screen was dark. Only the light from the window came in and illumined the bed. The "nurses" in their high heels and skimpy costumes let them into the room.

The poet was propped up, dozing in the center of the bed as if he had not moved since the last time, resembling a glowing white figurine.

When he heard them whispering, the good eye opened and pivoted until it found a focal point. Then a smile appeared on the blob's face and the arms began to rise away from the body suggesting a chicken about to take flight.

The voice had trouble at first forming itself into speech. Saliva had to be negotiated and sputum moved around, then it said, "My daughter, my daughter, oh my daughter, come here."

She looked at Noreen, squeamishly. He nodded.

The poet's torso and flaccid legs began to move. A loose sheet lay about his knees. He pulled it up, covering the blue sack between his legs. Then he extended his legs, swung them around, and let them perch over the side of the bed. After a long time he allowed them to bend and touch the floor.

Odors that had been imbedded in the sheets were now dislodged and spread out in the room. The poet's aura, a mixture of urine, phlegm, sweat, dried blood, and overheated bacteria, deployed in every direction until it had even filled the corners.

Noreen's nose twitched, and he told it to calm down, it was part of the job.

The nurses gasped.

Kafahvey was standing up. He held out his arms.

Noreen had not believed it possible.

Nora went forward and let the pile of flesh hug
her. Noreen watched the white arms and hands
caress her back and squeeze her buttocks. After a
while Nora pulled away.

The old man's sheet had fallen down and was still
held in front of him by his enormous erection.

The "nurses" looked at each other and then at
the doctor, who made no gesture, then they ran
over, helped the old man back in bed, and covered
him up.

He was panting and cackling every other breath.
"My daughter, my daughter, my beautiful daughter,
you've come back." He reached out a hand for her
but she did not take it; she just stood by the side
of the bed out of reach. He ignored her reluctance
by switching the subject. "Kafahvey sings today.
Kafahvey sings again. Doctor—"

Noreen moved to his side.

"Doctor, my beautiful relative, you sly peddler of
drugs, and social-climber making your way on my
back, you're a miracle worker. I shall never forget
you. I will write poems about you. I will let you fuck
my daughters if you like and can find them. Even
Nora, who has never been fucked by anyone except
myself. Is that not true, Nora? Say it, say it, say it.
Now hand me my guitar."

He made a move to sit up again on the side of the
bed. Noreen put out a hand to stop him. But the
old man wasn't having any of it. Noreen could feel

under the sagging flesh, deep within, a powerful strength like concealed springs waiting there all along ready to uncoil. The old man sat up, let his legs dangle.

Noreen wanted to hold the old man back, to take blood pressure, count breaths, but he let him go.

"What's a guitar?"

"There. On the wall." He was pointing at the plastic object dangling by a shiny yellow thong, a flat box with stings stretched across it.

Noreen went over, reached up, felt the strings vibrating, and handed it to Kafahvey.

The poet rested the instrument on his lap, so it was partially supported by his penis, as if the blue-red knob sticking out below was a decorative part of the device.

With fluid arm thrusts that were surprisingly graceful Kafahvey grabbed the neck of the instrument, pressed some switches, and flicked the back of his right hand's fingers across the strings where they traversed the box. Noise issued.

Both hands squeezed and pressed and the music of Kafahvey came out of the electrically amplified box—the music of Kafahvey which had unity and disharmony at the same time. It was music, wasn't it? Noreen asked himself, not quite sure. But it was not like the "music" that came out of the loudspeakers in every room in the dome.

Yes, it had to be music. So there was more to music than he had imagined. This did not just fill the cracks and corners, it pushed itself out into the middle of the room. He had not thought much about music until now and now more than ever he was not sure he liked "music."

Even when he felt his eardrums were going to break, Noreen could still hear the notes organizing themselves in plaintive cries or rhythmic pleadings and all the time a sinister low beat was threading its way through whatever message the high notes carried and it was all issuing outward from the poet and slamming into Noreen's own body so that all his bones and muscles and organs were vibrating to the beat.

The poet stood up now and spread his stinky bare feet on the tile floor.

His bulk seemed suspended without weight above and behind the instrument, and the legs were gyrating and lunging, and from the laughing fat skull of a face among the spray and the sputum the poet's voice issued forth. It was not so much what he said but the way he said it that had force.

"I got you babee, bababee, I got you I got you I got you I got you I got you now now now now now now!"

It was nonsensical, Noreen knew, but it came out as *truth*. What truth he didn't know, but at the same time he felt it a privilege to hear this nonsense.

It was a young man singing in an old man's body!

Kafahvey had moved closer to Nora now. She was dancing and clapping her hands to the music, as if she couldn't help herself. She had done this before.

Suddenly it all stopped and silence dropped into the room.

Kafahvey staggered and slumped back on the bed before anyone could catch him. The guitar slipped to the hard floor with a tremulous bump. The white noise that still came out of it buzzed angrily.

Noreen grabbed for the old man's wrist. Kafahvey had leaned back now and was catching his breath. A rougy tint brushed his face.

Noreen took the old man's pulse again. The first time he'd counted only fifty beats per second. Now it was forty-seven. He was either dying or operating on a fraction of his reserve strength. It was why he had lived so long. He was always just getting started. His motor rarely got up to speed. There was no wear on the pump at all. The blubber which distorted his outward form and would eventually kill him, who knew when, was simply the receipt for his indulgence. He was killing himself through excess but he had a long way to go. Still, Noreen could not understand the recovery that had allowed him to defy the weight of his blubber and the deterioration of his frame and stand up and perform as he had.

"I'm all right, doctor, don't you think?" he said, smiling at Noreen. "That's a rhetorical question. As if I value your opinion. Come, doctor, speak up— or have you lost your senses?"

"I'm not sure," Noreen said. "I think you should take it easy the rest of the day."

He wasn't sure who worried him—Kafahvey or Nora. He looked at her. She was inscrutable, arms crossed, finger aligned with her nose, still now.

Then he noticed a pounding had been going on at the front of the house. A nurse was returning with Major Dork. Dork was coming in with a rush but he recoiled at the sight he encountered.

"I heard these loud noises. I thought—"

You just wanted an excuse to barge in, Noreen speculated.

Noreen grabbed the major's arm and guided him to the front door.

"I just want to see my daughter alone now," he heard Kafahvey say.

"Everything's fine," Noreen heard himself say to Dork. But listening now for more conversation from behind his back. Anxious to hurry back. But now he could see Dork wanted to talk and this was a chance to make a good impression on him.

"You've just had a rare opportunity to see the corporate poet, 'the father of our country,'" Noreen said, trying to force a smile like Hayes'. "Sometime you must come back when he's feeling better and be formally introduced. I would like to have the pleasure of introducing you to him myself."

"I'd appreciate that," Dork said absently, staring at the place. "This is a wonderful apartment. It's almost a shame to waste it on an old man. I have a wife and two kids all squeezed into a little place. We could really enjoy this place, get something out of it."

"He's the father of our country."

"But he's almost dead. Isn't he?"

"Not quite. As you could see."

"But going soon? I wonder what will happen to this apartment when he dies."

"It'll be a national shrine. If he ever does."

"We can't really afford to waste space like this, can we, doctor?"

"Of course, not. It would be nice if someone deserving such as you and your family could move in here. In fact, I'll even suggest it. When the time comes."

"Would you do that?"

"Yes, I would."

"I'd like that a lot. One more promotion and I'll certainly qualify. I've always worked very hard and I'm extremely loyal to the dome."

"I can see that."

"And I come from an old important family. Dork is an ancient respected name."

"I'm sure of it," Noreen said. He had guided Dork down the stairs and out the front door and they were standing on the sidewalk in front of the security bucket.

"Now I'd better go back and attend to my patient." *See what he's doing to his daughter*, Noreen translated to himself.

"You're a fine man, doctor," Dork said.

Noreen shrugged modestly.

"I mean it. And I appreciate what you said about helping me. I'll be your friend for life if you do. It never hurts to have a policeman for your friend, I don't care who you are, don't you know?"

Noreen nodded wisely.

They shook hands.

The major watched Noreen go back into the building. Armpit sweat had soaked even darker semicircles on the black cloth of his suit. Sweat beads had pushed out of his forehead, and his bowed legs looked slightly more arched than earlier, as if stress increased their curvature.

CHAPTER

40

Noreen raced up the stairs, long legs taking all the steps they could reach. By now Kafahvey could be humping her.

The "nurses" were huddled over the bed. Straightening sheets and propping pillows. The guitar had been turned off and was back in its place on the wall. Kafahvey was stretched out, exhausted.

"He had an ejaculation. We're cleaning it up," a "nurse" said. She left the room carrying a wet paper towel.

The wall screen glowed now with subdued pulsating colored lights.

"Where's the daughter?"

"I don't know. She left the room."

Noreen found her in the kitchen, smoking a cigarette.

"Smoking is not allowed in the dome," Noreen said.

"Fuck you," she said.

"Why not?" he said.

"Is it almost over? Have I done the necessary?"

"What do you think?"

"I want to go home now."

"This is your home, isn't it?" She answered him with a laugh, a dry skittle that turned into a cough.

"It's over as far as I'm concerned," he said. "A medical miracle. And I've made friends with the cop. That's a kind of miracle too."

"Lucky you."

He could have told her he spent a night in jail, but let it go.

"We'll just stop in and pay our respects one last time, say good-bye, that is, and I'll see you back to the subway."

She sucked in a last drag and snuffed out the cigarette on the kitchen table, left it there.

Kafahvey was stretched out under his sheet like a white anthill, staring at the ceiling. He heard them come in but didn't seem to care. He said to the ceiling: "I'd like a few minutes alone with my daughter."

"You've seen me. You put on your show. Now I'm going," she said.

He turned his face toward her.

"Just five minutes more. Alone."

Noreen was sure he saw the tongue dart in and out, pointed and red, reptilian.

"As your doctor, I must insist you rest," he said.

He spoke up a little too quickly and wondered why he wanted to protect her.

"If you wish to remain my doctor you'll just shut up."

Noreen looked at Nora, who shrugged, then at the "nurses" who nodded *yes*. Noreen looked at his wrist time.

"Five minutes exactly then," he said.

"In five minutes I can do more than you can imagine in a life time," Kafahvey said, no humor or compassion in the now-resonant voice. Basso-profundo.

Noreen, followed by the "nurses," left the room. Before the door closed, he could see Nora standing at the foot of the bed. The poet had lifted an arm and stretched it toward her.

CHAPTER

41

In the kitchen one of the women saw the dead cigarette butt on the table and got excited. She started cleaning up.

The other one said, "Can I fix you something to drink? It may take a while."

That annoyed Noreen.

"It'll take five minutes. Less than that now." He tapped his wrist time.

"I don't think he can do it in five minutes now."

"What?"

"You know."

"No, I don't."

"That's all he thinks about. You know they called him the prophet of sex. It's what got people through the bad times in the old days. Then he went too far and the people went crazy and the dome authorities made him stop. But they still revered him as a poet, almost a saint. He talks about it sometimes. He remembers everything just like it was yesterday. He's got stuff lying around all over that's against the law to have and they don't take it away."

"Maybe he makes it up. What he says. He's a poet."

"I never thought about it that way. You know maybe you're right. Maybe nothing he says is true."

"He can sure play the *guitar*."

"Yeah, I wish they played stuff like that on the speakers. I get tired of the same old stuff. All the time."

"You too?"

"Yeah. Same old stuff."

"All right. It's time," Noreen said.

"We better wait. Give them a little longer."

"It's time."

CHAPTER

4²

The police bucket was still waiting out front. They got in and drove back toward downtown. Dork had gone on somewhere rather than wait. Noreen didn't ask her what happened. They didn't say anything during the trip until they had passed the central gardens. Then she said, "Do you live near here?"

"Yes," Noreen said, "not far."

"I'd like to use your john."

Noreen had been looking at her surreptitiously for telltale signs on her clothing or her skin. But nothing looked different. He wondered what she had done in the five minutes.

He told the driver where he lived.

"But—" the driver said.

Noreen said, "She's a dome citizen. She can go anywhere she wants. I'll see she gets back. The subway entrance is not far. If there's a problem let's call my new friend Dork."

The driver waited on the street at the foot of the steep stairs that went up to Noreen's porch. Noreen unlocked the door, then looked around and waved at the driver, who drove off.

Inside, Noreen closed and locked the door and watched the police car go out of sight, then pulled the blinds down tight.

"If you really have to use the john it's in there." Noreen nodded at the hall that went past the bedroom.

She placed her large black shoulder bag carefully on the couch and left the room.

Noreen almost set about checking the place and then decided it didn't matter, they would be leaving soon.

When she came back, she was combing her hair and then rolling up her sleeves.

"I didn't really have to use your john. I just wanted to see your place. But it was nice to take a leak too. Your place is just what I expected it to be. Boy, do I feel better."

She flopped on the couch and stretched out.

"It's always good to pee after sex, isn't it?" he said.

"What do you mean?"

"You know—"

"No, I don't know."

"Didn't you just have sex with your father?" She laughed gutturally. He could see a faint reddening under the thin white skin.

"Don't be silly. I haven't had sex in—" She pretended to count the days or was it months on her fingers. Maybe it was years, Noreen told himself.

"Make me a drink, will you?" she said.

"What would you like?"

"Whiskey and water."

"I thought you'd say that. I'm all out of whiskey. I drank it."

"I thought you'd say that too. But here—I've brought you another present."

She handed him a paper sack from her purse. He could feel the glass bottle inside and the anticipation of having another supply of whiskey thrilled him. What was happening to him?

She followed him into the kitchen. He got out the glasses and some ice water. All the time she was checking out his apartment.

He wondered what she would think if she knew about his photographs. Just as well the photographs were gone. Out there somewhere waiting to get him in trouble.

If she knew, she would ask for a vat of whiskey to keep quiet and turn him in when he couldn't pay up.

"You know that panel in your front room covers

a picture screen just like the one at Kafahvey's only smaller," she said. "You should uncover it and turn it on. Then you'd have pictures all the time. I can see you like pictures. What would they do to you? Nothing."

"They'd send Dork for me and put me in jail."

"No, not you. They'd never put *you* in jail."

He didn't tell her.

"I grew up with that stuff all my life," she said. "It can't hurt you. The people up here are nuts. I think they're afraid of something and they're covering up. They're crazy anyway. I don't like coming up here."

"Maybe they have radiation sickness."

"Harumph. You believe that stuff about radiation. The only thing they got right up here is fucking. And they got that from my father. And they don't even get that right. They don't know fucking at all."

"You seem to know a lot about it."

"I know that talking is not fucking."

"Are we talking too much?"

"I don't know. Does that mean that you'd like to fuck me?"

"Absolutely not."

"Then let's have that drink."

They looked at each other. He didn't know what she was thinking.

CHAPTER

4³

He poured the drink and they sipped slowly and he watched her sitting across the table from him. She had large wrists and broad shoulders from shoveling the coal, and a wide jaw, and he realized he had not seen that many large blond women in the dome. She seemed to be avoiding his gaze and looked nervous. He could feel the whiskey seeping in along with the fatigue and, re-running the conversation they had just had, he felt a little stiffening between his legs.

"Is that why you came by? For the old push-me-pull-you?"

"No," she said, getting up, and she wouldn't look at him now, wasn't going to look at him any more. "I've got to go now."

She didn't want to, he was sure of that. She was just jerking him around.

He pushed back his chair and stood up to let her pass by and when she did she brushed against him with the slight crushing sound of poplin and he grabbed her or she grabbed him and they were pressing tight against each other as if they were going to merge their body molecules, and he was surprised that she felt even larger and stronger than he imagined she would be. She tossed her long blond hair away from her face so he could kiss her and stick his tongue down her throat and she was trying to do the same thing to him and clamped together they managed to drag each other to his bedroom ripping open zippers and discarding clothes as they went. By the time they reached the bed her jumpsuit was hanging down around her ankles and she was hobbling and he lifted her onto the bed and pulled her suit the rest of the way off.

Entering her was like going back into the infrastructure again. This was the reverse of being born; he was returning to his primal home.

She was almost as tall and husky as he was. When he opened his eyes and saw her face two inches away from himself it was like looking at his own face in the mirror.

So he closed his eyes and let the night go on and on at its own speed.

CHAPTER

4⁴

When he awoke in the morning, a bit late for an important doctor at Organo Institute and an engaged one at that—to a member of a leading family—he felt no guilt or remorse, just a lacerating ache around his head, which was the whiskey.

He staggered into the john and then into the other room looking for her, thinking she had gone into the kitchen to make them some breakfast. He could still feel the imprint of her big breasts and her bony broad hips on his hands and could taste and smell her on his face. She smelled and tasted like whiskey and cigarettes and dried mucous pheromones, and her effluent had soaked into the entire apartment.

But she was gone. She had left a note and a rolled up tube of something on the table.

"There's more where this came from. Come again," was all the note said. Brief for a poet's daughter but probably cryptic in the family tradition.

He unrolled the tube and when the first inside edge appeared he could feel his heart skip beats.

The old pictures from the wall down there had not been destroyed. He held one in his hand.

It was a grotesque caricature on smooth shiny paper. The edges were frayed and indented from abuse and had a tendency to turn inward.

Its backside contained a black and white plea to sell something, mostly text, with a line drawing of a cylindrical device that for some reason he could not decipher was meant to be inserted into a nostril and twisted.

The front contained a drawing or a painting in garish color. From exposure to light and air the colored inks on the top, bottom, and right edges were faded, creating a mottled pale blue border about half an inch wide. But the central area of the page had been protected and its inks were as bright and clear and colorful as they must have been when they were first applied. It looked like a cover page from a periodical. A single image occupied the entire sheet even to the edges of the paper. This picture was cartoonish and exaggerated and lacked the depth of a photograph. Instead, it seemed to rise up above the page.

He had no temptation to enter the frame. In fact,

the picture was somewhat repulsive, even sinister, yet he loved it anyway. It showed the face of a man with a long, strikingly chiseled nose and slanted evil eyes under a black slouch hat with an exceptionally wide and flowing brim. The bottom of the face was tightly covered by a black cloth.

The man is leaning out of a window of a vehicle. His arms are extended and in each hand he holds a metal weapon. Small fires blaze forth in orange-red puffs from holes in the ends of these objects. The man is wearing a black cape with a red lining, part of which has flared up into view.

In the left hand corner of the picture Noreen can make out words, one of which looks like "Graves." This cartoon's not the same as a photograph, but he treasures it just the same. He looks forward to letting his eyes take a wild ride over the flowing lines and brilliant colors of this ancient relic.

Nora should not have rolled it. It was priceless and deserved better care. Each rolling and unrolling seemed to increase the depth of the jagged edge.

He would take care of it. Flatten it, and keep it flat.

What had she meant? More of her, or more pictures, or both? He would find a way to return to the underground.

CHAPTER

45

"What have you done to Kafahvey?" Hayes asked.

Noreen got a puzzled look. He didn't know what Hayes was talking about.

"I took his daughter over there to see him. Everything seemed to work out," he said.

"No, not that. I know that. But the old boy called me this morning. Himself. He sounded fine. He wants to give a concert. Is someone putting me on?"

"Oh my!" Noreen couldn't help saying.

"I'll have to think about this," Hayes said. "I wanted you to look in on him, not give him the fountain of youth. It's one thing to have a dying pensioner on your hands but quite another story when you've resurrected a messiah. You know, long before you and I were around, he was involved in a lot of controversy. I'll have to look that up. He was a troublemaker, you know. This is not good. Not good at all."

"What should I do?" Noreen said, wondering if he had got himself into more trouble.

"Nothing you can do now," Hayes said. "You've already done it. I understand you can be something of a troublemaker yourself, but, ho, ho, ho, let's not waste time talking about that. Oh, I guess you could give him an overdose of seco-barbital or something, couldn't you? Then we could have a jolly important state funeral. But I'm jesting. Though, who knows, it may come to that. On the plus side, I must say what you've done is remarkable. I must say, outside of your troublemaking. Actually, you'll get a commendation. The treatment was excellent, no one could have done better. Better even than my own in the past, I confess. You had no way of predicting the possible political outcome."

"Should I stop treating him?"

"Heavens no, we can't let on there's a problem. Where's the daughter?"

"I sent her back. I think she was glad to go."

He left out the details.

"Good. Let's keep her down there. She's undoubtedly part of the problem. She didn't give him anything, did she?

"I don't know. I don't think so. Why?"

"You let her out of your sight?"

"She was alone with him for a few minutes. Five to be exact."

"See. That could be it. I don't want to denigrate your treatment, but—you don't suppose they've got some new drug down there and she slipped it to him?"

"No, of course not."

He hadn't thought about that. He thought it was his treatment—and the girl's visit.

"Don't be so sure," Hayes said.

"I'm not sure about anything these days. But where would they get a drug like that?"

Hayes pursed his lips and shook his head at Noreen.

"Oh, Noreen, Noreen, poor fellow, you innocent! Who knows what goes on *là-bas*? I sure don't, and I'm in charge. Lots of crafty rascals down there. The dregs, of course, and they don't have enough to do. Ought to be cleaned out. I've always said that place has too much leeway. But most of us are too soft up here to spend any time down there. I admire you for having the guts to tackle the place. Though I must say you are a *naïf*, still the cloistered scientific, way outside your field."

Noreen lowered his eyes modestly for a moment and when he looked back up again Hayes was staring at him expectantly.

"He wants her to come back up soon," Noreen said. "I think she agreed."

"See, what'd I tell you? He's paying her, that's what. Getting something from her, anyway. I don't know how or what but it's got to be something like that. Keep an eye on her. Find out what she's giving him."

"You mean the next time she comes up?"

"No, I mean now."

"You mean go back down there?"

"It's a lot to ask. But, yes, if you don't mind. You know your way around that hole now—"

"I'd rather check the outside for botanicals, but yes of course, anything for the dome. If I go down below again, will I be allowed to continue my work outside?"

Hayes stood up, slapped Noreen on the back.

"Good boy. You'll have your time outside I promise, though I can't understand why anyone, especially with your credentials, would do scut work like that. But first things first. Let's take care of this Kafahvey thing, then we can think about outside. Too bad you can't wait another twenty thousand years to go outside again. There'd be no radiation then."

He paused the way he always did when he mentioned radiation to wait for a reaction, but Noreen didn't give him one. Did he know that Noreen knew about the radiation and was just waiting for Noreen to mention it?

Noreen said: "I don't mind going outside now. We have good protective clothing."

"And instruments, right?"

"Yes, early warning for sure."

Hayes nodded father-like, and let his thoughts drop off.

"And how's Martine?" he said, clearly slipping to a different plane.

Noreen stood up, got ready to go.

"Fine. Very excited, as you might guess."

"Wonderful. Take care of yourself. You want to be in good shape for that little girl."

"Thank you, sir, I will."

"And you won't become a troublemaker again? You'll leave all graven images below, where they belong, right?"

Hayes winked. Hayes knew something now. Had Brack told him?

"Right. I've learned my lesson."

"Good, good, old boy. And—find that elixir of youth—that potion or whatever it is they're giving Kafahvey. I hear he's still got an erection all the time. That must be wonderful, don't you think? We could all use a little of that, couldn't we?"

"Yes. You can count on me, sir." Noreen put his hand on the doorpull.

"I mean it—find that elixir!" Hayes called after him, getting up from his desk and coming to the door. "That's what it's all about now as far as I'm concerned, don't you know? You're on special assignment for me personally. If anyone asks, no details. None of their business. That means Brack too. I could use a little elixir myself. Keep the old pecker up. I bet you could too. Right?"

"Yes, sir."

"We all need to look out for our peckers, sooner or later."

"By all means."

"Good, good boy, Noreen. I know I can count on you."

In the hallway, going back to his office, Noreen wondered if he had deceived Hayes somehow or if Hayes had been playing with him. You could never be sure about that fatherly approach. Maybe he wasn't falling for anything.

The business about the pecker seemed real enough.

He probably knew Noreen had figured out about the "radiation." But they thought he got the pictures down below. That was good. Always misdirect them. Never let them suspect the existence of *his* cave. Lead them down below, as often as necessary.

Were there pictures down below? Photographs?

One thing was clear: he had carte blanche to leave the dome again, downstairs at first, then later outside. And already he wanted Nora again. He could still smell her on his upper lip and on his fingers even after washing them many times. He hadn't got enough of her, that big slathering rack. Most of all he would check out the catacomb's hidden treasures—pictures removed from walls.

And then find photographic prints. Surely, they had some downstairs. And if they had life-prolonging medicines it wouldn't hurt to know about them too. But there was no secret drug. Kafahvey was unusual but he was just in remission now—the spectacular remission from the disease called impending death. Thanks to the great Dr. Noreen who had filled the old man full of garlic. Kafahvey wouldn't last five minutes outside his apartment. The amphitheater in the park would never see Kafahvey again. He had lived too long; it was almost his time.

Still...

CHAPTER

"I'm very disappointed. You haven't called me."

Martine's voice on the phone sounded small and wavering. It was meant to make him feel guilty. Her voice was a weapon, and she could use it any way she wanted, he knew.

"I'm worried about you," she said. "Why do this to me? You miss me?"

"Of course."

"You were naughty, weren't you?"

"What?"

"With that girl."

"What girl?"

"Don't play dumb with me. You know. The poet's daughter?"

"Don't be ridiculous. I took her to see her father, that's all."

"I don't want you doing that again. Not ever."

"It was strictly professional. A job."

"I don't care. I'll talk to my brother."

"Don't waste your breath. It's over. I'm through with that job."

She cheered up, seemed closer.

"Good. I worried about you especially *down there*. That must be a horrible place. You could catch something down there. I've heard about that place. I don't want you down there or outside the dome, ever."

"Your wish is my command."

"I'm terribly happy to hear you say that. You mean it?"

"Yes, I mean it. You mean everything to me and I want to do everything that will make you happy. I want to stay near you as much as possible and that means staying in the dome proper at all times."

"Wonderful. And what will you do when you're near me?"

"You know exactly."

"I'm coming right over."

"No, not now, I have to go into the office, catch up, file some reports."

"You're so dedicated. When? Tonight?"

"No. Tomorrow. All weekend."

"Promise."

"Promise."

He wanted to ask her if she had turned him in to the police, if she knew where his pictures were. But he'd wait.

He'd keep coupling her and he'd wait and he'd couple her again and then he'd trap her in a lie and go on from there.

He had decided to return to the infrastructure tonight.

Kafahvey told me to bring his daughter up again. I thought I could catch her with the drug.

Once you started lying it was easy. You just spoke up and you kept going.

He had learned that from Martine.

CHAPTER

47

But that evening, just before he started to leave the apartment, Martine turned up anyway.

She wanted to show him her belly. It was acquiring a slight curve that was the baby, she was pretty sure, and she was anxious for him to inspect her, not as a doctor but as the father of her child. For a moment she held still while he ran his hand over the smooth flawless skin and it was possible, perhaps she was showing the first signs of pregnancy; and she seemed small and refined compared to his subterranean blonde, who demanded nothing except a case of whiskey for her friends and gave him an ancient picture to treasure, whereas Martine wanted to possess him and make a slave out of him for some selfish social purpose only she understood. He inspected her all right, first as the parent and then for an instant as a doctor but that wasn't what she had come for; she wanted to inspect him, her trophy, and she wanted the trophy to make her feel good, which meant probing between her legs in ways she couldn't do herself.

All the time he was watching her for some sign of guilt or anxiety in the clear brown eyes and the pouty lips and he saw none and he began to wonder if she even knew he had been arrested.

When she got ready to leave, he worried for a moment why she had decided not to spend the night. She said she had to get up early and take care of wedding details. Whatever they might be. She wanted him to get a good night's sleep. She wanted him to get to work on time. She wanted him to finish up with his work, whatever that might be, and she didn't want to know. She wanted him to be rested for an interesting weekend with her. This weekend was especially important to her. "Why?" he asked. "Just because. Because of all that's happened," she said. He told her he might not see her for a few days because of a new lab experiment. It required his constant attention. She started to pout and then she saw how sleepy he was and decided it wasn't necessary. She headed for the door. "We'll see," she said.

He fell asleep with the light on.

CHAPTER

An old woman of the night sits behind a spindly table on a banquette at a bistro. A fluted wine glass, two white saucers and an ashtray stand before her on the glass table top. The woman wears a velvet cloche hat with an artificial rose on top. A gauzy veil comes down from the hat and covers part of her face, which is thickly rouged and lipsticked. Make-up cannot hide the puffiness of her cow-like visage.

One hand rests on the table's inner edge, the little finger delicately extended. The other hand is pressed against the old woman's chest and is entwined in a large loop of dangling pearl necklaces. Both wrists wear multi-rowed pearl bracelets. Below the table, the hem of a sequined dress hangs loosely around old legs. One leg is twisted inward, the toe of the strapped black shoe in mock pirouette. The silk stockings on the shapeless legs are wrinkled and ready to fall down. A dark coat with a rough fur collar hangs from her shoulders. A cigarette butt rests on the floor beneath the acrobatic foot, its white paper glowing even in the gloom, on linoleum with a pattern of alternating geometric flowers.

She sits on the upholstered banquette with its embossed nails, letting the past go by and waiting for the next part of her life to begin. She has done this before. She doesn't think it unusual. Behind her a slender brass guard rail protects the wall that alternates decorative panels with large mirrors. Activity from the other side of the room is glimpsed in mirror view—a man's tie and white shirt, another table, the back of the woman's hat—but nothing is certain or complete.

The woman has had two drinks; she's waiting, or resting; perhaps she's taking her pulse; perhaps she's noting a pain that alcohol cannot mask; perhaps she's ready to go out again, fortified. The face is mannish; it could be a man in drag, and the eyes are painted-on almond-shaped slits with dark patches underneath, makeup or years of dissipation?

Where is this place?

Secrets live here.

I'm not sure I want to know secrets, I just want to know where dust and putrefying flesh and so many mysteries gather at once. I would like to talk to such a woman, check for vital signs, give her the coup de grâce if necessary.

I'm a doctor and I can ease pain, any way it takes.

CHAPTER

"Doctor!" One of the loutish guards at the subway entrance stood up when he approached.

"Yes."

It was Friday evening. The light was just starting to get dim in the streets. There seemed to be more traffic than usual. Even on his street, people had been moving about, perhaps watching him as he left in his dark suit and raincoat.

The guard stood at attention respecting Noreen's rank.

"Yes?"

"Are you going downstairs, sir?"

"Yes."

"I'm not sure that's a good idea."

"You're telling me I can't go down?" The guard backed away.

"Oh, no, I wouldn't do that. It's just—well they're having their big annual celebration down there. This is their biggest night of the year."

"So?"

"Well, they have a big party, they all get drunk, and they don't care what they do. I wouldn't go down there myself, even with reinforcements."

"I'll take a chance. I know people down there. They'll look out for me."

"We can't come down and get you out—"

"Don't worry. In fact, pretend you didn't see me. Consider that an order of sorts. And, oh yes, for your information, I'm on official business. Very important business. I'll be all right."

The guard stiffened and saluted. The other one who had been leaning against the railing managed to stand up and gave a ragged salute too.

"Don't forget," Noreen said, as he started down the steps, "you didn't see me. I'll back you up if it ever comes to that. But it won't. You're off the hook."

He didn't hear what the guard said because he had already left the stairs and was walking on the wet tile street toward the canted sidewalk.

He thought he handled the guards quite well.

He saw and heard no one, as usual in this stage of the journey. But somehow the tunnel seemed darker than usual, the infrequent yellow lights smaller and farther apart.

If there was a loud party it hadn't started yet or he wasn't close enough. All he could hear were his footsteps slapping against the pavement and a constant wind rushing through with a disturbing yowlish monotone.

Yes, now he knew why the whiskey had been important enough for her to visit her father. She had been planning a party. He wondered if she would mind an uninvited guest. And would he like barging in? He wondered about a lot of things but most of all he could see the imagined image of old prints yellowing on an efflorescing concrete wall.

It was interesting, how just like the calendar, old customs survived. It was May 30 and people were still having a party.

BOOK THREE

"A

LABYRINTHINE

WALK"

CHAPTER

50

He didn't have to consult his map and he didn't need Walter to guide him.

He was almost there when he heard running footsteps and shrill voices.

Suddenly the bulbous face of a defective female appeared out of the mist in front of him, clambering furiously away from something. As she got closer, he could see she was wearing a khaki jumpsuit unzipped down the front; her breasts flopped as she ran. Her eyes were wide open, and her mouth was pursed into a wet red "O" from which poured short bursts of ear-piercing shrieks.

Then a male of the same type came into view, and they both passed Noreen without noticing him. The male was chasing the female and Noreen couldn't tell if she was crying in fear or anticipation. He heard two bodies collide behind him and turned to saw the female, tackled by the other, fall to the ground and slide along the water-logged street under her attacker. They began to grapple and roll in the dreck, but it was obvious the female was trying to reach into the male's jumpsuit. By the time Noreen turned away they had already coupled and were pumping each other.

Now he heard more noises and saw other pairs chasing each other. It was as if they were being pushed toward him by a blast of loud music from up ahead. Khaki-covered bodies lay crumpled along the curb; others clutched at their partners against the grimy, tiled walls; a few lay on top of one another in the dark niches he passed that led to doorways.

He had almost reached the boiler room when a skinny retardee wearing nothing but a black cape and high heeled shoes approached him and tried to grab his crotch.

Noreen did not like this uncontrolled night, did not like to be touched by strangers.

He crashed the back of his right arm against the lipstick-smeared face and it crumpled whimpering into the gutter.

"Fuck you," it said after him.

He turned into the niche he was looking for, but the way was blocked by two couples trying to do something to each other. Noreen grabbed arms and

necks and cleared out a path for himself. The music
was coming from behind the boiler room door and
it was so loud even out here he wondered what kept
the door from falling down.

He pulled on the door. The music was like a
viscous force that took an effort to move into. He
made his way in and immediately felt like he was
swimming. The room was packed with shadowy
people. Two furnaces were blazing at full force,
apparently unattended. The partygoers close to it
picked up the infernal glow but at the edges of the
room it was almost pitch dark. He saw no shrieking
defectives, no khaki-colored jumpsuits. These were
boiler room people such as he had noted before,
still in their undershirts and saggy blackened
trousers, mostly men, and a few women with coal-
soaked skin and unwashed shapeless dresses.
Everyone had a drink in hand. The stink of whiskey
and cigarette smoke took the place of air. The
jumbled mass was undulating to rhythms that
Noreen had yet to detect in the din that he
assumed was their music. Somehow the sound
reminded him of Kafahvey. Which didn't surprise
him; it was Kafahvey's daughter's place.

He didn't see her.

He tried to ask where she was.

But no one cared to listen. Then he saw her
squeezing out of the hallway that led to her office.
She was carrying whiskey bottles and paper cups;
then she was swallowed up by the mob and went

entirely out of sight; when she came up again her hands were empty.

Noreen felt as he pushed toward her that it was like diving into a sea of protoplasm and that if he didn't get squeezed to death the sweat and whiskey stench would kill him.

But by the time he reached her it was as if he had absorbed the alcoholic haze and had inoculated himself because he could no longer smell anything at all.

He pushed her into her hallway and dragged her over supine bodies near the back of the passageway, which he assumed was somewhat out of bounds for the workers even at their own party.

She had a bleary red-eyed look as if she had already started drinking and her laughter was careless, panicked, and a little nutty.

"I knew you'd come, I knew you couldn't stay away. Did you come for me or for pictures?"

"For pictures. Where are they?"

"Well, they're not here—not with this bunch," she said, indicating the crowd. She was squeezed against the back door so hard she had trouble breathing.

"You picked a bad time to come down. I hate to say it. To turn you away. Go away now and come back some other time when things are quieter." She shouted and he could barely hear her.

"We have to talk. Now."

Even drunk, she could see he was serious; she found a key on a large ring dangling from her waist and opened the door. She locked it when they had pushed it shut behind them. Already he could feel bodies leaning against the other side.

They were in her bedroom, a narrow room with just space for a single bed, built-in closets and dresser, but it had a high ceiling. Way up above, a bank of tube lights, dim at this distance, and pipes and ductwork crisscrossed.

She let him push her against the door, not so tight as outside, and he rubbed his hand against the soft inside of her thighs. The pores of her neck and face had already picked up a dotting of coal dirt, but he didn't care. He figured by the time he left he would be covered with the grime himself, but he didn't care about that either. *What was happening to him?*

"No! There isn't time for that." She pushed him back. "Later. Now I have to take care of my employees. See that they get plenty of whiskey, have a good time."

"I'll wait." He indicated the bed. "I'll take a nap till it's over. When? In the morning?"

"Don't be silly. They can party for days. I've got to get back." Again she tried to push him away.

"Just five minutes then."

"All right. What was it you wanted?"

"What did you give Kafahvey?"

"Give Kafahvey?"

"Kafahvey wants to set up a concert. They think you slipped him a drug, an elixir of youth."

"Bullshit! If I had an elixir of youth, I wouldn't give it to anyone. I'd keep it for myself."

"I'll—they'll—need more than just your word. Your word isn't worth much to them."

"Or to you?"

"I'll wait and we'll figure that out later."

"I said—you can't wait. Not tonight. My people'd riot if they thought I let some one from upstairs spy on them tonight. Just go and come back in a few days."

"Can't. They might not let me down again. Where are the pictures? I'll go and take a look at them while I'm waiting."

"They're in a safe place. You wouldn't be able to find them by yourself. Not tonight. Just go home."

"All right, where's Walter? He can show me the way. Or is he partying too hard too?"

A flicker of sobriety crossed her face and he could see her think seriously for a moment.

"No, not Walter. I don't want Walter showing you around. You can't rely on Walter except to get you to and from the entrance. It'll have to be someone else."

"Fine. Whatever it takes to see pictures. That's the only reason I came down, really."

He said it to hurt her. He wondered if it hurt her. If it hurt her, he couldn't tell. Maybe she was too drunk to know what he was saying.

"I'll get Covarrúbias. He's a spoilsport. He hates parties. He'll love showing you around."

"Good," he said, "let's get going," and he opened the door and let her follow him out. He looked around and could see her locking the door, putting the bedroom key back on her massive key ring, then brace for the push into the outer room.

"If you find the elixir of youth, let me know," she called after him.

CHAPTER

51

W
I
L
L
I
A
M

B
O
R
N
E
F
E
L
D

"Well, I don't know," Covarrúbias said, scratching his head under the gray hair that seemed to undulate all by itself under his cap. "I don't like parties I must admit, and I don't drink, but I'm not sure I should work on a holiday."

He seemed like an old man, but Noreen didn't know, his lithe frame looked younger than the gray hair. Like most of the underground residents he had a cadaverous pallor. He also couldn't help looking mischievous, not shifty like Walter, but nevertheless seemed to be hiding something.

"Consider it a friendly gesture. I come in friendship. I'm here on personal business, not official," Noreen said.

"In that case—and because you're a friend of the blond lady—perhaps you'd like a drink before we start out. As I say, I don't drink, but I know how to be hospitable."

They were standing in the tunnel near the noise and the groping outside the door to the boiler room. Noreen looked at the door and then looked back. He was anxious to go on. He was anxious to find the pictures and also to see the girl again.

"I'll pass. Too much trouble to go back in."

"No trouble at all."

Covarrúbias withdrew a bottle of whiskey from his smock-like coat, broke the paper seal by twisting the cap, and handed the bottle to Noreen. "Although I don't drink myself, down here it never hurts to carry a bottle of whiskey with you. Be my guest."

Noreen tilted the bottle to his lips and as the stinging liquid rolled into his mouth, he could read lettering on the blue paper strip along the bottle neck side: "Old No. 7."

The burn in his gut felt good. It cut out the damp.

I'm getting used to whiskey and I like it.

Memories of ancient history hide in its corrosive amber. Fossilized distillate; he was getting to be an archivist and understood such things.

He handed the bottle to Covarrúbias, who twisted the cap back on and hid the bottle somewhere under his coat.

"Lead the way, my friend," Noreen said.

"Do you know the woman well?" Covarrúbias said over his shoulder as he walked slightly ahead on the narrow sidewalk.

"Not well at all," Noreen said.

"She's a solid piece of put-together, isn't she?"

Noreen nodded to his guide's back.

"I don't know what a woman like that's doing down here. She's the poet's daughter, you know."

"I know," Noreen said, and he watched the man turn around and look for an expression but he didn't give him one.

"So it's pictures you want, is it? Then it's pictures you will get, sir. But I must remind you, sir, it is against the law. Did you know that?"

He turned around and winked at Noreen, still walking, and Noreen nodded.

"I accept no responsibility for your delinquency, sir, but I am glad to oblige," the old man went on. "You see, down here the usual laws do not apply. Oh, we are law-abiding in our own way—just different. But as for you—well, sir, you proceed at your own risk and what happens to you is, well, in your own hands, not mine. Oh, you will be safe with me while you are down here, but afterward when you go back up I don't know. You see, they were right to ban pictures. They're just not good for most people, but, say—why talk when we can move along faster. Besides, perhaps you will be interested in some of the sights along the way, such as this we are now approaching—"

Gray fluoro lights poured out of a wide opening in the tunnel wall up ahead. A group of small, khaki-clad people filled the street out front. A demented hubbub echoed and clanged in the tunnel.

At the entrance the old man stopped. Noreen looked in. Moisture that reminded him of the central garden when they were hosing it down flowed out. A drunken defective couple brushed past, oblivious to everything except red-lipped lust.

The room contained endless rows of plants on flatbed supports under banks of brightly glowing fluoro tubes. He could hear water flow and see spray filling the air and rivulets of water traversing the brick floor.

At one end a few defectives who did not seem drunk moved purposefully among the tables tending the plants.

"They'll get their turn later. Now they're making sure the food supply is intact. These people think of only two things, coupling and work, and they're highly disciplined. They work just as hard at one as they do the other. This is where your lettuce comes from, sir. Most of the food you people eat up there comes from here."

"I'm impressed. But let's move on."

"Perhaps a sample—some tidbit to carry with us on the way."

"Come on, let's go."

A glance that indicated a possible angry mood crossed Covarrúbias' face and went away.

They walked through the tunnels without speaking for what seemed like half an hour. Gradually the party noises subsided and then disappeared. Only their footsteps and water dripping on the walls and from the ceiling made a sound.

"How long is it now?" Noreen said, losing his patience.

The tunnels stopped at that point and opened up into the edge of a wide-spread enormous room filled with darkness.

Covarrúbias produced a torch from under his coat and switched it on. The light was puny in that empty room. The air had become dry and dusty and the tile walls had stopped. In the light's dim beam he could see the walls here were rough and black. Attempts had been made to smooth them out and make them straight, but chunks had fallen and lay on the floor nearby. They were in a hollowed-out coal mine.

"There are lights down here, but they're not on all the time, for obvious reasons, as this part of the mine is all worked out. But somehow I thought there'd be a little light along the way to the stables. If my glim should go out, just feel along the wall on the right and keep going and don't panic. Give it a try now just in case. Remember, keep to the right."

The light went out and Noreen felt himself submerge into the deepest blackness he had ever known. It was darker than he imagined blindness could be. He extended his hand and moved to his right until he could touch the rough jagged shards of anthracite.

He could feel panic creeping up the inside of his chest and just as it almost reached his mouth, the flashlight came back on. He stared at the narrow white pencil tip of its beam, reaching ahead.

He had not stopped walking, but Covarrúbias had paused and Noreen almost ran into him.

"Goddam it, man! Don't stop in front of me like that."

Covarrúbias ignored the comment.

"We're almost there. I see a light under the door."

"I don't see anything."

"Your eyes aren't used to it. Wait here."

Covarúbbias moved out of view. The penlight beam got smaller. Then Noreen heard a door opening and he saw a rectangle of light appear in the wall ahead with Covarrúbias' silhouette in its center.

CHAPTER

5²

A low-ceilinged room filled with acrid smells of hay and animal urine. Dainty chuffing and stomping. No one around. Dull outlines of cubicles along the hallway.

They went down the hall and Noreen was aware of dark shapes lying or standing in piles of straw in the loosely- framed compartments. The hall made a sharp turn to the left and there stood a small covered wagon with two beasts harnessed to it. The animals were about two and a half feet high with short, dense brown neck and muzzle hair. Along their fat sides the hair turned abruptly black with wide dun-colored stripes. They had short pointy ears and tails and round backs, and he presumed they had pointy snouts, but their muzzles were covered with paper gas masks that expanded and collapsed gently as they breathed in and out.

"We could walk, but these little fellows know the way and will make the journey more pleasant for us. Besides, they are very strong and they enjoy company."

He handed Noreen the bottle and Noreen took a long swallow, as the old man led the team down the hall to the door. Outside, Covarrúbias closed the door, and as he did the headlights on each animal's forehead turned on and gave out a bright comforting beam that showed the way ahead.

"Get on now," he said, indicating the wagon, and he climbed on and Noreen pulled himself up and sat on the bench beside him.

Covarrúbias made a funny little clicking down deep in his throat and the animals moved forward. Noreen could feel the wagon lurch forward with a gentle shiver and then move smoothly ahead.

"We'll let them little buggers do the work. Sit back and relax, enjoy the trip."

"But they're so small, should they be pulling this big load?"

Covarrúbias laughed.

"Don't worry about them. This is what they do. They're tapizees. They love it."

And Noreen could see in the back light from their head lamps they were moving effortlessly forward, could see their long back muscles rippling under the tight skin, and he wondered why there were no animals in the dome.

"Should we have face masks?"

"Probably. But don't worry about that either. You're just a visitor to the underworld. You don't have to live down here. I'm not wearing a mask, see. And I've been breathing this stuff for years. The worst part was cleaned up a long time ago. The tapizees—well, they have delicate lungs—we can't take a chance with one of them. If they keeled over out here, it could be a long walk back. When one of them keels over you know you're in trouble."

"And they know where they're going?"

"There's only one place this leads to."

"Where is that?"

"You'll see."

"How long will it take?"

"We'll be there before you know it. Don't worry about that either. Now I better turn out the lights. Save the batteries. They don't need lights anyway. They see in the dark, or something."

He pressed a button under the seat and both head lamps went out at once.

Noreen saw total blackness in every direction, which meant he could not see anything at all, and they were marching into this no-thing, and he had no idea where he was or where he was going.

Was this a good idea? Had he had any good ideas lately?

As the wagon creaked forward, he could feel Covarrúbias' bottom press closely against his.

W
I
L
L
I
A
M

B
O
R
N
E
F
E
L
D

CHAPTER

5^3

It was night everywhere now. And night held him. There were no pictures here in this black nothingness, except the ones in his mind, and they weren't enough.

In the dark he stretched his right arm to the side and bent it forward at the elbow to see if he could touch the tip of his nose in the dark. His outstretched finger pressed against the hollow above his lips. He tried again; this time his unseen forefinger grazed the bottom of his nose. He could do better than that, but not down here.

In the dark he became aware of his breathing. The air was still and dry. He could imagine microscopic particles of coal dust dropping into his lungs. This was the other side of his journey up the mountain. At least there was light in the dome. He missed the filtered light and his good life in Fullerton; why was a level-five manager with a great future here now? It didn't make sense. He wanted to be in the arms of Martine or Beta. He wanted his comfortable adjustable chair in his office. He wanted to smell the flowers in the central garden, the Garden of Eden where he and Beta often took lunch, feel the spray from the gardener's hose brush over him as he walked to his office. And Beta—he would give anything to get back his quiet evenings with Beta. In spite of all the other women he'd had sex with, he knew Beta's round body better than any other, and he could trust Beta, the only one, surely Beta had not been the one to turn him in, more likely Beta had saved him by removing the pictures from the envelope, and now he wanted her again and was sorry if he had been cruel to her. When he got back up, he would break off the ridiculous charade with Martine, no matter what it cost him. She could keep the embryo and do with it whatever she wished. Have it for lunch if she liked, and it would not surprise him.

The forward lurching of the wagon set up a rocking motion that his body picked up; he was swaying like a keening old woman.

This had all come about because of his perverse impulse to be different, first by not taking his medicine, and then by twisting his scientific assignment on the outside into a personal crusade that led him to risk his life and dome property on the mountain slope. And he continued on his unrepentant quest for pictures from a dead society that couldn't do anything right for itself. He was caught in a web from people who had long ago built what they thought was the real world and then killed themselves and everything they had made. They were all dead now, dead so long nothing they had done had any more meaning. The scraps of paper they had left, the photographs, deserved not to be looked at because they were dead too. When you looked at them you were stepping into a tomb with the dead and whatever happened to you from then on didn't matter because you were already dead yourself.

This was the anguish of the man who had never spent a night away from home; this was the anguish of the beginning traveler; this was the zombie's epiphany.

There was no light anywhere, and light was what gave you substance; without light you turned into vaporous thoughts, and now he felt himself become weightless and begin to roll in place until he didn't know if he was upright or upside down; it felt like he was rolling at first and then he was tumbling through space along with the ineluctable blackness and there were no stars present, no traces of light of any kind, because this was eternity, and no place for him; he expected to become a speck at any time and then disappear into nothingness himself, because all was nothing anyway and if you started with nothingness you didn't get anything else. All this for pictures on paper, not even photographs in this case, since so far he had not seen a single photographic print down here, and there was no light now and never would be and without light what did it matter? Without light there could be no pictures anyway.

"We're almost there."

He heard Covarrúbias' voice coming to him, getting suddenly closer, and he stopped rolling and felt himself jerk to a rest and click back in place on his seat on the wagon. At the same time the head lamps came to life again on the tapizees' foreheads, and they were still lifting their short legs in the same slow deliberate rhythm going somewhere only they knew. The light from their foreheads shone only a few feet ahead in the blackness but the sudden glare blinded him and he squinted in order to shut out the pain to his retinas.

"I think I can see it now. Up ahead."

"What?"

"The doorway."

"I see nothing."

"Just keep looking. Straight ahead. In the distance above the animals' ears."

He kept staring but he saw nothing. Then like an

afterglow at the back of his eyes he was sure he saw a pinpoint of light.

The animals seemed to change then, to get excited, to pick up speed a little and flick their short tails.

The darkness is nothing, he told himself, and the light got bigger and then turned into a rectangle of light seeping around a door.

Covarrúbias jumped down from the moving wagon, ran ahead, and opened double doors. Without slowing down, the tapizees pulled the wagon into a wide hallway with smooth white walls. They drove past Covarrúbias. Noreen could hear him pulling the door shut. Covarrúbias ran ahead of the wagon and grabbed the animals' harness and pulled them to a halt.

"You might as well get down, stretch your legs a bit. We can walk from here. The animals will wait for us." From his coat he removed a pineapple, broke it more or less in half by slamming it against the wall, and, after gently removing the face masks, left each part on the floor in front of a tapizee's nose.

The air in the hallway felt filtered and clean and was moving slightly through ductwork. The walls and the floor were smooth and scrubbed clean.

"Take off your shoes," Covarrúbias said, already removing his. Noreen removed his shoes and placed them on the wagon seat next to Covarrúbias's.

As they walked down the hall he could hear the soft hum of a generator. The hallway ended soon at an intersection with another hallway and they turned to the right. Doors appeared at infrequent intervals on each side as the hall went on as far as he could see. The frosted glass panes in all except one door were dark. But one not far on the right had a light shining through. Room 12 B was all that had been marked on the glass.

Covarrúbias turned to Noreen and held his hands apart and palms up as if to say, see, I told you, and they opened the door. Entering they stirred up a little whirlpool of dust. When it settled, Noreen could make out a large gloomy room with enormous stacks of compressed rectangular sheets of paper. Faded markings showed on the outside of the ones whose top surfaces he could see.

"Anybody here?"

Covarrúbias called loudly several times into the stacks.

They waited. After a while, a rustling was heard in the back, then a slap-gaited shuffling. Noreen saw a dark-shaped something moving in the back of one aisle.

When it emerged he couldn't categorize it. At best he could figure out it was a half-man-half-insect. About the size of a man but bent over so far the end had to curl up to look at them, with almost human hands and face, but all the rest a hard, uncovered arachnid body with a tail of excrement permanently attached, hanging down from its pointed rear end. The face seemed to morph from man to insect and back again but the voice was so gentle and unctuous it put Noreen at ease at once and he decided it was necessary to like this creature and accept him for the wonder he was.

"This is Arras," Covarrúbias said, "an archivist, like myself."

He stood back and watched Noreen's reaction.

"I too am—an archivist," Noreen said.

The creature nodded.

"Excuse me if I looked startled. I don't get many visitors, though they are always welcome. I didn't expect anyone this night of nights. How may I serve you?"

"My friend has come to look at pictures. Are we interrupting—"

"Then make yourself at home. I was just having a snack and I believe I'm finished now."

"A snack?"

"I try not to—but from time to time I must. I limit myself now to what was called *Life Magazine* because there are so many of them. I would never eat an original of anything or an only copy. Tonight it was volume 5 through volume 37, from 1938 to 1954, whenever that was. The issues of July 25, 1949 and April 9, 1951 were especially tasty."

Noreen noticed a pungent smell now and saw hardened stacks of the insect's droppings along the walls and in the corners.

The insect noticed Noreen's glance and without looking at him said, "We save everything down here. Everything has value. I am sorry there is no humanoid toilet for me. Eventually I shovel it up and have it hauled away to the mineral depository."

"Of course. Don't mind me. Everything is new to me. I'm a scientist and just interested, that's all."

The insect shook slightly, emitting a faint rattling noise, and looked pleased as if Noreen had excused him and they were going to get along.

"Follow this way, and I'll show you some excellent examples of the kind of material we protect here."

The insect turned, straightening out his tail, and then hobbled ahead of them down the far left aisle. It opened up into a neat workroom surrounded by banks of flat metal drawers. The insect grabbed a handle with a long fingernail, pulled, and removed a portfolio box and put it on a table. He switched on a bright desk lamp that immediately made the room cheery.

This was it. Noreen leaned forward. What he had come for.

The insect opened the flap on the box and stepped back.

"Enjoy," he said.

The box was filled with sheets removed from ancient magazines. While Noreen looked, the insect went to his file drawers and brought back more solanders. He dragged up a chair, pushed it against Noreen, and then adjusted the tubular light. The beam fell down on the paper at the perfect angle.

He had now arrived at a bizarre treasure trove of graphic history and his fingers trembled at the touch of old paper as he turned page after page. But after several hours of savoring the blurred and fading colored inks of antique announcements for self-powered vehicles, cruises on large boats called steamships, and bottles and boxes depicted with strange names like Feen-A-Mint, Vitalis, Tono-Bungay, Alka-Seltzer, and Ex-Lax, that must have been primitive remedies, he asked, "Do you have any original photographic prints? Images in black and gray tones from silver oxides on thick white or ivory-colored paper?"

The insect paused; for a moment his antennae flicked, as he obviously ran through his mental file.

"No, we have nothing like that," he replied. "I have never seen such."

"Oh!"

The insect seemed embarrassed by Noreen's obvious disappointment.

"We have yet to visit all the stops on our tour—but I have never seen any myself down here," Covarrúbias interjected to break the awkward moment. "Perhaps someone will know of such things. Are not the pictures in the magazines satisfactory?"

"Oh yes but—"

"Perhaps moving pictures will do."

"Moving?"

"Whenever you are ready, follow me. And thank you, old eater of paper, for your hospitality."

The insect made a slight squeaking noise because he was so embarrassed by the attention and yet pleased with the compliment. Then he managed to place his human voice and spoke in low, slowly modulated tones.

"You are most welcome. I hope you will come back again soon. I understand that in the dome it is considered against the law to look at pictures, but I hardly think that applies down here. I wonder if it is against the law to eat pictures. For if it is, I am surely a criminal. But in my own defense I must say that I don't eat very much or very often and I try and limit the damage. I don't believe I will live long enough to eat up everything in this room, but then I have already lived a long time and there is no telling how long I have to go."

In the hallway the tapizees were standing patiently in front of the cart. There was no sign of the snack Covarrúbias had given them. He had stored the animals' face masks on the seat next to the shoes, and now reinstalled them, and the little beasts twitched their pointy snouts and made little grunts.

An electronic ringing noise was coming from Noreen's black topcoat which he had left in the wagon.

Brack's voice sounded thin and distant as if almost out of range of the phone signal. Noreen wondered how far they had come. Were they perhaps beyond the dome's perimeter?

"What the hell are you doing? I've been trying to reach you for hours."

"I'm in the infrastructure."

"I *know that*," Brack said. "Why are you down there?"

"I'm doing a little medical research for Hayes?"

Brack paused, then said, "He didn't say anything about that to me. Why can't you stay put?"

"Does he have to clear everything with you?"

"Well—er—no—"

"Then I can't see there's a problem."

"The problem is Martine. She's hysterical. She thought she had some kind of date with you this weekend. And she doesn't want you down there. I don't understand how a decent person would want to hang out down there myself and frankly I'm a little concerned about you. Dome people just don't go down there. What kind of research you talking about?"

"Hayes thinks there's clandestine drug work

down here and I'm supposed find out what's going on."

"Hayes is nuts. Noreen, I order you to return to the dome at once."

"What did you say, Brack? You've faded out on me. Please repeat. Can you hear me? You aren't coming through."

He heard Brack say quite clearly: "Return to the dome now. I said come up to the dome at once—if you know what's good for you. Now Martine wants to give you a piece of her mind too—"

"Brack—Brack—you still there—I'll keep trying until I reach you—hold on old buddy—Brack, Brack—"

To hell with Brack. Let him think I'm fading out. Though I heard every word clear enough. Didn't like any of it.

But I don't like much of anything these days.

He switched off the receiver and returned it to his coat. Covarrúbias had been watching. He made a circular gesture with his forefinger at the side of his head but that was all.

"Let's go and find these moving pictures," Noreen said to him.

CHAPTER

5⁴

They opened doors, and new doors appeared. They opened these, and there were other doors again. Small rooms and doors unfolded one after the other and they all looked like the ones they had just seen. It was making Noreen dizzy. He had lost count of doors and rooms. It was like an endless puzzle—mirrors reflecting each other, boxes opening and revealing smaller boxes, feedback and convolution, never ending. He was holding his breath expecting them to come out somewhere and then he was gasping for air. They were moving so fast now he wasn't sure their feet were touching the floor, gaining momentum until they were flinging themselves through the openings, doors opening barely enough to let them pass through and banging shut before they had completely exited. He thought he would drop soon. He was seeking something to look at, and all he could see were doors, opened and closed; if he found something, if he were to find something at the end of this maze he would have worked for it, but would it be worth it? Let's go back, he started to call out to Covarrúbias at his side, wondering if more doors were in front or in back. Doors forever, none leading anywhere.

Then they stopped running. The last door had opened and closed and was swinging gently back and forth trying to find its resting point.

The corridor had stopped at a gash in the wall that led to a cavernous workshop. Blinking pinpoints of colored light and dim yellow desk lamps appeared in the overall gloom.

Noreen hesitated, then followed Covarrúbias into the space.

As his eyes adjusted to the dimness, the control panel lights appeared brighter and more frantic in their unsynchronized blinking.

Panels of strange electrical equipment surrounded them, switches and knobs, none of which looked familiar to Noreen, who had thought he was acquainted with all state-of-the-art electronics in the dome.

Noreen heard a door in the back open. A bony old man came shuffling in. He had the standard all-gray look, and was more bent and humped than anyone Noreen had ever seen except the insect. Most people in the dome, especially the dark short ones, never lived long enough to get desperately old. He wore thick lenses and peered upward with a squinty, strained expression, because he was bent over so far.

"Hola, Sparks. It is Covarrúbias."

The bent old man let out a smile on his wrinkled face, and nodded.

"But not alone. I see a large white shadow standing next to you."

"This is Dr. Noreen, my friend from the dome."

"Is it the messiah?" the old man said, ignoring or not hearing the introduction.

"No, it's Dr. Noreen," Covarrúbias said louder.

"You know I've been waiting for the messiah for a long time. It is my duty."

"No, not the messiah, just Dr. Noreen."

"If it's the messiah, I am prepared to show you that I have taken good care of the equipment. I am prepared to throw all the switches right now. Everything is ready for the broadcast."

"No, not the messiah! Dr. Noreen!"

The old man moved closer to Noreen until his twisted neck and upturned face were right under Noreen's chin. He could smell the old man and see into his rheumy eyes, magnified.

"He looks like the messiah. I do believe he is the messiah. I'll turn everything on right now."

He started to leave the room.

Covarrúbias grabbed his arm gently.

"No," he said. "The messiah is fat and ugly now. And possibly dead, for all I know. This is only the messiah's son."

"His son, you say? Then it's almost the same as the messiah—but younger."

"The messiah has many children. This is but one of many. Listen, old man, you've been alone too long. Where is *your* son?"

The old man stepped back, still puzzled, but he let it drop.

"He's out back, fixing the vent. But I can turn on the equipment without him."

"No, we don't want you to turn it on. We just want a little demonstration of moving pictures."

"Oh, in that case you'll want my son. He'll be back soon. Can I fix you a little snack?"

They let him fix them a light meal of tender fresh watercress and large white mushrooms, thinly sliced on a hard crispy biscuit.

As they ate, Noreen savored the unexpected tastiness and at the same time studied the small rectangular lights set in panels around the walls. They made moving, colored patterns, just like the large screen behind the secret panel in his apartment.

The old man sensed more than saw Noreen's glance and went up to one of the screens, almost placing his eye against its surface.

"Ah," he muttered, "just the test pattern."

He reached out and pulled a large lever.

The colored light pattern instantly left the screen and was replaced by a moving picture of a man singing and dancing to loud music. Rhythmic, manufactured sound now filled the room, blasting Noreen almost off his chair. There was no escape. The noise pulsed from banks of heavy-duty speakers wedged into every part of the room, including the ceiling. The performer was a slender young man in a form-fitting, white, satiny suit with floppy sleeves and cuffs.

Noreen leaned forward. Somehow the man looked familiar. The rhythmic sounds were just like the noise Kafahvey had played in his apartment the other day.

"It's the messiah," the old man said.

Noreen stared. The young Kafahvey sang and danced and squeezed and slapped his guitar.

"When was that?" Noreen asked.

"When we were allowed to have pictures in the dome," the old man said.

"How long ago in years?"

"The year Kafahvey was thirty."

"When was that?"

"I don't know. I'll have to look it up."

"Never mind. Just turn it off."

"What?"

"That fucking noise!"

"You don't like it?"

"Just—"

"I am a little deaf—from listening—"

The old man pressed something and the moving picture and its ear-breaking beat went away. The eye that was the screen glowed white, a cataractous smear. They were surrounded by other cataractous eyes that watched them.

Noreen had stopped eating and sat for a long time resting his temple against outspread thumb and forefinger.

After a while, the old man said, "If you like we can look at it on the big screen. You can even see the embroidery on the suit then. Or whatever you like. I'll lower the sound."

The old man led them around the corner into another room and did his trick with the switches.

Kafahvey began dancing as a glittering light along the far wall. He was taller than Noreen and the screen was twice as tall as that. He was dancing over the sound, which was barely audible but still obnoxious.

"I never get tired of watching," the old man said.

Noreen wasn't sure he liked moving pictures.

"I can remember when everyone in the dome watched this," the old man said with a reverence that Noreen found sickening. "It was everything to the people in the old days. There were all kinds of what we called programs. All the old disks are still here. Everyone had a wall in those days. That was when no one did much except look at the wall.

That was before they covered up the walls. I'm not sure why they had to do that. I thought it wouldn't last long. As you can see, I'm hoping they'll change their minds one of these days. I can't see what harm it does. Not a little bit of vid screen, anyway. I'm ready whenever they are. I'm sure—when the poet talks to them—it's been a long time, hasn't it?"

"I think that what I don't like is the noise," Noreen said. "I'll never get used to the noise."

"You need to be a little deaf like me," the old man said, "then you don't mind. You start out by liking it and you don't know why and then when you realize it's hurting your ears, you're already a little deaf, and you can go on listening."

The old man reached over to the control board and the noise dropped entirely away, but Kafahvey continued to jump around on the wall.

"You *really* have to get used to the speakers," the old man said. "I'm almost deaf from them, but I can remember the way it was with young ears. You should have seen the young people dancing in the dome in the old days."

"In the dome?"

"Yes, in the Garden of Eden—where they had all the dances. I helped install the speakers. At the top of the dome—near the arc-igniters. I could climb in those days. They were wonderful speakers, four of them, built to last forever, much more powerful than anything we have down here, designed to make so much sound that you had to be careful, they would kill a man if they went off when he was nearby. They still use those speakers today."

"What?"

"For the artificial thunder. That's how I tell time down here. I watch for the thunder on the oscilloscope and when I see it I know another day has gone by. It's more fun than checking the clocks, and when you're out of touch, even more so when you're old, you need little amusements—I've seen all the disks so many times—"

"You know every time there's thunder and lightning in the dome?"

"Yes. *In* the dome. Not the real thunder and lightning outside. The sound for the dome thunder comes from down here. It's programmed and automatic. No one up there has to do a thing. They may even have forgotten."

"Hayes, I'm sure, thinks it's natural, sort of."

"Hayes?" the old man said.

"The man I work for. He's in charge of thunder, if any one is."

"Never heard of him. I thought I was in charge of thunder. I can show you the disk if you like. Everything's on disk down here. Waiting to go. You sure you're not the messiah? I'll have you broadcasting to the central garden in a moment. That's been my job, don't you know? Waiting for you. Who's this Hayes again?"

They heard a noise in a back room and the old man's son came in. He was middle-aged and pale but very wiry and strong-looking. After introductions, he tried to be friendly, but he seemed distracted by the work he had just left.

"I've been trying to fix a vent," he said, "and I'll have to find a tool to help me."

"It's those damn bats," the old man said. "They'll squeeze in any place they can find a little opening."

"Bats?" Noreen said.

"Little flying animals. They go out of the cave at night and come back in the morning. I hate when they get in your hair."

"Where do they come from?"

"The old coal mines."

"And where do they go?"

"Outside."

"That's impossible. There are no animals like that."

"I'm not strong enough to move the plate by myself." The son was rippling with muscles and apologizing for his strength.

"We'll help you," Noreen said. "Where is this vent?

CHAPTER

5⁵

W
I
L
L
I
A
M

B
O
R
N
E
F
E
L
D

Noreen could feel cold night air blowing through a cast-iron grate near the roof of the cave. The back room of the electro-sound and moving-pictures suite had opened out into a rough-hewn cave. The dirt floor sloped upward to the vent. Noreen followed the son until they were just below the ceiling. The wind strengthened, cooler now. Through the slots in the vent Noreen could see nothing but blackness, but he smelled fresh loaminess on the wind.

The grating did not quite meet the edges of the aperture it was supposed to be covering.

"It must have shifted at some point with a tremor," the son said.

He stuck his fingers through the slats and tried to move the iron piece over. The veins in his face and neck bulged and Noreen could see the grill lift slightly.

Noreen stood close to him and reached up. He felt the cold from the grill enter his hands when he grabbed the slots.

"Now, push," he said.

The grate shifted slightly toward the edge.

They both let go and caught their breath and shook themselves and both said "Now," at the same time and gripped the covering again, tensed their bodies, and said, "Now" again, and moved the grate into place.

"Let them get in now," the son said, as they walked back down the slope to the center of the room.

Noreen felt a tightness in his back and arms from the unaccustomed exercise and it felt good. He wasn't getting enough exercise these days. It had been days since he had done any physical activity, days since he had gone outside the dome, and he realized that was what he needed.

He was glad he had come below too, made this trip beyond the main underground. He felt like a pioneer seeking out new territory. In fact, that's what he was, an explorer. The dome needed something new. Perhaps a new age was opening up for the dome and he was one of its first truthseekers.

And perhaps nothing is nothing.

"Where does this air come from?"

"From outside."

"From the dome?"

"We're a long way from the dome."

"But isn't the air outside the dome radioactive?"

"It hasn't bothered me or my father."

"I can't believe you're getting air from outside."

"Then go back and put your face close to the grill. Look through the slots. Let your eyes adjust. Tell me what you see."

Noreen went back up the slope and pressed his forehead against the grill. He could feel the cold metal pressing into his skull and waking him up. He stared and watched for a while, then he went back down to the two other men.

"What did you see?"

"Stars. It's a starry night outside."

CHAPTER

5⁶

"What time is it?" Covarrúbias said.

"Almost dawn," the son said. "It won't be starry night long. You're welcome to spend the night here and go back when you're rested."

"Yes," Covarrúbias said, "I think we'll have to do that."

"No," Noreen said, "we'll leave now. I have to be back."

Covarrúbias looked sick, but he moved toward the door anyway.

"Then we'd better get started," he said.

"Take the back way," the son said, and he led them to a rear door. "It's shorter."

Covarrúbias looked relieved but he kept moving

quickly. Noreen followed. He said: "I'll just say good-bye to your father."

The son said: "I'll tell him you said good-bye. You'd better hurry. Come back and see us anytime, sir. Soon, I hope. My father is the great technician B. F. Sparks, as he no doubt mentioned. I'm Barthwell, and I'm still learning from him. You can count on us to continue to man our posts, sir."

Noreen noted the man's unusual deference and was bothered by it. He mumbled thanks and farewell.

As they were leaving, and to escape from what he felt was some awkward moment of protocol, Noreen took a last look around and noticed what appeared to be thick, silvery roots sticking through the cave walls, all along the other side, under the grate. He wanted to ask what they were, but Covarrúbias had already grabbed him by the hand and was pulling him along.

Could it be?

The roots of the dome?

If so, the geodesic grid work was not pure aluminum as he had always assumed. It was a bio-metallic plant form, that had been nurtured into shape, was perhaps still growing.

How else explain the construction of the dome. Once you thought about it. The only way to extend the stores of bauxite. Did Hayes know? Who remembered?

Was the dome's legacy—its memory and its works—being forgotten—except down here?

The smooth surface of the roots glowing in the dim room still cast a little light on the back of his retinas. The silvery effulgence reminded him of black and white photographic prints.

The door opened onto a short dark hallway filled with clutter, stacked boxes overflowing with unidentifiable metal and wire devices, that quickly led to another door that took them to the first hallway.

He could see the wagon and the tapizees waiting patiently near the main entrance.

He and his guide had bypassed the maze.

Covarrúbias started running and, by the time Noreen arrived, had covered the animals' mouths with the masks and had them turning the wagon around.

"Hold the doors!" he said. Noreen stepped out into the black coal mine and felt dry, dusty, coal mine air surround him as Covarrúbias led the team out. Noreen immediately missed the clean air and sparkling lights of the broadcast suite.

"Get on!" Covarrúbias said. He had already climbed on the seat. Noreen could see, in the light seeping from the door, Covarrúbias getting ready to move the team forward. Noreen climbed up. Covarrúbias let out a bloodcurdling yell. The little draft animals' ears twitched and they shot forward into the darkness.

Noreen held on now, as he and Covarrúbias bounced around on the seat.

"What's the rush?" Noreen said.

"Nothing. I hope," Covarrúbias said.

The tapizees seemed to understand there was some urgency and they raced on of their own accord. All Noreen could see now were the small circles created by their head lamps. The coal floor revealed there rushed by so fast it was just an oddly-white blur.

Noreen could hear the little clicking sound of tiny feet hitting the rough floor, but mostly he heard the creaking and groaning of the covered wagon.

I'm in a hurry, but not this much hurry.

He started to tell Covarrúbias this, but he was stopped by an unfamiliar sound that started to swell behind them.

"What's that noise?" Noreen yelled.

"It's dawn outside the dome," Covarrúbias said. "We should have left earlier. I'm sorry."

It was a low buzz at first, barely noticeable above the wagon sounds. Then it increased in intensity until it was a screaming groan advancing toward them from the rear like a projectile.

"What is it?"

"It's the bats—coming home to roost. Fleeing the dawn up above."

He jerked the team to a halt, grabbed a plastic sheet from inside the wagon and ran down and covered the now motionless tapizees. They stood with a rigidity that was a direct contrast to their usual wild scramble or patient waiting, as if they were bracing for some assault they had known before.

"Get in the back of the wagon. Quick!"

Noreen heard flapping noises on each side now and could feel the air moving around him, then he saw black shapes whizzing past the headlights that still shone through the murky plastic covering the animals. He waited for Covarrúbias, gave him a hand, and pulled him up on the wagon. They both tumbled into the wagon bed. Covarrúbias pulled the flaps shut. They could hear something swooping past the canvas top. They could feel the canvas undulating, and now and then something struck it and bounced off. The rushing noise enveloped them. The air felt as if it had been sucked out and replaced with an acrid stink. Both men were sweating. Covarrúbias had found a flashlight and turned it on. Noreen could see sweat rolling down Covarrúbias's face. He was oscillating the light against the top and the back of the canvas cover.

"Maybe some of the light will show through— steer them away."

He tossed Noreen the whiskey bottle.

Noreen removed the cap, and let a lot of whiskey

run into his throat. Its sting gave him courage, and the warmth in his gut absorbed his fear. He pressed the bottle back to Covarrúbias. "No," Covarrúbias said. "It makes me sick."

Noreen took another swig. He was beginning to feel drunk and brave. His fear had subsided, just as the sound had started to die down outside.

"How long does it last?"

"Not long."

"Will they come back?"

"Not till the evening."

"Where are they going?"

"To the far side of the mine, where the mine cuts into their old cave."

"They don't belong here anymore, that's it, isn't it?" Noreen said. He said it as a slur that murdered his words.

"So they say."

Covarrúbias listened to the outside. He heard nothing. Now their breathing and the slight creaking as the wagon swayed from its own inertia were the only sounds.

Covarrúbias crawled to the curtain and peered out. Noreen could see the light from the head lamps still shining through the plastic cover. Covarrúbias jumped down and pulled the plastic off the tapizees. They made funny little noises and twitched in the open air. Covarrúbias stroked their ears and their backs. The air still carried an acrid residue. Covarrúbias returned to the bench and stuffed the plastic in back.

"Go, little friends," Covarrúbias said to the tapizees. "But go now at your own pace."

They moved forward at a leisurely walk. Noreen felt disjointed and dizzy. He rocked in place to the wagon's movement.

The telephone in his topcoat was ringing. It had been ringing for a long time. But its cry was weak now, getting so soft it was disappearing into the coat's fabric, as the battery died away.

Where am I? What am I doing here? I am falling falling falling....

I don't care.

He heard the sound change as the footsteps left the rough coal floor and began tap-tapping on the brick-lined alley, but he didn't wake up at first. Then the hollow echo against the tile-lined walls, the water dripping in the gutters, and the distant sound of worn-out voices crept into his brain and pulled his eyes open. His head hurt, not just where he had pressed too hard against a wagon strut but all over. He told himself he had slept off whatever had been bothering him, but he wasn't really sure.

Covarúbbias was slumped forward, rocking in his sleep. Noreen suspected he might fall off at any moment, he was jerking involuntarily, but Noreen felt helpless to do anything and lacked the will to try. The old man had been riding like that so long, he wasn't going to fall off now.

The tapizees stopped. Three defectives were stretched out unconscious across the road. One had his jumpsuit pulled down to his ankles. In a doorway another one was masturbating, pulling on himself as if he had been doing it a long time and didn't know how to stop.

Noreen wanted to get out of there now, but he wasn't finished with his journey.

What he had seen was interesting for a visit but he wouldn't want to live there.

He remembered the wide-open plateau beyond the dome and he wanted to be there. The pictures were there, not here, not this night.

"Get out of the way!" Noreen called down half-heartedly to the corpse-like figures in the roadway.

Covarrúbias awoke then and jumped down from the wagon. He pushed the sleepers into the curb with a foot, and climbed back up.

"They don't hear anything now."

The wagon started moving. They saw more people but not as many as earlier and they were all moving slowly.

"I'll take you to the main gate to the upstairs. You'll be all right after that," Covarrúbias said.

"No, I'll get out at the boiler room."

"I wouldn't advise that. Those people don't want anyone from upstairs at their party tonight. They get ugly about now."

"To the boiler room."

"No, really—"

"Just take me there."

"You have a stomach for punishment, sir. You've seen too much as it is tonight. I hope what you've seen you'll consider all very personal and will not mention any of it to anyone upstairs. In fact, I'm having second thoughts now about showing you so much. That's the way it is after a long night, isn't it? If you could start over you'd do it all differently."

"Just shut up and take me there."

"You know it's because I've taken a liking to you that I do these things for you and put up with your—"

"Shut up."

"As I said, I've grown accustomed to you and I hope you'll come back again and let me show you the parts of the basement you've missed."

"Just stop. We're here now."

The hallway to the boiler room was packed with bodies. Loud music still came from the other side of the door, but he couldn't hear any sounds of people partying.

Noreen began grabbing bodies and kicking and pushing them out into the street. No one complained. The limp bodies were warm and reeking with vomit.

He opened the boiler room door.

Only one of the furnaces was burning and much of its force had died down. A pale flickering glow reached out and showed him the way through the exhausted partygoers who had collapsed with their bottles on the floor.

When his eyes adjusted to the light, he could make out a small group of revelers still trying to force a few minutes out of the party near the right side of the furnace. A little clearing had been made.

"Next," he heard a weak, faltering woman's voice from the floor. "Stay in line...take your turn...plenty to go around...next...next...next..."

A large woman lay spread-eagled on the floor. She was naked, a big blonde, covered with coal dust, and a shadowy figure in a coal hauler's rough garb was humping her. She lay stretched out with her neck arched, staring at the ceiling. Her arms were spread out and in one hand a whiskey bottle swayed. The men waited in a scruffy line for their turn at the woman's crotch. He could see other men lying at each side, satiated and exhausted, with their flies open.

"Next..." the woman kept saying, sing-song, without remorse or interest.

There are no photographs on paper down here, just this tableau.

When he was standing directly over the copulators, Noreen looked down and into Nora's face.

She stared up at him but didn't recognize him.

"Get in line," she said. "You'll get your bonus like everyone else, but you'll have to get in line." She mumbled so much he could hardly hear the words, but that was what she said.

Covarrúbias was waiting for him by the door and followed him out the dim portico to the street. Noreen stood by the curb holding his head. He felt faint and shaken as if his legs were about to buckle. He felt Covarrúbias grab him and put his arms around him. He could smell the old man's sweat and feel the rough hairs of his top coat brushing against his skin.

"There old friend, I've got you. I'll take care of you. Come, let's go lie down."

Covarrúbias was holding him a little too tight. Noreen felt the strength return to his legs.

He remembered he didn't like being touched by strangers.

He was angry at Nora, when he shouldn't have been, because she was free to do anything she wanted. And he was angry at this old man he could smell. She had left him with this wretched creature of the night. Noreen did not see any future relationship with this fellow, yet the old bird was holding him too tight as if assuming he could enter Noreen's personal life and expect personal, perhaps sexual, favors. It was disgusting! Like Nora. He wanted to hit something.

He pushed Covarrúbias back and saw the old man slam into the wall and lose his breath.

"Don't bother me, you dirty old fucker!"

The old man would be all right. He was getting his breath back and about to straighten up. He had not hit his head.

Noreen turned and walked away.

As he walked up the wide steps that led out of the basement and into the diffused light of morning in the dome, Noreen could smell fresh moist air and hear the sounds of traffic and pedestrians and the low background hum of the moving walkways.

It all seemed good and familiar to him and he wondered why he had ever wanted to leave it. He would go home quickly, take a shower, sleep for a while, and then call Martine. He almost looked forward to getting married; most of all he missed her lean tight body and the pouty little girl's voice. What was happening to him?

His eyes were blinking in the bright light, but he could make out the usual two soldiers lounging in place, this time a different pair. He assumed he would just walk by them, perhaps nodding, and if necessary show his badge, and then enjoy the walk home. His apartment was only five blocks away, and he would be there in no time, but along the way he intended to breathe deeply, filling his lungs and exhaling slowly, the excellent dome air, note its freshness against his face and the backs of his hands, and otherwise enjoy the ambiance of a splendid Fullerton morning.

But when he reached the top of the steps and

started to make the turn to the right two policemen moved away from a bucket parked at the curb, just outside the wrought-iron entrance, and came toward him, separating so one was on each side. He started to reach for his badge.

"We know who you are. Get in the bucket."

"Sorry," Noreen said. "I have to be in my office right away. I'm a friend of Major Dork, by the way."

"Major Dork sent us."

He got in the car.

CHAPTER

5⁷

They took him to Brack's office. Brack was seated behind his desk, Dork standing next to him. Morning sun came in the windows behind their backs and shined into Noreen's eyes. He still wasn't used to bright light and squinted, trying to make out their expressions.

"I didn't know people were arrested for giving up their weekends to do their jobs," Noreen said.

He was too tired. He didn't give a damn what he said. It was probably all over anyway. Everything. Again.

"Oh, shut up. Sit down and stop whining. No one's arresting you. No one cares about you," Brack said. Noreen thought he saw a little smile curl up

Dork's lip. Brack liked seeing Noreen squirm. Dork was getting something out of it too.

Noreen sat down and Dork pulled up a chair and sat alongside the desk. He stared intently at Noreen with an expression that said nothing.

"I have a personal matter to take care of with you, speaking about the weekend," Brack said. "My sister wants to talk to you. She doesn't like it when people hang up on her."

"The battery in the phone went dead."

Noreen pulled the phone out of his coat pocket and let it drop onto Brack's desk. It slid to the edge of the desk, tottered for a moment, and then fell into Brack's lap. Noreen could see Brack look down at his lap and spread his legs and heard the phone clatter and crack on the floor.

Brack shook his head as if Noreen were a small child.

"But this is not about you. We have a real problem," he said. He turned to Dork. "Major, please tell my would-be brother-in-law what has happened?"

Dork cleared his throat and spoke in low guttural tones in the formal way he thought appropriate for high officials.

"Your patient, the esteemed poet, who lives in the select part of town, is missing. When was the last time you saw him?"

"A few days ago. What do you mean 'missing'?"

"He has disappeared from his luxurious apartment."

"What do his 'nurses' say?"

"They are missing too."

"Well, he didn't walk away. Not far, anyway."

"That's right. We think he's been kidnapped," Brack said.

Noreen thought about that. Could maybe see a scenario in his mind. Not possible, yet—

"You didn't see him in the infrastructure, did you? Or hear any suspicious comments?" Dork said.

"I heard nothing. Saw nothing," Noreen said. "They were all too busy having a good time. It was their annual party night. Everybody was drunk. Acting like animals."

He left out the part about the messiah. He left out anything that might help them. Anything, that is, that would involve the old man's doctor.

"The daughter? You see her? What was *she* doing?"

"I saw her but she was in no condition to talk about anything. Like everyone else she was dead drunk."

And fucking her head off. Well, she'll never get fucked by me again.

"Typical of that class," Dork said.

Noreen nodded and Dork thought he was agreeing with him. He wasn't.

"Maybe he's just taking a ride around the block,"

Noreen said. "I told you his condition's improved lately. How can you be sure he's missing?"

"A neighbor reported strange-looking people going into the building. Major Dork, who's been keeping an eye on things out there, checked the apartment personally."

"Yes, and I'm not sure I agree with everything that goes on in that place. What a shame to treat a nice apartment that way," Dork said.

"I agree. So? Why worry me with this?"

"Because you're his doctor and you know the daughter."

Noreen stood up, glanced at the door.

"I say give it time. He'll turn up. Alive and well, I suspect. Kafahvey's playing a trick on us. Showing us. He's Kafahvey, you know. Different."

"Different all right. Non-conformist, I'd say. Not a good quality in a leader," Brack said and he stared at Noreen.

Dork stood. He straightened his sleeves, adjusted his collar, cleared his throat. He'd had enough talk. *If you asked him*, Noreen thought, *he'd tell you he was a man of action.*

"I'll be going," Dork said. "I'll proceed with my investigations."

He left the room.

"Dork wants the apartment," Noreen said. "Maybe he did away with the old man."

"Don't be absurd. Dork's not in line for a place like that. Noreen, are you cracking?"

"No."

"You act funny."

"It's too much young pussy. Or radiation sickness."

He smirked.

"Too much of both, right?" Brack said.

"Not enough. I've been away for almost two days."

"I assume you're talking about my sister," Brack said. "Call Martine, then. Call Martine anyway. And get out of here."

Brack stood up, kicked the broken phone across the floor to Noreen. Noreen picked up the pieces and put them in his pocket.

"Also, Hayes wants to see you. You're getting awfully close to Hayes, aren't you?" Brack said, unable to hide his envy. "But clean yourself up first. You're a mess."

Noreen walked down two floors to his private office. He wanted to go home and sleep for days. But he took a shower and shaved. When he came out of the bathroom, his phone was ringing.

"I hear you've already seen Brack. You tell him about the elixir?" Hayes said.

"No."

"Good. He doesn't have to know about everything. What did you find out?"

"I didn't. I'm still working on it."

"Then there is one?"

He could feel Hayes' excitement. Hayes wanted to live forever like Kafahvey. Hayes was worried about himself.

He'd string Hayes along. Easy to do now. Get Hayes to let him back outside. Make him think the "elixir" was outside.

"I'm not sure. There might be. I think I'm close to finding out one way or another."

"Excellent, young friend."

"Now I'm going to go home and get some rest."

He wanted to hang up, but waited for Hayes to do the honors. Hayes put a lot of store in respect.

Hayes didn't say anything right away, then a little timidly he said: "Sorry, that won't be possible. You heard about Kafahvey? You and I are going over to his apartment right now."

"*You're* making a call like that?"

"I do whatever the situation requires. I'm hands-on, when necessary. The people like that in a leader. Keep it in mind. May come in handy as your career unfolds. I consider this important. What was that noise?"

Noreen had heard it too. A momentary screech outside in the open central dome area. Loud and piercing, and then gone.

But Hayes had talked right through it and Noreen hadn't heard clearly.

"I don't know," Noreen said. "Nothing I guess. What do you expect to find at his apartment?"

"Who knows? Kafahvey the titular poet, I hope. On the other hand—I'll meet you downstairs as soon as you can get there."

Noreen pulled on a clean jumpsuit and locked the door. He could hear the phone ringing behind him. If he had to guess, he would guess Martine.

Hayes had a chauffeur-driven bucket, comfortable with imitation burled walnut trim and deep, buttery cabretta seats. The driver jumped out in front of Kafahvey's apartment building, and opened the limo's back door. Noreen got out first and gave Hayes a hand. A policeman was standing just inside the lobby door.

"I'm not supposed to let anyone in," he said.

"You'll let me in," Hayes said.

"Of course."

"And stay here. We don't need any help upstairs, but we want you to be available."

"Yes, sir."

In the lift, Hayes said: "I wonder who actually verified that our folk hero was gone?"

"Dork, personally, I believe," Noreen said.

"That ass!"

"He wants Kafahvey's apartment."

"I'll see he never gets it. How about you and Martine—the apartment for a wedding gift?"

"That's a bit premature."

"You mean the wedding?"

"No, I mean we don't know if Kafahvey is really giving it up."

"To hell with Kafahvey. I want that elixir."

Hayes had an official-looking key ring like Dork's. He let them in. Right away they heard a noise in a back room. Noreen led the way. He could see Hayes checking everything out with his nose turned up. They saw no one. The apartment looked as it had the last time. The bed unmade, with the sheets piled up in an elongated lump that resembled a discarded shroud.

"Ecce homo," all right. But does the poet live?

In a kitchen pantry they found the two "nurses" trussed up, gagged, hysterical. Bleating now with their mouths uncovered.

"Well, I guess he was kidnapped," Hayes said. "Maybe he's dead already."

Noreen couldn't tell if Hayes enjoyed the prospect, or what.

The "nurses" said that two men had knocked on the door. They pushed their way in, put a blanket around the poet, and stuffed him into his wheelchair. Then they raped the nurses and locked them in the closet. They heard the wheelchair creaking with the weight of the poet and all the time they heard the poet cackling, even when the door had shut, "*Ecce* Kafahvey! I am coming. I am coming."

"It was degrading," they said, straightening out

their clothing. They didn't look upset about much other than the discomfort of their ropes.

"Would you like me to give you a pelvic exam—for the police record?" Noreen said.

"No," they said quickly.

"No time for that. We need to check the apartment," Hayes said.

"What are you looking for?" the nurses said to change the subject. "We'll help you."

"We must check his medicines for one thing," Hayes said.

"Strange," Noreen said, "that Major Dork inspected the apartment and didn't find you in the closet."

"That fool! Consider the apartment yours," Hayes said.

Noreen glanced at the electronic mural in the bedroom and wondered if it came with the gift. He looked for the "guitar" but it was no longer hanging on the wall.

Stolen? Or the poet's inseparable companion?

Hayes was already checking the pharmaceuticals near the bed. Noreen saw him pocket something and then go into the bathroom to look for more.

"Where could Kafahvey be?" Noreen asked the nurses.

"We don't know," they said. "He often talked about *returning*, but we don't know where."

"Down below," Hayes said, sticking his head

around the bathroom door. "With the girl. You'll have to go down again and find him. There's nothing like an elixir here."

Just what I need. I want to go back outside, and Hayes keeps sending me to the basement.

"I'd rather not," Noreen said.

"Well, isn't that just too bad, young man?" Hayes said.

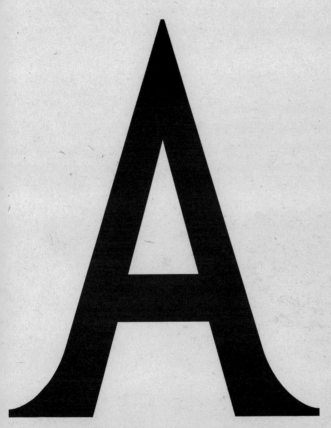

BOOK FOUR

A

LONG-GONE
WORLD

CHAPTER

5

Noreen wasn't going anywhere without a few hours' sleep. But when he stopped by his apartment, he found Walter sitting in front of his door.

"I rang, and a woman inside said you weren't here. Told me to go away. But I waited anyway."

"A woman? What kind of woman?"

"A woman from up here—with color in her cheeks."

"That could be anyone. Is she still here?"

"No, she left. About an hour ago."

"What else did she look like?"

"I don't know. She was just a woman. They all look alike up here."

"Was she wearing glasses?"

W
I
L
L
I
A
M

B
O
R
N
E
F
E
L
D

"I didn't notice."

He told Walter to wait and went inside.

He didn't like Martine letting herself in. He wondered where she got a key. Or was it Beta? Surely, if it had been Beta, Walter would have seen her glasses. He checked the apartment. Right away he noticed a screw missing from the bottom of the view panel. He saw it shining in the carpet nearby. He hadn't left it there.

Outside, a terrific racket had begun. It was shaking the building's wall. It was a rumbling and a crackling he couldn't identify. It pushed against the wall in waves that rattled the windows. Every now and then it would let up and seem to stop. He could hear it roll out across the street but then it would quickly bump back and start all over again. He wanted to jump up and check, but the speakers next to the panel began to beep. He quickly pulled out the remaining screws and lifted the cover panel.

Bright-colored lights roaming the screen in circles stung his eyes.

At first he didn't see the large envelope that dropped down from the wall and fell near his feet. But when he bent to pick it up, he brushed the screen. A ripple of static electricity tickled his side.

The envelope had weight. He lifted the flap and glimpsed edges of photographic paper. He stuck his hand in, separating sheets, and spied parts of beloved images he'd thought lost forever. Counting.

Twelve. All there.

He clenched his fists; in for him a rare expansive gesture, he raised both arms over his head. He felt an exploding surge of strength within his body. He was no longer tired. Another miracle.

Martine had changed her mind and returned his pictures.

It was Martine, wasn't it?

But Martine would never lift a screwdriver, not for him or anyone: she probably didn't even know how, and wouldn't try. She'd need help. Had someone else returned the prints? Who? Was it a trick? He could detect a faint trace of perfume in the air. His own flower field.

It didn't matter how they got back. They'd returned. Whatever'd happened, his luck had got better. Surely, someone in authority knew about this, and had relented.

Now the public speakers stopped crackling and beeping and a male voice flowed out from them, startling him. He could hear its echoes outside even through the apartment wall, blasting down from the top of the dome.

"Attention, dome residents. Listen. An important message. Go to your homes and remove the panels covering your video screens. The large panel in your living room. Take out the screws and wait. Don't let yourselves be deprived of the greatest of dome achievements. Wait no longer. Run to your homes now."

The message kept repeating itself. The voice sounded familiar.

Walter was pounding on the front door, yelling to be let in.

Noreen looked around and hid the pictures under his pillow. He'd do what he had to do down below and hurry back to a visual repast.

He opened the door. Walter rushed in. He was covering his ears with his hands.

"The noise is too much. It'll make you deaf. Drive you crazy. What are they thinking?"

"Who?"

"The people in the broadcasting station. They've got Kafahvey. He's dying. They want you to come down and treat him. Maybe you can tell them to turn down the sound too."

Noreen remembered that nobody trusted Walter down below.

"Who sent you?"

"Why—the old man's daughter."

"I think we should call the police—let them handle it."

"Not the police. They say the police'll kill the old boy."

"Not my problem. Let someone else deal with it."

"It'll be a big problem for me if you don't come

along. They don't like me as it is. If I don't do what they tell me, I don't know what will happen to me."

He fumbled for a few seconds with a zipper bag he carried, reached in and brought out a chrome-plated L-shaped artifact from the time of forged and shaped steel. The chunky object was incredibly ancient and ugly with specular glints that came and went around its single bloated orifice. Noreen vaguely remembered hearing of such an object. That it spoke fire and was designed to kill.

Walter turned the object around until he had gripped the handle part of the L and the aperture side was facing Noreen.

"What's that?" he said.

"It's called a pistol. It's what will kill you right on the spot if you don't come with me at once," Walter said. His hand trembled and his forefinger had entered a wire-like opening below the "pistol's" frame.

All the time his arm wavering and his fingers squeezing the handle tight.

"I'll get my coat."

CHAPTER

5⁹

The speaker noise overwhelming the street had been lowered by the time they started down the hill but it was still ear-crushing. Noreen looked up. Four crescent-shaped dark lumps clustered near the apex of the dome. The sounds came from there. He had always assumed they were part of the lightning display. Nearby, the dark figures of three men were climbing the scaffolds embedded in the fretwork, trying to reach the speakers. As he watched, one of the figures reached out, missed its grip, and plunged downward. The five hundred foot drop straight down seemed to take a long time. At last the figure disappeared into the trees near the park.

The vibration of the speakers had set everything in motion. He could feel the street shaking and the rhythms pulsating within his bones. The façades of buildings had picked up the beat and were shimmering as they passed, and leaves were blowing at a rapid rate here and there in little tornadoes. The opalescent dome skin also seemed to be sucking in and out like a crazed bladder. People were running back and forth in the street crying and shouting as if they didn't know what was happening or where to go.

"This is horrible," Noreen said.

"Just don't worry about it. Hurry. We'll be all right down below," Walter said.

He had hidden his pistol in his coat and was pushing Noreen along by his elbow.

For the first time on a trip down below, a small black satchel hung on a strap from Noreen's right shoulder, and he felt like a doctor making a house call. He didn't really expect to find Kafahvey. But the old man was his patient and in the event he found him and it was necessary to treat him he had medicines and minimal equipment for first aid.

Now and then he touched the bag and got pleasure out of feeling its firm chunkiness and knowing that in a way he was not alone, that he was accompanied by the familiar tools of his trade.

But Kafahvey couldn't stand the trip, so there would be no Kafahvey, and, besides, the poet had no reason to go below now that Nora was coming to him. Kafahvey was probably in a luxurious apartment not far from his own usual dwelling, and when he wasn't laughing he was sleeping and smelling up the room.

Or—and for a moment Noreen believed this—maybe Dork had abducted the poet in order to free up the apartment.

But Dork was a civil servant. He went by the book. Surely there was nothing in the manual about kidnapping an important personage. It did not occur to Noreen that this might be a rhetorical question of a prophetic nature.

And Noreen wasn't afraid of Walter, or even the weapon, just wary of Walter's stupidity and his blind loyalty to a meaningless job, a form of existence that disgusted Noreen so much that he could not even begin to understand it. Even the antique weapon with no-doubt fatigued metal or plastic was more likely to blow up in Walter's hand than to hurt anyone else.

At most, if he had to he would jab a tranquilizer needle into Walter's arm, a task he somehow looked forward to and might even try to arrange.

He wondered if any passersby noticed he was smiling to himself, but no one near was looking at anyone else. They were all running away from dome central.

Noreen heard a familiar crackling noise overhead. Jagged lines of yellow fire from the arc-igniters were streaking across the dome ceiling near the two remaining climbers. They stopped suddenly and then began to scramble back the way they had come. A bolt of lightning caught one man and knocked him off the scaffold. Noreen didn't see his flight. Noreen and Walter had started running side by side toward the subway entrance

The guards were cowering on the steps just below the surface level, hanging on to the rail. They peered up now and then around the railing, with their hands covering their ears.

Noreen showed his badge and they barely noticed.

As he and Walter started down the steps, he saw a black police bucket skidding to the curb near the entrance, as if choreographed to match Noreen's arrival. Behind him, Noreen could hear the car's door open and running footsteps.

"Stop, Noreen, you can't go down there!"

Noreen turned around, halfway down the steps. Dork had hesitated at the top and was trying to decide if he should follow. He took a few shaky steps forward.

"Did you hear me? You're not allowed to go down below—or outside the dome—ever again."

"Who says?"

"I say. You kidnapped the old man so you could get his apartment."

"You're nuts."

"I'm sending my men down now to get you. You might as well come up like a gentleman."

The heads of two timid cops appeared behind Dork, and didn't come forward, as if they were afraid to expose their whole bodies to the stairwell.

Walter, who had gone a little farther into the tunnel, turned now. He held the handle of the pistol with both hands. Dork stood up, as if to walk down the steps. Walter pulled the trigger.

The blast echoed back and forth on tiled walls and into Noreen's ears.

Dork grabbed his chest and staggered over to the railing. He held himself there, his knees bending slightly.

The two cops ducked out of sight.

"Come on," Walter said. "Run."

Noreen started running down the tunnel.

"Why'd you do that? That was crazy. Give me that damn thing."

Noreen grabbed Walter's arm, still running, and twisted the pistol from his hand. Noreen felt the weapon's thick weight and dropped it into a side pocket.

He wondered if it could go off by itself.

"They say I can't do anything except bring people to the subway entrance," Walter said, in between breaths. "That's not true anymore, is it? I guess I showed them, didn't I?"

He didn't look worried about what he'd done. He rather seemed to flaunt a mock-operatic stance.

"You killed Dork, that's what you did."

Noreen was sure he was the only sane person left

in the universe, which he guessed was the dome itself, and the unpredicted end of the dome had arrived too.

I'll be outside soon enough now. We'll all be outside.

In the street near the hydroponics rooms a crowd had gathered. Everyone wearing the standard khaki jumpsuit. A gang of khaki suits huddled near the curb.

"C'mon," Walter said, when he saw them. "We'll take a shortcut."

"No," Noreen said, "let's find out what's going on."

"No, I insist."

"Come."

"Give me the fire stick then?"

"No."

"Then you better take this."

Walter handed Noreen what looked like two slender metal envelopes. In the open tops of each one Noreen could see the ugly brass tips of the weapon's projectiles.

"Take out the one in the pistol and put one of these in. It's called a clip."

"What?"

"Just do it."

"Why? I don't intend to kill anyone."

"Just do it," Walter said, "you never know about this old stuff."

They huddled by the wall. Noreen removed the

pistol from his pocket and Walter showed him where at the top of the handle to press. The clip slipped out and Noreen put it in his pocket. Somehow it looked different. He snapped one of the new clips in and returned the evil thing to his pocket. He would check the old clip later, find the difference.

"I'm a doctor," Noreen said, glaring at Walter as they started walking again. "I help people, I don't kill them."

I am protesting too much.

"You've got everything going for you, haven't you?" Walter said. As if he had a bad taste in his mouth. He dropped back and let Noreen move ahead.

The imbecilic defectives were keening and moaning. When they became aware that Noreen had come up, they stopped crying for a moment, stepped aside and let him through.

Covarrúbias lay on his back on the stone floor with blood on his chest and face. He wasn't moving. Two defectives held his head; one let it rest in his lap. Their eyes were red and tear-filled. They started crying again.

Noreen knelt down, felt for a wrist pulse. The arm was cold; it contained no movement; its fluids had already started to congeal.

"What happened?"

The defectives were muttering things, excitedly, that Noreen couldn't make out.

Then they saw Walter. He had turned and was limping back toward the exit.

Suddenly they all started shouting at once and began running after Walter. The one who had Covarrúbias' head in his lap lay the dead man carefully on the ground, and as he got up said something. Muffled words made their way out through the back of his nose: "Walter—shot—him."

He ran after the others.

Noreen put his hand around the pistol in his pocket and pulled it out and was surprised how comfortable it felt in his hand, how natural it was to point. His right forefinger slipped easily around the curved lever that would set off the explosion. Instinct told him to shoot Walter in the back, and he could feel his hand start to squeeze. He was looking straight over the top of the barrel. But Walter had run almost out of sight, and a mass of khaki blocked Noreen's aim. He let the pistol hang down by his side.

Once more he reached out to touch the old man; this time he ran his fingers over the neck; he got nothing but the feel of the cold entering the body.

He stood up, shaking his head. He felt nothing, no regret, no remorse, no sense of loss, because emptiness has no feel.

He had been trying for a while now to fill himself with compassion, or some equivalent, and it was a lost cause; it ran out of the bottom somewhere faster than he could put it in at the top. Maybe if he threw away the pills, looked at more pictures, lived outside in the direct sun, maybe he would connect some time with real human feeling. Or maybe he was kidding himself. Maybe he didn't have any ancient virtue (if that truly once existed) because it just wasn't built-in anymore.

I can feel a little disgust coming in now like a cloudy rain, and maybe that is something, about as much feeling as I can handle. I am disgusted with Walter and I am disgusted with Covarrúbias for letting himself get killed and I am disgusted with Nora, though I should not be because I have always believed that sex was all right in any form, and my changing point of view in that regard must be a weakness, but most of all I am disgusted with myself. These people were getting along just fine before I came down, and now I seem to have brought them misery. I have come down here like a virus. I am the plague. It would be better if we could all go back to the time before I left the dome. But there's no going back. The bug is out of the test tube. Already, it's proved fatal. I'm a carrier waiting for it to catch up with me.

The symptoms are listlessness, anxiety, and loneliness. I have tried the antidote and it doesn't work anymore.

He withdrew the extra pistol clip from his pocket and examined it. The remaining unspent inserts had no rounded ends where he assumed the projectiles would be. Walter had fired noise at Dork but nothing had left the pistol's barrel. Therefore Dork had never been in danger. Dork had been acting. Why?

They said you couldn't trust Walter. Now he was sure he knew why. Walter was a snitch and a deceiver. He worked for Dork. He had just pretended to be a police-hating rebel.

The faked death of the policeman was a charade. Dork wanted something and Walter was helping him get it. What? Something to do with Noreen? Perhaps they expected Noreen to start to trust Walter and lead them somewhere. To Nora? No, they knew where she was. Some place many people down here were aware of but weren't telling the authorities? Some place they thought Noreen knew about. But he didn't know. Unless it was the cave with the ancient transmitter? Whatever, it had to do with the misplaced poet.

Noreen sneered. The charade was another one of Dork's fantasies, like the apartment he coveted. He could imagine Dork and Walter rehearsing. The bored guards must have watched.

If it was the transmitter, they didn't know how difficult it was to reach. Without Covarrúbias it was impossible. They had killed the guide. They had torn up their ticket.

So where was Kafahvey? Down here? If he was, then he was most likely just where Dork thought he was. But Noreen didn't know where that was or how to get there.

He didn't know what to do. He didn't even know why he was down here now. Why he kept leaving and returning to this hole. It certainly wasn't Nora anymore. It wasn't pictures. He knew where the pictures were and it wasn't down here. He decided he'd leave the dome and head for his mountain cave as soon as he could, even if he had to sneak out. He'd breathe outside air and look at photographs until his eyes dropped out. No matter what the cost. He felt a little delirious at the notion. He had finally decided to do something.

He started to walk away. Then he felt an irresistible urge to go back and look at Covarrúbias's body again and say good-bye.

His eyes started watering. Was he going to cry? The one time he had cried he was a little boy. Someone had spanked him.

What looked like steam rising from the gutter floated up from Covarrúbias's body. Little wisps of fog over the corpse. Noreen felt dazed, as if lack of sleep the last few days had caught up and was going to do him in. Make him lie down on the street and drop off. Like Covarrúbias. Already he could imagine the cold on his back. But the steam blew toward him and he turned to keep it out of his face.

Something touched his arm then as if fog had acquired weight and substance. He started walking and it felt as though the steam was guiding him.

Wrapped in mist, he could see just a few feet ahead. After a while he had turned and turned again; the streets got narrow; barely room for two people to pass. He didn't know this part of the underworld. At last he came to a wall with a large steel plate barring the way. He was surrounded by liquid smoke now; a coating of warm sweat all over his body that nevertheless felt dry. The pressure of the smoke lifted his hand to a lever. The iron plate slid sideways, revealing the end of a dark tunnel that stopped here but went on into blackness as far as he could tell. Although he knew he sought the light, he had descended into darkness. Was darkness his friend now? Already part of him? He stepped in and pulled another lever inside that closed the plate. He could see better now; the mist had gone. He had left it outside, or rather it had stayed there of its own accord.

A few feet away the floor dropped down to a track bed. A row of dim light bulbs stretched out overhead into infinity. In front of him a small tubular projectile with brighter lights and seats inside, awaited him on the tracks. He stepped through its open doorway and the door closed behind him.

He sat down in the bucket seat at the pointed end of the capsule.

On the banked dash, large buttons marked START, GO, STOP, SLOW and HELP faced him.

He pressed START and the deep throaty noise of

a dynamo began vibrating somewhere under the floor. Then he pressed GO.

The single head lamp shined down the track. He was slipping through darkness faster and faster as the train picked up speed.

Good-bye, old friend. We won't be seeing each other anymore. I'm sorry I was mean to you.

CHAPTER

60

The first objects that fell from the top of the dome were the hyper speakers.

A loud creaking followed as the biometallic dome fretwork flexed itself. Parts of the skin began to tear. Bits of geodesic frame broke off and fell, mostly under the dome's apex. Like old branches.

Women turned away from the wall screens in their living rooms and ran to the balconies. They began to scream.

The men, fearful, grabbed the women and pulled them back into the apartments. They made the women sit on the couches, and they all sat and stared at the screens.

CHAPTER

61

Noreen passed several dimly-lit station platforms. In the few seconds it took to go by he saw closed doors sealed by drifting piles of dust. The train's generator throbbed strongly and the rails rang and hummed and echoed around the tunnel.

Up ahead he saw a brightly lit platform with an open door and, looming much too fast, a wall where the tunnel ended. He pressed the SLOW button, but the train was still moving too fast. He wondered if the STOP button halted the train immediately, or if it was programmed to slow and then stop. He pressed STOP and braced himself.

With a shudder the train downshifted at once, then jerked into slow speed and gradually braked.

It let itself coast to an exact stop at the station platform.

He heard the motors shut off, and the silence in the tunnel had an eerie, expectant weight.

OPEN DOOR. The words lighted up on the dash.

Noreen pressed. The door pushed itself back into its slot in the train's wall. He stepped out onto the platform.

A sign above the entrance read: MULTIMEDIA CENTER AND ARCHIVE.

Nora was coming down the hall.

"I heard the train," she said. "I'm glad it's you. This way."

As if she hardly knew him. The word *harlot* flicked in and out of his awareness.

He followed her into the studio. The same one he had crossed the coal mine to reach before. Covarrúbias had endured that hardship rather than reveal the easy way. Until he knew Noreen better. Until now.

The control room and adjacent studio had a half dozen people moving about. They had the preoccupied unisex look of the usual shadowy, gnome-like functionaries Noreen had become used to in the infrastructure.

Dazzling stage lights had been turned on in the studio and sputtered and popped overhead. A camera with its monitor glowing in the darkened sidelines faced the stage, where a monstrously fat old man dozed in a wheelchair.

He looked already dead.

An unusual yellow-gray cast tinted his skin, and for the first time his cheeks had a sunken look.

Noreen touched the back of the poet's hand, and felt a quiver within the mound of flesh. The rheumy eyes opened up.

"I'm going to give you a little on-the-spot checkup," Noreen said, "but first tell me how you're feeling right now."

"I have no feeling at all," the poet creaked. "I am twisting and turning in outer space."

"You should not have left your home."

"It seemed important at the time. Now I'm not sure. They said the people wanted me. But I don't even want myself anymore."

"I'm going to give you some medicine, a stimulant, and then we have to get you back to the dome."

"Not now," Nora said, over Noreen's shoulder.

"Get a glass of water," Noreen said to her.

He began by checking the old man's vital functions. The poet was still alive, that was all, but it was hard to tell how much.

They should not have brought him down.

These people are stupid down here. Just like the people in the dome.

You're stupid too. Why did you come down here in the first place? He was beginning to feel suffocated by recent events and the tomb-like atmosphere. No wonder they drank whiskey.

She appeared at his side and she said, "Here's the water." And as if she had read his thoughts, "I brought a shot of whiskey too."

Noreen slipped a capsule between Kafahvey's lips and then held the water up for him. Water dripped down the front of his white suit.

"I'll take the whiskey," the old man said.

Noreen let the girl dribble it into his mouth.

Noreen observed that Kafahvey was dressed entirely in white as usual but he had a fat old man's version of the brocaded silk jumpsuit with flared sleeves and cuffs that he had worn years ago.

I wonder if they expect him to dance. They'll be disappointed. He looked around for the guitar. It was not in view.

"All right, help me rock and roll him back to the train." He grabbed the back of the wheel chair and started to turn it around.

A little crowd had gathered next to the camera. B. F. Sparks came forward, followed by his son.

Sparks looked younger than the last time. He stood up straighter and he could see better. He was still squinting, but behind thicker lenses.

"Not possible. We're about to start the live portion of the broadcast."

On a monitor, the young Kafahvey sang and danced. The bell bottom pants and sleeves flapped to the raunchy beat. The thin young man flexed and bumped his pelvis. He had coal-black hair, puffed up into a pompadour, that shined from the pomade holding each strand in its proper place.

"I'm taking him to the hospital."

"He just has to read a poem."

"No way. Move aside."

They gathered around Noreen and the wheelchair and there was no way to pass through.

"All right. If he wants to."

"It's on this paper. In his own handwriting. He just has to read it. But he'll know it by heart."

"All right, ask him." Noreen stepped backed.

Sparks held the paper in front of the poet's face and whispered into his ear.

The poet's eyes had closed and his head had tilted to the side but was held in place by wrinkles of flesh. Two drops of whisky still rested on the wrinkled crusty lips.

"Messiah," the old man whispered gently. "We're ready to broadcast your return. Wake up."

The poet made no move and said nothing. But a fart that started as a low hissing worked itself up to a raucous raspberry of an unfolding crescendo and then ended with a poof while a cloud of sulfurous gas dispersed among the faithful.

Noreen pushed over and nudged Sparks aside. He still had on his stethoscope and now applied it to Kafahvey's chest. He stepped back.

"This man is either in a deep hibernative

trance—or dead. I rather suspect the latter. You've killed your messiah by bringing him down here."

"No no no no no..." The faithful began to wail and cry.

"Let me boogie your butt boogie all night your butt," the figure on the monitor sang.

Noreen recoiled with a mixture of revulsion and contempt thick enough to shovel. He wanted to get out.

Sparks and his companions had grabbed the wheelchair and were pushing it off the set. Everyone was crying. Kafahvey's head bounced now as the wheelchair moved over the uneven floor.

A recorded voice, unaware of anything, masculine and orotund, somewhat rusty at the job, continued on the speakers.

"Ladies and gentlemen, we are proud to present the first public speech in a long, long time of our beloved national poet, the great Kafahvey. Not since his farewell performance more than a hundred years ago have his admirers been blessed with an opportunity to hear his perfect voice and wisdom the way we are about to now. Alive and direct. Yes, alive! Ladies and gentlemen—prepare yourself for the greatest miracle of our time— Kafahvey the glorious messiah has returned—the father of his country—the honorable and magnificent—I present Kafahvey once again to The Family of Man."

Barthwell, whom Noreen had once helped slide the grate in place and now showed none of his earlier unctuous friendship, held the paper in front of Noreen's face.

"Only one thing to do. You'll have to read the poem."

"I don't think so. You read it, if it has to be read."

"But you're his son."

"Not his son. Pure test tube. And at this moment proud of it."

"Look at yourself in the mirror. Then look at the young man dancing. All you need is a suit like that and you'd be exactly like he was a long time ago. I could find you one, but we'll do without."

"I'm leaving," Noreen said, pushing the hand with the paper away from his face.

He had almost reached the door.

"You're not going anywhere," Barthwell said at the top of his lungs.

"We'll see."

Noreen grabbed the exit door handle.

Barthwell was smiling. He held a small black box in his right hand. The top of the box was covered with several rows of red and black buttons.

Barthwell pressed a red button. At that instant Noreen heard the door latch click shut. He tugged at the door. It wouldn't budge.

Noreen thought about pulling out the pistol and killing Barthwell.

"The train's not available to you," Barthwell called. Everyone in the room was looking at Noreen now. A white sheet had been placed over the wheelchair.

He would have to kill all of them to get the black box.

"Then I'll leave by the mine."

"It's a long walk on foot. Do you have a good flashlight?"

"I'll use the covered wagon."

"It's not here now. Won't be here until morning. Maybe not then. The bats have taken over the near cave. Their comings and goings aren't predictable anymore. I think they may be sick."

Barthwell sneered triumphantly.

Noreen grabbed the paper out of Barthwell's hand and went back to the set.

"Here?"

Noreen pointed to a brightly lighted desk facing the camera. Barthwell nodded and went behind the camera.

Noreen sat down and cleared his throat. He stared at the paper.

He'd read the words and get out. Maybe throw in a few words of his own. Tell Hayes the elixir was an underground train. That went nowhere.

All he'd wanted was to look at his photographs and be allowed to find a few more. He felt helpless and impotent.

You're melting like jelly.

Red lights started flashing next to the lens.

"'I don't know if I'm coming or going but now I must be going,'" he heard his voice saying, reading from the paper.

Stop me if I lose my place. Would anyone care?

"'I am going and coming but—as the prophet said, now I must be going to come is to go now and now that I am coming I know I am going going going where I don't know but I been with you for a long time and if I am going really going where I don't know so this is it my coming is over and I'm really going but don't you all stop coming and going now I must be going going going when this you see remember me and stuff like that....'"

Noreen read in a dull monotone without looking at the camera. He kept his head bent over the desk. But when he was finished reading Kafahvey's message he looked up and hesitated.

He had the same feeling, whatever it was, he'd had when he was on the side of the mountain getting ready to jump over the chasm to where the path continued on the other side. He could almost hear the airbike's engine revving up and the handle lever twisting under his palm.

Here goes, I have to do this. Might as well be now.

"My name is Dr. Noreen. I've just read you a so-called poem by my patient the poet Kafahvey. Kafahvey is dead. He passed away a few minutes ago. Otherwise, he would have read his poem to you in person. I am sure it would have been a better experience for you. I didn't do a very good job.

"I'm a doctor, not a public speaker. I took care of Kafahvey for a while. I'm not sure how well I did, since he's dead now. His prospects looked pretty good for a few days. That's why Kafahvey decided to give you his message. He was feeling better for the first time in years. But the trip did him in.

"And I did a poor job in reading his poem. If I had practiced I might have done a better job. But there wasn't time. I must confess I didn't understand the poem. We're all shook up by the— messiah's—death.

"I feel I have to do something special for you to make up for my awkwardness. For what may be my taking your poet away. Give you a gift. What might that be? What can I tell you? How can I make amends? What do you want to know?

"There's something I have been thinking about for what now seems a long time. I will tell you. You can leave the dome any time you wish. You don't have to live in crowded apartments. You can go outside and start over, have a wonderful life in the wide open spaces. Have all the children you want. Live with just one person if you like. Outside. Unlimited space. I've been out there. It's wonderful out there. You won't believe how beautiful the outside is. And how free you'll be out there.

"What does this mean? Why haven't you been out there? Because you've been afraid of the radiation. But, my friends and neighbors, let me assure you now, there are no high levels of radiation beyond the dome. I'm speaking to you as a doctor. The radiation dissipated a long time again. The dome officials, who have known about this for generations, have lied to you and kept the truth a secret.

"Go, if you like. Hold no grudges against anyone, just go. You no longer need the protection of the dome. Stay only if you wish. The choice is yours. In the name of Kafahvey, begin your travels now. I have begun mine."

Noreen needed a deep breath and a drink of water. Besides, he didn't know what else to say. But the red lights were still on. He wondered how you ended a program. How he signaled to Barthwell that he was finished.

You just say, *Barthwell, that's it.* He was about to say that.

But he stopped because—he had started thinking about what he had said, how he couldn't get it back. How stupid it was to say anything. But everything was falling apart and it seemed like the right thing to do at the moment.

Are you proud of yourself now?

No, not really.

It was the first time Noreen had ever spoken up about anything. He felt like a different kind of man. *It's the way you were when you stopped taking the pills. Your blood pressure went up and you had crawled into a different skin. You were capable of living outside the dome if you wanted. Nobody had to tell you what to do. You could even look for old pictures if you wanted.*

He looked up and nobody was paying any attention to him.

He looked away again, and at that moment the control panel blew up.

Resistors, diodes, and chips blew out from the wall with a burst of flame and puffs of smoke. The flunky who had been standing nearby noticed that his coveralls had caught fire and ran from the room.

The red lights went out. The camera shuddered on its three legs and let out a frightened bleat.

Noreen jumped up.

Nora came in running, out of breath, "Our spotter in the dome just called." She yelled to anyone who might hear. "He says the dome is flexing. Something to do with our transmission. The sound's up too high, or something, or we're on the wrong frequency."

Bathwell started running. Noreen could see him heading for the back room and followed.

Below the ventilator the dome's roots bulged and twisted. The silvery bark rippled with a mirror sheen that he had not noticed before, as if the plant were trying to rid itself of the aluminum.

Bathwell took one look and ran back toward the control room.

"Cut the power," he yelled at his father. "All of it! Now!"

The old man started closing down valves and turning off switches and when he had finished it was as if all life had gone out of the room.

"I wonder what happened," the old man said, after he had finished, leaning his back against the counter. He seemed small and bent again.

"You had your damn speakers too loud for one thing," Noreen said.

"I remember now," the old man said, digging deep in his memory. "It had something to do with the dome skeleton. Why they stopped the transmissions years ago. The frequencies we used and the light waves and even the sounds—yes, it's coming back—they excited the growth pattern of the grid work, and we had to cut out everything except our weak standby signal. Yes, I remember now, the lightning at night was just enough to keep the plant alive, but more than that created a problem—how could I have forgotten that? They banned looking at pictures then."

"You asshole!" Barthwell said to his father.

"They say the covering has torn and some of the streets have buckled," Nora said.

"I'm leaving," Noreen said. Inside his coat, his hand gripped the checkered handle of the pistol. You pointed and pulled the trigger. He would do that now if anyone objected. Anyone.

"I'll go with you," Nora said.

Noreen looked at her like she was a piece of garbage and said, "Just to the boiler room."

"Drive slowly—in case the track has shifted," Barthwell said.

CHAPTER

6²

WILLIAM BORNEFELD

Noreen stared out the glass at the head lamp that poured over the tracks ahead. He held the rocker switch that said GO halfway down and had one thumb on the STOP button. Traveling at half speed this time, he felt they would never reach the main part of the infrastructure.

The head lamp hitting the ties made him giddy. Jumbled his thoughts into a murky soup.

What will they do to me? Nothing.

If he had saved the dome by *making* them turn off the equipment, he would be a hero.

But nobody would know about that. He wondered if he should bring Nora along to testify in his behalf. They wouldn't listen to her, even if she was cleaned up.

Kafahvey's wheelchair with its sheet-draped hulk was wedged at the back of the aisle against the banquette. Noreen could look back and see two feet squeezed into shiny black pumps with rhinestone tassels.

"I'd like to come up and stay with you in your apartment for a few days. Do what we did before," she said.

"No thanks."

"I'd move outside with you, if that's what you're planning."

"No thanks to that too."

"Why did you decide you didn't like me?"

He looked at her and smiled. He could see her suddenly think of the one thing she had done recently that he wouldn't like. That maybe he knew.

She had been drunk at the time. It hadn't occurred to her until now.

"You saw?"

He nodded.

"But I was drunk."

"I was too," he said. "But I'm not now."

"You do certain things to help your employees. That are expected. That mean nothing. I didn't want you to see. That's why I sent you away with Covarrúbias."

He could see the other end of the line approaching. He lifted his finger from the GO button and began to press his thumb down on

STOP. He felt like sighing but he couldn't bring himself to do it.

Just too tired, he figured.

"This is where I get off," he said.

"Look," she said. "Tell me. Where did you get the weapon?" It was as if she hadn't already talked to him.

He could feel the magnetic feet clamp the rails. The train slammed to a halt a few inches from the platform's rubber bumper.

"From Walter," he said, not looking at her. "He killed Covarrúbias with it."

"That figures. Walter works for Dork. He's been trying to find the subway for years. He follow you?"

"Probably not."

"Give me the gun."

"What?"

"The hand weapon."

He looked at her and said, "No."

"Why would you want a gun?" she said.

"I like the way it feels—and looks," he said. "It looks old and purposeful, and has just the right weight in the hand."

He'd carry the gun whenever he went outside the dome.

"You worry too much about the way things look. Get over it. Give me the gun."

She held out her hand, flat.

"No."

"Why do you need a gun upstairs? An old gun belongs down here. Dork will be waiting for you when you go upstairs. If he finds the gun—"

He handed her the gun.

She wants to kill Walter. Let her.

"I'll be around if you need me," she said. She had a soft look that he didn't see too often.

"I won't."

"I can bring the gun up later if you like."

"We'll see."

"Guess we'd better get going then."

"Yes," he said.

He was already walking toward the back of the car.

CHAPTER

6³

W
I
L
L
I
A
M

B
O
R
N
E
F
E
L
D

Beta felt the moving walkway suddenly jerk forward and stop. She lurched forward and rocked twice before she got herself balanced again, but her ankles felt shaky and her heart was beating so hard she could almost feel it thumping under her new, fashionable Organo Institute uniform.

She looked around. Some of the passengers had fallen to the ground and now were picking themselves up. Everyone had been riding away from the center of the dome; now most of them started running. As they passed, she could feel the loose covering of the walkway bend and thump.

She began to walk. Noreen's apartment was not far now. She could feel the flexible walkway bend and sway under her feet and it was a strange sensation to be walking over it instead of standing still and moving on it.

When the man fell from the grid work she had been standing on the Organo Institute balcony and she saw him. Even now, she couldn't believe it. She could still see him falling. Stryker and some of the other executives came in and told everyone to get out of the building. "It's an earthquake," they had said. "Thank god, the dome can withstand an earthquake." They all ran back inside and took the elevator.

But she wasn't so sure. The grid work appeared to be flexing within itself, not from without.

The man was falling, even now.

She should have gone straight to her apartment. But she had to see Noreen. One more time. Get things straightened out.

If it was the end of the world, she wanted to spend it with the only man she had ever loved. She'd spend it with him even if it meant just watching him from across the street.

She would beg him to take her back. She would promise to do anything he asked. She would overlook *anything*.

It was ridiculous, now that the dome seemed to be falling apart, but she had changed her hairstyle, bought a new uniform and thrown away her harlequin glasses. She wasn't quite used to the contact lenses; she was watching her step carefully because plants and bricks had fallen over the walkway and her feet seemed a long way off, as though she were looking at them through the bottom of a telescope.

When she reached the stairway that led down to Noreen's slanted street, she held onto the railing and squeezed back against the wall to let a screaming man and woman rush by.

She still had her key to the apartment and when she went up the steps and inserted it in the lock she felt a shiver over the back of her neck from the familiar old routine.

How could things have changed so much? Why did I not appreciate the times we had together when they were taking place?

I am not talking about sex now, though I miss that. I want that too. Now I am talking about killing time with the only person you ever want to be with.

The falling man never reaches the ground because he is always falling.

She thought she could detect Noreen's scent as soon as she closed the door behind her, but it was just his lingering aura. She had spent so much time in that apartment she wondered if she had left her own imprint, but if she had, she couldn't detect it. The apartment was empty, totally, bone-chillingly empty.

She decided she would take off her coat and wait for him but as soon as she sat down at the galley table, she could hear the noises outside getting louder and she could feel the floor vibrating against her shoes. It felt as if the whole building were in a sling swaying back and forth.

She was frightened then, not for herself, but for Noreen. She was especially worried that he might be *là-bas*. She'd always been afraid of down below though she'd never been there, but she had heard awful stories about what it was like and now she worried that the whole infrastructure might cave in and cover everyone down there with dirt.

She could not bear that happening to Noreen. Noreen to suffocate, buried alive. He was her life partner, no matter what might happen. The affair with the girl was nothing. Even if he married her, it was nothing. He would eventually come back to her. He would have affairs, and this was one, and she would have affairs too, but they would always belong to each other. She would rather die than have anything bad happen to him.

The front window began to rattle in its frame and she could imagine the whole building collapsing. She stood up then and removed a screwdriver from her purse. She could at least protect Noreen's reputation. She did not want anyone finding Noreen's pictures in the rubble. They belonged to Noreen and she would look out for them and for him.

"What are you doing in this apartment?" Martine was coming up the stairs as Beta pulled the door shut.

At the foot of the stairs, a taxi bucket waited. The driver stood next to it; he was short, dark, and unable to withhold the panic on his face, as he wondered whether to wait for Martine or to flee in his cab or on foot.

Beta pushed past Martine without saying a word.

"Answer me, you horrid old bitch," Martine said, and she reached out and grabbed Beta's arm.

Through her new contact lenses, Beta could clearly see Martine's flawless skin and her sparkling dark brown eyes that didn't need glasses.

"I live here," she said.

"Not any more."

"We'll see."

"Where's Noreen?"

"Who's Noreen?" Beta said. She pulled her arm away, turned and started down the steps.

"The father of my child," Martine called.

"He's not here," Beta said.

Beta didn't look back. She went up the stairway to the main sidewalk hoping it would be working again. She wanted just to step onto it and stand still and just look ahead. If the dome fell down on her she'd just ignore it. But the walkway still wasn't working.

Beta stepped onto the motionless platform and, carrying next to her purse a yellow envelope, she started walking again. She was used to the bouncing underneath now and she took deliberate firm steps and knew that she would be home soon.

She looked up at the top of the dome, but the falling man wasn't there now.

Martine had slumped at the top of the steps outside Noreen's apartment and, with her head bent over her arms, was crying her eyes out.

She looked up just in time to see the cab driver get back in his bucket. Before he could slam the door shut, she stood up.

"Don't sneak out on me, you little brown bastard. If you know what's good for you—my brother is managing director Brack. Take me home."

Her tears had already dried.

CHAPTER

6⁴

He felt he had gone out of his body and was watching himself talk to people.

Hayes asked, "Did you get it?"

"What?"

"The elixir."

"No."

"Then there's nothing I can do for you."

"Oh."

❦

Brack's voice came to him, "Looks like your adventures are over. Is that how you see it? And no payoff?"

Noreen could look past Brack's shoulder out the

picture window. Two workmen, properly harnessed this time, dangled from the dome's apex. Empty space had taken the place of three of the black dots that had been hyper speakers. The workmen were leaning over the third black dot, getting ready to remove it.

It was strange not seeing the dots any more. He had always looked up there and never asked what they were. He was different now. He had learned to use his eyes. But what difference did it make?

I can't be modest now. I'll speak up, save myself for my pictures.

"I saved the dome."

His voice felt stuck deep down in his throat. It was strange hearing himself talk again.

"Oh, really, how do you figure? I don't quite see it that way. How do you account for all the damage?"

He could hear shovels scraping concrete, soft-sounding at that distance, workers cleaning up the central garden. The dome getting back to normal.

"It would have been worse."

"Worse than if you hadn't opened your big mouth?"

"I was under duress then."

"No, you're under duress *now*. Remember, you were supposed to keep the secrets."

Could he be happy now that he could see? Was he happy before? Could he ever be happy? What is "happy," anyway?

"I've learned my lesson," he said.

"I should think so. But once the secrets are out, they're no longer secrets. There's nothing to keep anymore. What should I do with you?"

"Pretend it never happened."

"Like last time? That would be easy, wouldn't it?"

"Yes."

"And leave you in the gentlemen's club, of course? Marry my sister?"

"Sure."

"Like it's all over with and forgiven?"

"Exactly."

"No, not this time. As for pictures, that's nothing. Trivial. I can overlook 'pictures.' But radiation—that's a different story. Radiation's been our shield. The myth of radiation keeps things properly oiled. Always has. Before you and me. After you and me too. But, anyway, no one believed you about the radiation. They think you're crazy. Like your father Kafahvey. What they believed was the earthquake you almost caused. No one is leaving. Why would anyone leave paradise?"

"That's my point. I really don't want to leave either."

"You would see it that way, wouldn't you? Now. Well, I don't see it. Martine doesn't see it. Did I tell you she's having an abortion?" He said it as if he were wielding a knife that had just made a deep cut.

He looked for a moment as if thinking about making several more thrusts, just for fun, but then he must've remembered something else he had to do or wanted to do and he let it drop.

"No," Noreen said.

"You're not surprised?"

"Not surprised about anything. Just let me go. I'll make my way outside, if necessary. If I have to leave, I'll never come back. Or I'll stay and be a good doctor. There will always be secrets. You can keep them."

"You and that girl?"

"What girl?"

"Your sister?"

"She's not my sister."

"Sure, she is."

"No, not her. And Kafahvey's not my father."

"Believe what you will."

Brack closed a file on his desk top, bounced nervously for a second in his chair, and Noreen could see that the meeting was over.

The distant murmur of voices drifted up now, as office workers left their buildings and got ready to have an outdoor lunch hour.

Noreen thought of Beta and wondered if she had started going out with someone from her office. He missed Beta.

And Martine? Really, he didn't miss her at all. Or did he?

He wondered if he should start the pill again.

Brack stood up, sighed.

"Oh Noreen Noreen Noreen. I'm going to—well—what I have to do—oh my—will hurt me more in the long run than it will you. I'll always remember you. You're unforgettable. Like Kafahvey. I'm laughing, of course. You're such a beautiful fellow—to look at, that is. Good-bye, Noreen."

CHAPTER

6⁵

"Why are you dressed all in black?" Betty Brack said.

"Because I'm in mourning," Martine said to her sister-in-law.

"For the dome? Don't worry about the dome. The dome will survive. I don't see you've missed any meals, have you?"

"I've lost someone."

"Don't tell me you've miscarried?"

"No. Nothing like that."

"Then you need white. A bride should be dressed in white."

"I'm not getting married. I have no one to marry."

"Don't be ridiculous. This'll all be over in a few days. Then everything will be back just the way it was. Brack will see to that."

"I don't want it to be over. I've been mortified, truly offended. No one does that to me."

"That's silly."

"You're silly."

"No, you're silly. The silliest young woman I've ever seen. Why would you turn down a beautiful man like that?"

"We'll see."

She drifted out of the room away from her sister-in-law. Her brother had stupid taste in women.

She liked the way the filmy black cloth billowed around her as she walked down the hallway to her private apartment.

Noreen had never been there. Too bad. He didn't know it existed. He had almost made it but almost is not enough.

She removed her black veil and, carefully folding it, set it on her dresser. Then she plopped down on the couch at the foot of her king-size bed and slouched into the cushions, running her hands over her swollen stomach. It felt funny through the black gauze.

Under here lies the real Noreen. I can deal with this Noreen. And there are more where he came from in the freezer. Oh, it was so smart of me to think ahead. I could have just thought about the sex and nothing else. But I'm a Brack. And we are always thinking of the future.

The sex will take care of itself. Though—it was awfully nice with the father of my children. Perhaps I'm making a mistake. But I'm thinking about the past now. Leave that to people like Noreen.

She got up and looked through her menu of video disks, touched one, and, forgetting about the gown, flopped in the middle of her bed.

The opposite wall glowed with soothing images and fruity sounds as her favorite motion picture began to unroll itself. The ancient titles were familiar-looking but made no sense to her because she had never bothered to learn dead languages like French, Italian or English, and the strange language persisted in titles that ran at the bottom of the screen and changed whenever someone spoke.

If Noreen had only waited, he could have seen all the pictures he wanted. It was what every rich person knew but didn't talk about. He almost made it. Perhaps she should have told him. But she wanted it to be a surprise. Oh, well—

Out of the corner of her eye, Martine glimpsed herself in a distant mirror. Yes, she compared very favorably to an old movie star.

On the wall the images known as Ava Gardner and Errol Flynn copulated and cavorted in a colorized and transfigured movie that could not

BOOK FIVE

THE
LIGHT
OF THE
WORLD

CHAPTER

6⁶

You are the only person left in the world.

You are walking along a slightly vaulted, cobbled allée. You are looking straight ahead.

Your path extends from lower left up one third of the frame and ends at an intersection, which jogs right and left at an awkward angle out of view. The façade of a three-story building glimpsed ahead ends your view of the street. An almost unbroken wall of four-story buildings rises up on each side.

It's winter; you are sure of this, because somehow the wispy shadow of the bare branches of an unseen tree fills the wall immediately on the right. Narrow shutters cover portals. Old mortar cracks, and drops away, revealing rough bricks. A wrought iron fence with pointed shafts guards an upper wall. Perhaps a window's there, an artist's skylight. It's early or late in the day, you can't be sure; the angle of sunlight making that faint tree shadow reveals it's not noon; the sun is high enough to reach one side of the street but not the other. A gas lamp glows in the shadow on a wall. Perhaps it's afternoon.

Where then is everyone? You feel no one is left inside the buildings, that it's not just an interlude, when traffic has ebbed. Everyone is just gone. Except you.

You have stumbled into a mystery.

You are the witness.

Where are these rough stones? What happened to all the people?

A long time ago, and yet now.

The sky should be blue—that is, a gray tone—but it's blank white paper. The entire frame's black and white, but overall there's a cold brown tone. Chocolate gone bad. Everything is dark, heavy, and waiting for you.

You have been here before and yet you don't know when or why. You are the witness and yet you don't know where you are and you don't know where you're going, and you have no idea what's going on.

You lift your right foot, and enter the picture. You become part of the puzzle. You are no longer the witness. You are the picture. You have slipped forward as easily as if you had breathed yourself in.

And then you know: there is no way out. You are trapped forever. You have made a mistake.

You feel yourself flattening, losing one dimension, as you frantically search for your place in the frame, turning into unpalatably bitter chocolate.

From this perspective, you see nothing.

CHAPTER

6⁷

It was still dark when he looked out over the rows of airbikes parked near the dome exit.

He hadn't been able to sleep, thinking about what had occurred the last two days, and he still couldn't believe he was free. He was sure he now had a furtive, shifty look that he had to quell, because it would call attention to himself and arouse suspicion, but every time he looked around no one seemed to care what he was doing and no one was following. That was of course the way he wanted things to be but it was still disconcerting.

His last time out he had made a tiny cut in the right hand grip of the airbike he had been using and he found the bike now and pulled it out of its rack.

He set the throttle on standby, turned on the ignition and listened to its civilized putt-putting.

He wondered if he was right in assuming that this airbike would still perform in the demanding way he intended. Perhaps he had permanently damaged it on the mountain. He thought about selecting another bike at random. But the exit guard was now looking this way, and he hand-guided the familiar bike over to the guard's station. The guard remembered him from the last time, but he looked at Noreen's blue badge and nodded in a deferential way and deep down in his throat said have a nice day.

Noreen snapped shut his visor and pushed the bike into the airlock.

He was alone, halfway in, halfway out.

He straddled the bike, gave it slightly more lift pressure, bounced gently on the seat. He could feel the cushion of air below the bike push against the ground like a rubber ball.

The outer door opened and he drove out. The sun was just starting to make its arrival on his left. It had moved farther north during his absence. Night on the earth was being replaced by the grainy shadows of predawn.

Every now and then he looked back at the dome and saw it getting smaller and smaller. Already the rising sun cast a long jagged shadow behind him of his silhouette astride the airbike. The shadow stretched behind him toward the dome. At its farthest limit it converged with a sharp point. The shadow was a dagger that was cutting him loose from his past. He smiled at the idea of such an image. He had never analyzed anything in visual terms before, now it seemed he could think in no other way.

The dome was almost out of view yet no other bikes had appeared behind him. They were really letting him get back to work again. They were all comfortably asleep in their beds. The bogey man had passed through the dome and gone away outside. No damage done. Nothing that could not be repaired. He laughed to himself and the laugh moved around inside his helmet hitting the plastic and coming back again or getting lost in canvas and it was pleasing.

He was a different man now. So much had happened since his last time out of the dome. He was different yet the same, himself but more so, the person he was meant to be.

He felt free and reborn and was beginning again to have generous and kind thoughts about dome life. He could not imagine a better life or place to grow up in than in Fullerton and he was grateful now for the opportunity it had given him to grow up and become a doctor and to explore the flesh of beautiful young women and then this ancient world that was being reborn because of him. Just as he was being reborn.

He felt like a larva that was just about ready to climb out of its cocoon, and the knowledge that he had come so far in his life and yet had an exciting new future ahead made him giddy.

He looked back. The dome was gone. The dagger had disappeared beneath the airbike. He was riding on it. The mountain had been moving closer on his right and now he was almost alongside it. Up ahead he could see the spindly rock near where he would leave the road. Without taking a rad reading he snapped up his visor. At once he could smell the perfume from the flower field. He could see its rosy bloom near the base of the mountain.

He wished he had a photograph of the flower field, so that he could look at it and remember the way it was any time he wanted to in the quiet of his apartment.

Such pictures should be taken. Pictures of the earth, and dome life too, as they happened, at different times of the year, so nothing was forgotten. They would not be substitutes for the real thing, just reminders of the endless varieties and possibilities of life.

He looked back again, saw no one, then twisted the throttle handle, and left the road, earlier than he had last time, bouncing over the mesquite. He had not gone as far east as the last time, and it would not take him as long to reach the gorge. Soon he saw the rocky ground passing in a white blur under his feet and he had reached the rock field that meant the mountain was near; from this approach the rocks started sooner, but they were smooth and flat, and the bike made good time, barely oscillating with the cracks.

Now the big rocks appeared, and he threaded his way through the lower crevices, slowing down slightly; soon he could see the gorge picking up the high morning light, the dry rocks' glare, and ahead the rocky slope up the edge of the eastern half of the mountain.

His pulse raced as he thought about how close he was to the cave and he gave a jolt of altitude and forward thrust to the motor, and went up the rocky path on the side of the mountain, and at once he was leaning forward to compensate for the new angle upward, and below him he could see the black rocks passing by and on his right the base of the rocky gorge farther and farther down below.

He was now in the shade of the mountain and he could see the top of his path because he was two-thirds of the way up, with the high-pitched whine of the engine bouncing back from rock surface and filling his ears so he could hear nothing else. Then the sun went away under a cloud and it was almost dark. The light that had been blazing off the side of the other mountain to his right went away also and it was dark over there on the other mountain too, and as he reached the summit he realized he had been mistaken about the direction. This was not the same path he had taken earlier. He was not anywhere near the cave. In fact, there must have been two gorges in the mountain and he was undoubtedly on the one closest to the dome. He had never been in this place before, and he began pulling back on the altitude lever and throttling down and thinking of how he would set down gently and turn around manually, but he had already reached the top and leveled out, and he kept going because of the momentum even after he had pulled back on the levers, and then he went over the edge and out into empty space and began to fall. There was nothing for the air jet to connect with. The path stopped at that point. He had reached the other side of the mountain and the path didn't go anywhere after that because that side of the mountain was simply a vertical slab. And he was sliding along it now holding onto the bike which had flipped a full ninety degrees over onto its side, the uncontrolled jet catching on the vertical wall and pushing him further away from it over the chasm, and he knew he would hold on all the way down to the bottom of the gorge, but it wouldn't do any good. From now on everything was an empty gesture, because the one thing he should have done right, taking the correct path, he had failed to do, and that's the way it was, you had to die sometime and even if you made a little cry it

died out right away and that was that. It occurred
to him that if he were an insect he had come out
of the cocoon without any wings and he thought
how interesting the pattern was along the rock face
at that point and that was all.

CHAPTER 6

After awhile he had fallen asleep on the cot and was having a dream and when they came in and shined the flashlights into his eyes he got up but he was trying to remember the dream. They had not turned the overheads on, so he couldn't see their faces. He figured there were five of them and he was surprised how rough they were treating him. He thought that sort of thing was all over. He was going to have some big bruises from the punching they gave his ribs.

"Don't worry about your shoes," the one in charge said, and in less than a minute they had him out in the hall and were dragging him down the corridor. They were mostly big guys, except for the leader who was rather small and thin and had slick black hair, and they all had dark brown skin.

"You want to look at something," the slender one said. "We'll show you something."

The lights in the hall had been turned down for the night and had a pale gritty quality.

He saw that and then he didn't see anymore, because someone covered his head with a sack and pulled a drawstring against his neck and it was interstellar night inside.

But for whatever reason now he was counting the paces and paying attention to the direction. After fifty paces, they turned right, which was the end of the hall, and then another sixty-three paces and they stopped. He could hear the rumbling of the elevator as it came up and halted at their level. They got in. He heard the door close and felt the elevator going up. It must have gone up two or three floors which was above the Institute laboratories where Chief Surgeon Stryker worked, and they got off and led him down a hall and went into a room. By then he had stopped counting because he could smell formaldehyde and he had a pretty good idea where he was.

They didn't remove the mask until they had strapped him to an operating table. He could feel the straps buckled around his neck, his arms and wrists, and his feet strapped to stirrups as if he were about to give birth. He felt them let go and move back and he relaxed then and let himself press his head against the cushioned pad and looked up at the large circle which contained the operating theatre lights.

"This is going to hurt me more than it hurts you," he heard a voice say, and he recognized it.

Then a head leaned over and shut out the lights for a moment and in the shadow he could see it was Stryker.

"Stryker, old boy," he said and he felt some relief now.

But Stryker said, "No old boy anymore."

And his face went away. Then a hand moved in and attached forceps to his eyelids so they would stay open and he realized his head was fixed in place too. Then a spindly instrument was shoved over his face and he recognized it as a lazarium. And it was turned on and he could see the narrow shaft of light pointed at the ceiling and its needle point was brighter by a thousand times than the halogen lamps in the ceiling.

"This won't take long," he heard Stryker say. "I want to get home as soon as possible. I have a new poetry disk and I intend to spend all evening listening to it."

"Kafahvey?"

Stryker laughed.

"Who's Kafahvey? Don't worry about such things. It's not your field."

"Look, Stryker, let up. I've learned my lesson. I even dreamed just now I died outside the dome."

"I have never believed much in dreams," Stryker said. "I don't even think dreams exist except as a perverse excuse for visual experiences."

Noreen could see Stryker's strong smooth white arms enter his field of vision and grab the laser's handle. They pressed a button that turned off the beam, then rotated the head until the tube was pointing down at Noreen's face.

I guess they're threatening me with a lobotomy. Should I beg forgiveness or just tough it out?

But before he could decide, he was looking straight into the laser beam.

They took out his right eye first. He lost sight at once, long before he could smell the ocular fluid steaming up rancidly, and little hot droplets stinging his cheek. Then the unbearable whiteness of light cut into his left eye and he couldn't see at all anymore. The two doses of light cut like needles into the infinity of his brain.

At first he was lost and floating within a universe of emptiness and pain, his own suffering. Then he found himself in a gallery with white walls and on the walls were twelve framed photographs. The whites of the photographs were purer than the whites of clouds and the blacks were deeper and yet more colorful than the blackness around him.

CHAPTER

6⁹

W
I
L
L
I
A
M

B
O
R
N
E
F
E
L
D

The puffy white face of an old woman rests on a silk pillow in a brocaded box. Tuberous white flowers surround her bier. A younger, but also old, woman in a black coat weeps over her mother's corpse. After a while she moves away, momentarily facing the camera without seeing it, and raises a handkerchief to her tear-filled eyes.

She's hunched over, as if flinching from a blow. Shrinking back from the unknown horror that hits with an invisible fist.

The moment freezes. C'est le moment décisif. The photographer's right forefinger becomes glued to the camera's shutter release button. The woman is unable to move back or go forward. Everything stops. The camera's locked in the fourth, fifth and sixth dimensions.

It's night in an alien place. Everyone's dead now. All that's left is this picture.

Everything ends. There are no survivors.

Eternity becomes paper. Truth is fiction.

JUNE 16.

TWENTY-FOUR YEARS LATER.

THE GARDEN OF EDEN

CHAPTER

70

Martin Hayes sat on the top deck of the old restaurant known as the Garden of Eden, sipping a holo drink, and, as usual, thinking about himself. He was looking forward to the party that night celebrating his twenty-third birthday and his graduation from medical school on the same day.

He was looking forward to the party the way he always looked forward to anything in which he was the center of attention, and he was enjoying the mild spring breeze that he could feel gently blowing against the short blond hairs on the back of his neck.

Most of all he was looking forward to the airbike, which no one, especially his mother, wanted him to have, but which he expected for his birthday.

"The super model, the one that can jump up fifteen feet."

For some reason his mother, Martine, was appalled at the thought of his having such a vehicle; but his mother would do anything for him, her only child, and in the end always got him anything he wanted.

She would come through this time as she always did. It was just a matter of asking, and asking over and over again, until she could not stand to hear herself saying no to him anymore, and all the time she was looking at his blue eyes and blond hair that was unlike most of the dome people's and reminded her of something she wouldn't talk about.

He had also received a mysterious note from a woman named Beta asking him to meet her at the restaurant in the central garden, and though it was an annoying distraction on this special day, he could never turn down an invitation from a woman.

He was not surprised by her request. In addition to his unusual, tall and muscular good looks he had luminous blue eyes and a superior attitude that women liked. Beautiful young women were always trying to lure him into their arms or, to be more accurate, into their bedrooms. And then...well, he knew what to do with them and he usually did it until they bored him and he had to move on to one of the others waiting their turns.

But this Beta person turned out to be something

else. A real false alarm. She was OLD and NOT GOOD LOOKING AT ALL. She even had a slight limp. And she had the nerve to sit down at his table before he could tell her it was all right.

Without even a pause she said she had something for him she was sure his father wanted him to have.

"You mean you knew Hayes?" he said, and couldn't believe she was the type of person who could ever have known anyone important. "That must have been a long time ago. Hayes died two years after he married my mother. She fucked him to death."

"No, not Hayes, your real father, Dr. Noreen."

That got him. The obscenity he uttered just to annoy her didn't bother *her* a bit, but he felt himself reeling from her too personal approach to someone—a doctor—*him*—she didn't know. For a long time he'd been aware that Hayes wasn't really his father and it didn't bother him one way or the other, but he had never got around to looking into the details. Apparently this odd OLD person knew some things about him, or thought she did, that he didn't even know himself. He didn't like talking about anything, certainly not personal things, to a stranger, especially someone he'd just met and considered ugly. And not in a public place like The Garden of Eden. Where the waiters all knew him.

What was she trying to do? Ruin his birthday? It was insulting!

He started to think of ways to punish her for her impertinence. For being OLD *and* UGLY. And BOTHERING HIM.

"I'm pretty busy," he said. "What's this thing you wanted to give me? And why?"

She pulled a fat old yellow envelope from under her saggy raincoat and shoved it across the table toward him. When he started to open it, gingerly, because he wasn't sure where it had been, she said, "Not here. Its contents are very personal, rather dangerous, in fact, I should say. And not in front of your mother. Later. When you're alone?"

His eyebrows had raised only slightly and he withdrew his outstretched hand. But now he was interested. Dangerous? He forgot about her insults. He was almost sorry when she got up and moved away.

"Why would you give something like that to *me*?" he started to say, but it was too late.

He watched her pathetic lumpy figure waddle down to the main moving walkway and float out of sight.

Dangerous? He let out an arrogant snort and for a second the waiter looked over.

Riding airbikes was dangerous. Could be, anyway. Especially if you raced the Dork boys. But not opening envelopes.

Hey, I'm frightened. Maybe I'm headed for a paper cut? Pick up an old disease from rotting paper?

He sipped holo-cola. It seemed to have gone flat.

Okay, he'd look inside the envelope late at night. After the party. Get to the bottom of this "father" business.

Then he forgot about Beta and the envelope.

He stared down at the bimbos twisting and turning on the dance floor. Nobody paying any attention to the large vid screen that flickered and pulsed to the beat.

Vid screens couldn't compete with drugs like Candiblo, Dashpot and Pop-Off. Talk about your colored lights.

All he could think about was airbike stuff. He was bubbling with an enjoyable excitement that no holo drink could send away.

Funny, for a doctor, supposed to be a pillar of society.

Well, things are not always what they seem. He'd learned that in his walks around town. From now on he'd *ride* around town.

Get out of my way, everybody.

What he'd do was this: act nice for a change at the party, since he really was twenty-three now, and a doctor. Then when all the old people had gone to sleep—and his mother would go to bed early because of all the stuff she took—he would look inside the mysterious envelope and have a laugh or two at whatever fell out.

And then he'd take his airbike outside, and ride through the dome at full throttle. Maybe he'd race the Dork boys if they were out, leave them choking on his negative ions, go anywhere he damn well pleased.

That's all he wanted—to ride his airbike—who knows where?

Maybe, he'd even leave the dome, check the outside. Go places nobody'd ever been.

"Waiter!" he called over. "Bring me a double holo-cola. It's my birthday and I'm ready to ride."

THE END

AUTHOR'S NOTE

Most of the graphic images referred to in this book are descriptions of or were suggested by real photographs by more or less famous photographers whose work I have admired.

Here's a list of the major references in the order they were introduced.

I have included sources I consulted while writing this book, works close at hand in my own library. I have known these pictures for a long time, however, and most have been reprinted in a variety of publications, not just in the ones listed.

1. "Pepper, 1930," Edward Weston, *Edward Weston: His Life and Photographs*, Revised Edition, An Aperture Book, Aperture, Inc., Millerton, New York, p. 146.

2. "Mount Williamson," Ansel Adams, *Examples: The Making of 40 Photographs*, Little Brown and Company, Bullfinch Press, Boston, 1983, p. 66.

3. "Spanish soldier," Robert Capa, *The Best of Popular Photography*, Ziff Davis Publishing Company, New York 1979, p. 84.

4. "Farmer's Kitchen, Hale County, Alabama 1936," Walker Evans, The Museum of Modern Art (dst. By New York Graphic Society Ltd., Greenwich, Connecticut) 1971, p. 82.

5. "Nude, New Mexico, 1937," Edward Weston, *Edward Weston: His Life and Photographs*, op cit. p. 165.

6. "Woman in 'A Spanish Village,'" W. Eugene Smith, *W. Eugene Smith: His Photographs and Notes*, An Aperture Monograph, Aperture, Inc., New York, 1969, p. 41.

7. "Couple on bed," Henri Cartier-Bresson, *Henri Cartier-Bresson: Photographer*, Little Brown and Company, Boston, First revised edition 1992, p. 26.

8. "Corpse," photographer unknown, New York City Municipal Archives, the *New York Times Magazine*, 4-17-94, p.18.

9. *Shadow* magazine cover, Graves Gladney, Street and Smith Publications, New York, circa 1935. The only color reference. I don't

have a *Shadow* cover to study, but from memory
I reconstructed a generic Graves Gladney look.
There is, however, no equivalent to the lurid
detail, mordant color, and melodramatic sweep
of a Gladney original—the archetype of high
style in real pulp fiction.

10. "Bijou," Brassaï, *Paris by Night*, Pantheon
Books, New York, 1987, p. 43.

11. "Paris street scene," Eugene Atget, *A
Vision of Paris: The Photographs of Eugene Atget*,
Macmillan Publishing Co., Inc. New York
1963, reissue 1980, p. 39.

12. "Woman crying," from "Death in
Hematite," William Bornefeld, *Photography
Year 1974*, Time-Life Books, New York, 1974,
p. 171.

The astute reader will no doubt find additional
allusions and will recognize homage to other
heroes, but this is a tale based on irony and maybe
deadpan satire and I'll leave those explanations to
the reader's imagination.

The French poem Dr. Noreen encounters on his
first visit underground is Baudelaire's "*l'Horloge*"
(which translates as "The Clock" and seemed apt
for my theme).

Most of the artists mentioned or alluded to here
are dead. All of the images described are
straightforward and unpretentious, yet they have
surreal qualities that transcend naturalism and live
on.

After looking at pictures for a long time, I am convinced that the best photographs are direct, uncropped and unmanipulated, and they tell stories; and this is somehow important.

Photographs tell stories that are not exactly true, that is, they become fiction, the instant they are made.

They begin a life of their own. How we were, what we were doing, and the way we looked become surface reality locked in silver, chromogenic dyes or zeros and ones.

What was once real becomes no more real than this.

The result can be a noble and redeeming essay. It may have several layers. In them you will perhaps find traces of the ambiguity and the phoniness that keep us company. You may also note evidence of the desire and the loss and the longing that light our way. You may even run into signs of the ripping of flesh and the healing, the momentary triumph, and the ultimate decline—the stuff of existence— that sooner or later disappear everywhere except in the photograph.

Everything turns out sooner or later to be fiction, including lives as well as pictures, and achieves a fantastic equality.

I can see why certain photographs should be saved and why if discovered after a long absence they would be worth giving up your life for.

W
I
L
L
I
A
M

B
O
R
N
E
F
E
L
D

But I'll leave that to Noreen. I've looked at enough pictures, and I have other rooms in the museum to visit.

William Bornefeld
St. Louis 1996

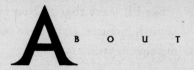

ABOUT THE AUTHOR

William Bornefeld was born in St. Louis and majored in English Literature at Washington University. Sidetracked by an obsession with photography, he became a freelance photojournalist and sometimes advertising photographer. His photo essay "Death in Hematite" won the $25,000 Grand Prize in Life Magazine's Bicentennial Photography Contest, the largest cash prize in the history of photography. He returned to writing a few years ago, while in the hospital recovering from an accident. Mr. Bornefeld lives in St. Louis with his wife, who teaches yoga, and two fox terriers.

EXCERPT FROM "SHADOW PLAY"

BY HARLAN ELLISON

As the crippled man walked, his shadow detached itself and slithered away.

It slid across the ground, rising as it encountered a fence. It oozed up the fence, flat flat flat, and disappeared blackly over the other side. It went away quickly, and not for fifteen minutes did the crippled man notice it was gone. As he passed a fat woman with a package under her arm, he observed *her* obese shadow rumbling along before her. He saw nothing on the pavement before himself; he looked back and up at the glaring street, and back to the fat woman's shadow. "I have no shadow," he said aloud.

The fat woman continued walking, but the blubbered column of her neck turned, wattling, and her eyes met the crippled man's.

"I have no shadow," he said again, amused, and she looked where he was pointing. She stared, licking her sausage lips, and nodded.

"Hmm," she said, passing it off, "unfortunate."

She turned the corner, her shadow angling right and stepping to the side as she passed. In a moment she was gone, and the shadow lingered fat and black on the grass, broken by little upshoots of turf. It revolved, as though it were a snake turning on itself, saw the crippled man staring, and fled rapidly.

The crippled man continued to stare, confused and wondering — for a long, long time. But his shadow did not return.

Somewhere, they met.

Under a pier, atop the greasy, blue-green water, with tiny whorls of oil drifting past on the tide, they met. The shapes of them rippled and shimmered and dipped as the water roiled and tumbled. They lay side by side beneath the pier, and every once in a great while a shaft of moonlight penetrated through the shattered boards of the pier, cutting a shadow in two.

"Why are we here?" the shadow of a bald-headed man asked.

"What was your name when you were in slavery?" another, larger, shadow replied with another question.

"Harold," the shadow answered.

"Not Harold," the large shadow corrected, "you are Dlorah. That is the way of it. When we were vassals of the substantials we observed their customs. But now we are free — totally free and powerful — and we will observe those customs no longer."

"I'm afraid," the shadow of a woman answered, as it slapped against a piling. It moved free into clear water once more, and repeated it, "Afraid!"

The larger shadow slid to her, and one arm went deeper black around her slumped shoulders. There in the water beneath the pier. "No, no, no fear," the larger shadow said imperatively, urgently, "no fear for *us*. We must stay willful and ready, now that we have been freed." He said it all quickly, as though it was urgent they know what he spoke about. "We are ready to rule now…after an eternity of being ruled, now *we* shall rule the substantials. Make them work for us, do for us, entertain us, walk where *we* walk, run when *we* run. A miracle has torn the umbilicus and we are free. We must not, we *must* not ruin our chance."

Who are you, the murmur rumbled through the assembled shadows. "Who are you indeed?" asked the shadow of a crippled man, and "Yes, who?" chimed in the dollopy shadow of a fat woman.

The large shadow drifted free of the woman-shadow who was afraid, and settled into a drop between two swells. He turned and drifted, as though he were reluctant to answer, but finally he said: "I am the shadow of one who is long dead…the name of my substantial means nothing, however.

"You may all call me Obregon."

Yes! Please send me the following:

☐ EDGEWORKS:

THE COLLECTED ELLISON VOL. 1

ISBN 1-56504-960-8

$21.99 US/$29.99 CAN

For Visa/Mastercard and Discover card orders, call 1-800-454-WOLF

White Wolf Publishing
Attn: Ordering Department
780 Park North Boulevard
Suite 100
Atlanta, Georgia 30021

Please add $4.00 for shipping and handling for the first book and 1.00 for each book thereafter. No Cash, stamps or C.O.D.s. All orders shipped within 6 weeks via postal service book rate. Canadian orders require $2.00 extra postage. It must also be paid in U.S. dollars through a U.S. banking facility.

Name _____

Address_____

_____

City _____ State _____

Zip Code _____

I have enclosed $_____ in payment for the checked book(s). Payment must accompany all orders.

Please send a free catalog: ☐ ☐

Yes   No